FOOL'S FIRE

Pete Mesling

Other Kingdoms Publishing, Seattle

ISBN-13: 979-8-218-01669-2

Cover design and artwork by: Alan M. Clark
Additional cover design by: James T. Egan of Bookfly Design
Library of Congress Control Number: 2022910386
Printed in the United States of America

PUBLICATION HISTORY

PRAISE FOR *THE PORTABLE NINE*

"A compelling tale of vigilante hit men that'll keep readers on the edge of their seats."—**Roy Lee**, producer of *IT*, *IT Chapter Two*, *Doctor Sleep*, and *The Stand*

"A dark blend of *Ocean's Eleven* and *Mission Impossible*, Mesling's *The Portable Nine* pits a team of mismatched miscreants against a nefarious villain in an age-old tale of intrigue, betrayal, and revenge. With whip-sharp characterisation and a network of plotlines, Mesling proves his mettle in this cinematic thrillride."—**Lee Murray**, three-time Bram Stoker Award nominee and author of *Into the Mist*

"Pete Mesling has gifted us with an intriguing cast of characters and a complex, fast-moving plot in *The Portable Nine*. This one gets off to a fast start, and never stops to catch its breath. (Borderlands Press Writers Boot Camp lightning strikes again!)"—**Tom Monteleone**, five-time winner of the Bram Stoker Award

PRAISE FOR *JAGGED EDGES & MOVING PARTS*

"Pete Mesling leads the reader through many a harrowing tale in this collection of short fiction. The wide variety of stories, long and short, grabs the reader and holds on. Be prepared—the going will get tough. You are not getting through this book unchanged."—**Alan M. Clark**, author of *The Prostitute's Price*, *Mudlarks and the Silent Highwayman*, and *Fallen Giants of the Points*

"The writing was as beautiful as the stories were uncomfortable. Pretty pictures of ugly things."—**Well Read Beard (a.k.a., Kevin Whitten)**, reviewer and BookTuber

"Each short story is a new and exciting world ... A brief glimpse into a horrific painting before being ripped away at the conclusion ... Pete Mesling can write. Wow."—**Steve Stred**, author of *Father of Lies: The Complete Series* and *Mastodon*

PRAISE FOR *THE WAGES OF CRIME*

"First, Mesling's writing is crisp and fine-tuned, channeling the best of 1950s and '60s crime writers. The voice fits with the wonderful style of a magazine like *Manhunt*. Second, Mesling is master of the short story form."—**Coy Hall**, historian and author of *Grimoire of the Four Impostors* and *The Hangman Feeds the Jackal*

MISCELLANEOUS PRAISE FOR PETE MESLING'S WORK

"A creatively conceived, over-the-top thriller with plenty of room for more delicious treachery."—*Kirkus Reviews* (from their review of *The Portable Nine*)

"Claustrophobic and terrifying; you'll be holding your breath."—*Rue Morgue*

"Pete Mesling's *None So Deaf* gave me a serious dose of the creeps. Herein lies an assemblage of horrors that, when it isn't reminding you of Bradbury at his grimmest, will have you double-checking the locks and turning on all the lights. Wonderful stuff indeed."—**Kealan Patrick Burke**, Bram Stoker Award-winning author of *The Turtle Boy*, *Kin*, and *Sour Candy*

"Reminiscent of the best and darkest work of David Morrell and Dan Simmons, the new collection by Pete Mesling, *None So Deaf*, crackles with malignant life and death. You can smell and taste these stories, which are written with a surgeon's eye for detail and a mortician's sense of drama. Highly recommended!"—**Jay Bonansinga**, *New York Times* best-selling author of *The Walking Dead: Invasion*, *Self-Storage*, and *Saint Oswald*

"We've got the genealogical report in on Pete Mesling. There's some Fredric Brown. Some Kafka. And even some Brautigan. But mostly there's Mesling. And that's 100% unique and original.

As is *None So Deaf*, this memorable collection."—**Mort Castle**, author of *Moon on the Water, New Moon on the Water*, and *Knowing When to Die*

"With his debut collection of mad scientists and classic monsters, childhood wonders twisted into nightmares, and *Twilight Zone*-style morality plays, Pete Mesling reminds us what's fun about horror—and adds serious chills along the way."—**Norman Prentiss**, Bram Stoker Award-winner, author of *Invisible Fences*

"Flashes of darkness ... moments of the macabre captured like the snapshots of a scream ... or an impaling. Short, fast, and deadly moments of discovery!"—**John Everson**, Bram Stoker Award-winning author of *Covenant* and *Sacrificing Virgins*

"Pete Mesling's *None So Deaf* explores the darkest regions of the human soul in readable tales that take no prisoners."—**Nancy Kilpatrick**, *Nevermore!: Tales of Murder, Mystery & The Macabre*

"A terrific new author. His work is fresh and different."—**John R. Little**, author of *Miranda, The Memory Tree*, and *Soul Mates*

"Lean and masterful prose. Buy this book."—**Wayne Allen Sallee**, author of *The Holy Terror* and *Proactive Contrition*

"Pete Mesling's fiction is definitely the kind of old school horror I grew up with. Short, sharp shocks that touch on the fears we all have—stuff like claustrophobia, the anger of strangers, carnivals, spooky houses. Definitely give them a whirl!"—**Paul Kane**, Bestselling and award-winning author of *Pain Cages, The Hellraiser Films & Their Legacy*, and *Lunar*

"Pete Mesling is a brawler of a writer. Whether his touch is light as a feather, like Bradbury, or a hard left hook, like Lansdale, he has you exactly where he wants you."—**John Bruni**, author of

Tales of Questionable Taste

"Pete Mesling's *None So Deaf* takes the reader on a whistle-stop tour of American gothic, traditional and modern, with unsettling carnivals, kids breaking into decrepit houses on a dare, and corrupt preachers in the Wild West. Nasty new stings in the tail alternate with tilted perspectives on horror tropes for this box of entertainingly poisoned chocolates."—**Narrelle M Harris**, *The Opposite of Life*

"Just when you think you know what's going to happen, Mesling pulls the rug out and down the trapdoor you fall, spiraling into expertly crafted nightmares. I'm already looking forward to Pete's next offering!"—**Robert Essig**, author of *In Black*, *People of the Ethereal Realm*, and *Stronger than Hate*

"*None So Deaf* spans the horror spectrum from fearsome to fun in the spirit of *Skeleton Crew* and *Strange Highways*, making it a great read for any fan of the genre!"—**Matt Hults**, Author of *Husk*

For the foolish, and for the fire that sometimes burns them.

The noise of one car passing in the night can drop a hundred sleepers into the deep part of themselves. It's funny to think of that one car racing through the dark, trailing so many dreams.
—Truman Capote, "Master Misery"

The fire glows brightly, crackling with a sharp and cheerful sound, as if it loved to burn.
—Charles Dickens, MASTER HUMPHREY'S CLOCK

Fool's rush in where angels fear to tread.
—Alexander Pope, "An Essay on Criticism"

CONTENTS

PREFACE

Welcome to the fire, fools and savants. This might be my last story collection for a while, so it seems fitting to me that it's a full-blown return to my horror roots. The genre is most often at its best in the short form, if you ask me, and I hope the tales collected here do more to support that opinion than otherwise.

But why the threat of tapping the brakes on my short-story output? It's what I'm most appreciated for, I suppose; however, some of you may recall that I published an assassination novel last year called *The Portable Nine*, and hinted at a forthcoming sequel called *The Portable Eight*. If you detect a pattern in those titles, you're on to me. I do in fact plan to write a series of *Portable Nine* books, with one less member of the band of mercenaries extant in each successive entry. With the gods on my side, there will even be a tie-in collection of stories down the road. That's what's known in the biz as a heavy lift.

Will I live long enough to see the *Portable Nine* series through to completion, not to mention the other novels I have bubbling away on the back burner? I hope so, but finishing the series will mean keeping this nose of mine to the grindstone and avoiding literary distractions as much as possible. I hate to think of short stories that way. I love them every bit as much as novels and poetry, but the Portable Nine have a dossier on me, I'm afraid, and there could be dire consequences for leaving the record of their adventures incomplete.

Enough on that, though. What kind of preface would this be if it dealt mostly with books other than *Fool's Fire*? Let's start with the paint job on this baby. Wow, huh? If you haven't worked it out for yourself, Alan M. Clark is the artist responsible. I've wanted to work with him for a long time, so this really is a dream come true. And to think he's also a world-class writer! It hardly seems fair.

Unlike my previous horror collection, *Jagged Edges & Moving Parts*, *Fool's Fire* is loaded almost entirely with supernatural tales, and even the stories that are more realistic in their makeup have kind of an otherworldly feel to them. Hence the title of the book, and hence the cover art (*fool's fire* is another term for *ignis fatuus*, or will-o'-the-wisp). I think you'll find as much a sense of wonder as of terror in the book you're about to read, but I'm not picky. I'll take either one.

There's one last piece of business I'd like to button up before I send you into the wilderness ahead. Those of you who have been paying close attention to my work for a while will notice that we return, in "An Occurrence at Kendrick Outdoors," to a family we first checked in on in "The Worst Is Yet to Come," a story of mine that has appeared, among other places, in *Jagged Edges & Moving Parts*. "An Occurrence at Kendrick Outdoors" is also noteworthy because it was suggested by a true incident that a good friend of mine found himself involved in not long ago. Quite a bit of detail has been turned on its head per the demands of fiction, of course, but the mood and tone of the story come from the dark fascination that grew within me as I listened to what my friend had to reveal.

There, now you're provisioned with all that I have it in my power to bestow. Godspeed as you venture forth, and please do your best to make it through the woods before dark. The trees at night sing a plaintive melody that's been known to drive travelers out of their minds. There's also talk among the locals of strange lights that float above still waters.

Are you sure you're up for this?

—Pete Mesling
Seattle, Washington

IMPOSTER SYNDROME

"**M**a, it's gonna be dark soon. Can't we go back? Please?"

She wanted to say yes, that they could give his father one more chance. It didn't seem much worse than continuing on in this rainstorm—a radar-indicated threat, the lonesome voice on the radio had called it before she switched it off—with darkness less than a half hour away. June days were long in the Pacific Northwest, but never long enough.

"I'm afraid not, Dom." She eyed him in the rearview mirror. "Not for a while, anyway. Maybe we'll let him cool his heels for a bit."

Unbelievably, the rain began pelting the windshield of the dilapidated pickup with even more force. She eased up on the accelerator and redoubled her grip on the steering wheel.

"He wasn't gonna hit me with the bat," Dom said from the backseat of the cab. "He's never hit me with the bat."

"No, never with the bat. With a boot once, and a cargo strap, I remember. But never with the bat. Unfortunately, there's always a first time."

"Ma, look out!"

Standing in the middle of the road, waving his arms in long, opposing arcs, was a man. She zipped around him, half planning to continue on and leave the poor soul to the elements, and the deepening dusk. Fleeing an abusive husband and father didn't exactly fill her with the milk of human kindness. But she'd caught a glimpse of fruit salad on the upper left area of the man's jacket. Having a Marine colonel for a father, she recognized a decorated Army man when she saw one.

She pulled to the side of the road and watched in the side-view mirror as the man jogged to the passenger door and stooped over so he could see in.

"What do you think, Dom? Should we let him in?"

"He looks okay. Got to be cold out there."

"You're a good boy."

She powered the passenger window down a few inches.

"Hello, ma'am," the man in the uniform said, squinting rain out of his eyes as much as possible. "I hate to ask, but we've got a bit of a situation up ahead. I sure could use a lift."

The sound of rain through the open window drowned out the drumming on top of the cab.

"Well, you wouldn't be hitchhiking in this weather, I guess, least of all in that outfit. Hop in."

"Thank you."

Once he was settled and the window was back up, she eased the truck forward again.

"What kind of situation are we talkin' about?"

"Some of it I can tell you. Some I can't. Some I'd rather not. But lady, you need to get this rig pointed in the opposite direction, because you're headed for the eye of the storm."

"Sir, the name's Shakayla Watkins and I'm not turning around. You got something you want to get away from. I appreciate that. But my boy and me, we're gettin' away from something, too, and it's behind us."

The man looked back at Dom and smiled. "Okay, that's the way it is, then. That being the case, why don't you turn right at the sign for Great Rim Lake. We need to duck and cover for a spell. I'm Sergeant Major Rich Bilkins, by the way."

"That's my boy Domenick. Goes by Dom."

It was full dark by the time she turned onto the two-lane road leading to the lake, a curious moon spying over the treetops in the distance. A glowing blur among clouds one moment, nothing but a rumor the next.

"You're going to want to take a left up there by the

barbwire fence." The sergeant major removed his hat and wiped it on his leg, which Shakayla didn't think could have helped dry it any, as soaked through as he was.

She followed his directions without question or complaint. The pickup's headlights soon led them down a curving slope and up the other side, where they shone on a small but neat complex she would have guessed to be military, even if she wasn't being guided there by Sergeant Major Bilkins.

"That where we're headed?"

Bilkins nodded.

"I gotta pee," Dom added from the backseat.

"Okay, sweetie." She pulled onto a service road and stopped before a chain-link gate on rollers. "I'll find you a bathroom in a minute, but first the sergeant major here is going to tell me what he was running from up on the highway." She turned an icy gaze on the man.

"I'll have to run my card." Bilkins stepped out of the pickup. "Be right back."

Shakayla watched him swipe a card across a reader on a metal post, and the gate rolled open. Once he was back in the truck, she passed through the open gate but stopped some distance from the only building on the property.

"Ma'am, I'll be happy to fill you in on as many details as I can, but time is of the essence, and every minute we spend out in the open puts us at risk. That'll have to do for now." He opened his door and stepped once more into the punishing rain.

"Mo-om!"

"Okay, okay."

"You don't have to join me," Bilkins said as Shakayla and Dom stepped out of the truck. "I appreciate the ride, even if it didn't get me as far from base as I would have liked. But the time to make your decision is now."

"Because of that situation you mentioned earlier?"

"Yes, ma'am."

He had to try a few different keys before the front door unlocked. Shakayla and Dom followed him inside and he quickly bolted the door behind them.

"Bathroom should be down that hall." Bilkins pointed off to their right.

Dom ran in that direction.

"It's not much to look at," Bilkins said to Shakayla, "but it's good to be out from under all that wet."

"Yeah, I'll give you that much." She traced her gaze along the walls and ceiling. Long overhead fluorescent fixtures ran the length of the large room in authoritative rows, and all of them were blazing, motion activated. "What is this place?"

"Training facility. This room can be outfitted as a classroom. When it's empty like this it's used for drills, mostly."

"But it's not where you're usually stationed?"

"No, the base is up the road a piece."

"And something went wrong there?"

"Yes, ma'am. And maybe it's just as well if I tell you this while your boy is down the hall. We've been running some experiments up there. Top secret stuff, honestly, but I don't suppose it's going to stay that way for long. See, one of them got out."

"Got out? My God, are you doing things to animals?"

"Not exactly, no. See, we've got—"

"Hey, Dom," she said as her son reappeared. "You all good?"

"Yeah."

"You wash your hands?"

"Yeah, kinda. Where are we?"

"It's a place for military training. Sounds like we might be stuck here for a bit. Why don't you read a book on your phone or something. I'm gonna try to make a call."

"No use." Bilkins removed his hat and turned it in his broad hands. "You won't get a signal in here. That's by design. No cellular signal and no Wi-Fi. Keeps the recruits focused. There's a landline, though. Let me get some chairs out of the storage closet first. If a body has a place to sit, things could always be worse."

"Sir?" It was Domenick.

"Yes, son?"

"Is there anything to eat here?"

"See, things are looking up already. That's another thing I can do something about. Let me get a few chairs set up and then I'll show you where the kitchen is."

He went to a part of the wall that Shakayla hadn't even realized was a door and opened it to reveal several stacks of conference chairs. Once he'd placed three of them in a rough semicircle in the center of the room, he showed Domenick to the kitchen.

Shakayla sat down and checked the time: coming up on 9:30. Fear was beginning to etch its fine lines on her ceramic resolve. The more lines, the more fragile she became. Eventually, one light tap with a mallet would send shards flying in all directions. She'd learned that she could erase the hairline cracks if she concentrated hard enough, but it became a question of which was faster, the sure hand of dread or the effacing powers of her fortitude.

Maybe if she could get the sergeant major to open up about what exactly had gone wrong up the road ... Having all their cards in front of them might help. At least they'd be able to collaborate on a plan. Bilkins being the only one in the know made her feel even more like a damsel in distress than running away from her asshole husband. She was growing tired of the feeling.

She also hoped Bilkins would have someone to call, because she sure as hell didn't. No one who would be any use to them, anyway. And the cops? What good would they be, if the Army itself was in some kind of panic?

"I think he'll be back there for a while." Sergeant Major Bilkins took a seat next to Shakayla. "The fridge and freezer are packed with food and drinks. There's every variety of junk food in the cupboards, too. Your son has Major Kinsky to thank for that. Must have the metabolism of a field mouse, I swear. The man eats like he just emerged from the desert and never seems to gain a pound. Probably works at it some, but that hardly—"

"Sir, I don't mean to be rude, but Dom and I have had a trying day, and you've got me pretty shaken up with this business at the base. I'd appreciate some answers. And maybe we can work on a plan to get away from here?"

He stared at her without saying a word. Maybe he was racking his brain to be sure he didn't wander too far into classified territory with her. But that wasn't the impression she got. It was more like he was assessing her in some way.

A sudden pounding saved him from having to give an immediate response. It took Shakayla a moment to realize it was coming from the other side of the door they'd entered through. She sprang to her feet.

"Help!" a man's voice cried out, dampened by the steel door but obviously desperate. More pounding. "For the love of God, let me in!"

"Mom?"

Shakayla spun around and saw Dom standing by the corner of the hallway that must have led to the kitchen.

"What's that noise?" he asked, his voice a little shaky.

"It's nothing, sweetie. You go back to the kitchen. I'll come and find you in a bit. Sound okay?"

"Okay." He disappeared again.

"Well?" Shakayla said to the sergeant major. "Are we going to let the man in, or are you going to give me a reason why we shouldn't?"

He got up and walked to the door. The pounding and hollering resumed.

"I'm not sure I even want to confirm that we're in here." He turned to Shakayla but shook a finger at the door. "That might be a man in distress. Probably that's what it is."

"But it might not be? Is that what you're saying?"

"Yes, it might not be. We've been working on something at the base. A military project. You shouldn't know any of this, but I don't see how I can keep it from you, now that you're involved. Some of it, anyway.

"We've been working on the ultimate soldier for some

time. Until fairly recently, the fundamental approach to the problem has been to medically alter men already inclined toward violence. Enhance their musculature, inflame the rage center in their brain, but make it controllable. Ethics started to lead us more and more toward robots and invisibility fabrics, but we had a lucky breakthrough before changing course completely."

"Jesus Christ, am I in the Twilight Zone?"

"Afraid not. Anyway, I'm not going to tell you the exact nature of that breakthrough, but we should talk about the outcome, because it might be out there pounding on that door and crying to be let in."

"What in the hell—"

"Please, bear with me. It sounds like a man out there. If we decide to open the door, it will probably look like a man. But it might not *be* a man. It might be ... a shapeshifter."

All she could do was stare in disbelief until he continued.

"It must sound insane, but it's not. We've developed a creature that can take on the form and attributes of almost any living thing—nothing too small or too large, but just about anything else."

"And this ... thing simply got loose?"

Bilkins nodded.

"And that's why you were hitchhiking in the rain."

"It set fire to all the vehicles on the base. Someone did, anyway."

"But if that *is* just a man out there ..."

"Then he's in trouble. AO1 will destroy him.

"AO1?"

"The shapeshifter. It's code for Army of One. The only way to stop it, other than killing it, is with a verbal command. As you can imagine, the proper command is changed from time to time and treated with the utmost confidentiality. Above my pay grade, I'm afraid."

"So you're telling me we have a killing machine on the loose out there and there's nothing to stop it from changing shape and taking out everyone it comes in contact with."

"You have the general picture. The change tires it out a little. It needs to recuperate after assuming a new form."

"Isn't the change controlled by anyone?"

"It will be eventually, we hope. *Hoped.* We haven't had any luck in that area. It seems to change at will, and always into a human, even though there shouldn't be anything preventing it from turning into an animal of some kind."

"Sir, we have got to let that man in. I'm not going to make him into some kind of sacrifice. Can we protect ourselves, in case he does turn out to be this AO1? Don't tell me bullets won't stop it. Or do they have to be silver?"

"No, regular old bullets will stop it, but we don't keep any weapons or ammo here in the training facility, and I'm unarmed, as you can see."

Shakayla had a little piece of self-protection in the glove compartment of the pickup, but that might as well have been a hundred miles away. *Shit and dammit.*

"Will you meet me halfway on this?" Sergeant Major Bilkins asked. "Can we rest up and then see how we feel?"

"See if the problem has taken care of itself by then, you mean? Jesus, what if that was you out there? Wouldn't you want to be let in? He seems to know that something's after him. It's cruel to leave him out there."

"Fine. You want him in, we'll let him in. But by God, you might be signing your son's death warrant."

Trying to rub a chill from her bare arms, she took a step toward the door. "I don't hear him."

"Mom?"

She jumped and whirled around. "Dom, sweetie, what is it?"

"There's a man knocking on the kitchen window."

"Oh, shit." She tore off down the hall.

"Don't worry," Bilkins call after her, "it's fortified glass."

She had drawn the curtain across the kitchen window by the time Bilkins arrived, her son at his side. Dom ran to her and she cradled him as if he were half his actual age of ten, her back protesting more than it would have five years ago.

"Okay," she half whispered to the sergeant major, seeing her breath pass through Dom's hair before she stood back up, "he knows we're here. You still want to leave him to chance?"

"No, I suppose not. I'll go get him."

Bilkins was gone before she could mention the weapon in the pickup, and Dom sat down at the large table that dominated the kitchen.

"Who's outside?" he asked.

"We're not exactly sure, hon." Shakayla sat down across from him. "Looked like he was wearing fatigues, though, didn't it? My guess is that he's another Army guy."

"What's fatigues?"

"Kind of like casual military outfits. Not fancy uniforms like the sergeant major is wearing. You know, there's a chance this man you saw has something to do with an experiment that went wrong at a nearby base. I've always been straight with you. Ain't that right?"

He gave her a scared look. "Yeah, I guess."

"Well, he could be dangerous. He probably isn't. That's why I can't leave him outside if something might be after him. Does any of this make sense?"

He nodded but didn't look her in the eye this time. The front door could be heard opening, letting in a piece of the storm, then closing again.

"Do you think you could find a place to hide until I know for sure what to make of this stranger?"

"Okay."

"Then do it, now. And don't you make a move or a sound until I come looking for you. For the time being, I'd rather not know exactly where you'll be. Now get moving."

He bolted out of the kitchen and down the hall, away from the training room and the hallway that led to the bathrooms.

Now it felt real, and Shakayla Harriet Watkins was truly afraid. There was no sign of the two men, so she wandered across the hall to what appeared to be a mail or photocopy room, absently hoping to find something she could use as a weapon if it came to that. The handle of a paper-cutting guillotine caught her eye but looked too difficult to remove. A pair of scissors lay on a counter. Better than nothing. She snatched them up and slid them into her back pocket, making sure to cover the tip with the fringe of her top.

The display of her phone read 10:12. Checking it made her think about communication with the outside world again. There was a desk phone in the room. Would 911 be any more effective than having a military officer in her corner? Well, an unarmed military officer, yeah. She wouldn't give them the truth, of course, but she could say enough to get them to send help.

It turned out not to matter. The line was dead. Probably the storm. Just like the soldier who'd knocked on the front door and the kitchen window was probably a man. Then again, maybe it was the soldier who'd cut the phone line. And maybe he wasn't a soldier. Which meant maybe she'd sent Sergeant Major Bilkins on a dangerous errand.

She hated the idea, but maybe it was time she checked on things outside. Before doing anything rash, she crossed back over to the kitchen and peered behind the curtain into the dark, wet, howling night. No sign of man or beast. The thought made her shudder. Still not wanting to rush into harm's way, she decided to scope out other windows, hoping not to uncover Domenick's hidey-hole in the process. It probably didn't matter all that much, but she didn't want to risk an unconscious tell if someone—or some*thing*—asked where he was.

Jesus, she thought, *all I want is for him to be safe and I end up moving him from one threat to another.*

But there'd be time enough for regrets later, if she was lucky. Right now she wanted to know what the hell was going on outside. The building had only one story and there were surprisingly few windows. Proceeding down the hall toward the bathrooms, she encountered no windows until she reached a small office. The only window in that room looked out on the same general area behind the facility as the one in the kitchen.

Walking back the other way, she glanced at the main door, which was closed tight and appeared to be locked. Beyond the kitchen and mail room was another common area of some kind, and more offices, one of which had a window overlooking a narrow strip of land between the building and the chain-link fence that skirted the property. She saw nothing but whipping rain outside, and only that thanks to a nearby sodium lamp.

A nondescript door in an alcove off the main hallway caught her attention as she left the cluster of offices behind. It was an odd place for a door, she thought as she gave the release bar a push. The door surprised her by opening. It looked like the kind of door that might only be used in emergencies, even though it wasn't marked in any way. She feared it might open onto the outside world as she cautiously pushed it open, but instead it led to a small enclosure, lit dimly by a caged red light on the far side of a hole that claimed the exact center of the floor. A ladder, not caged, descended into the hole, and suddenly Shakayla wondered if she'd stumbled across the very entrance to Hell. If so, she'd probably be able to find her way around pretty well down there, with all she'd been through.

It would be the perfect hiding spot for Dom, she realized, wondering where he'd ended up secreting himself. Maybe it was worth finding him and bringing him here.

There were a handful of interior rooms she hadn't bothered checking out because they wouldn't have windows. Domenick must be in one of them, she figured. Walking the short corridor that ran perpendicular to the main hallway, she saw that the first two rooms were dark, and whispering Dom's name brought no results. In the third office, a fluorescent light flickered from the undercarriage of a desk-mounted shelving unit.

"Dom?" she whispered, her quiet a habit developed over the course of a lifetime of punishments small and large.

"Mom!" he sprang up from under the illuminated desk and ran into her arms. "Did you let the other man in?"

"Not yet, honey. But I may have found you a better hiding place. Say, what's that?"

Leaving him for the moment, she stepped across the room to where a detached cabinet stood against one wall. It was locked but, but only by one of the handles, and the mechanism and doors appeared flimsy. She retrieved a three-hole punch from a nearby counter and proceeded to slam it against the locked cabinet handle. After half a dozen blows the handle gave way and hung limp. She eased the door partway open.

"Dom, get the lights."

Before he could switch on the overheads, the sound of the main door opening and latching shut again startled them both.

"Okay, the cabinet can wait. Let's get you out of sight. Follow me."

She led him the short distance to the oddly situated door and pushed it open again.

"What's this?" he wanted to know.

"It's a safe place. Now listen to me." She got down on her haunches and held both of his shoulders. "I don't know where this ladder goes, but you'll be away from whatever happens up here. If you don't hear from me or Sergeant Major Bilkins, you stay down there until morning. Then you make your way back up and get help if you need to."

"You're scaring me."

"I know, sweetie, and I think everything will be okay, but we have to be prepared. Can you go down there for me?"

He nodded but looked on the verge of tears.

She stood up before she could catch his troubles. That was something her mother used to say. *You won't catch nobody's troubles if you know when to look away.* Her mother would have belt-whipped the living tar out of Terrence by now if she were still alive, and she would have done it by knowing when to look away from his troubles. Shakayla had never learned the trick of that. Not completely.

Or maybe she had at last.

"Love you, squirrel," She gave Dom's head a quick rub.

"Love you, too."

As soon as she was back in the hallway she could hear the voices of the two men. Touching the scissors in her back pocket, even though she could tell they were still there, she started off in that direction. The two men didn't seem to be arguing, just talking. That was promising. Still, she lingered at the juncture where the hall opened onto the training area, peering around the corner at Bilkins and his new friend.

"No, honestly." Bilkins said. "You know as much as I do now, corporal. Here, have a seat."

The man in fatigues, wet like an otter from head to toe, sat down and nodded. Convinced they had a regular old human being on their hands, Shakayla stepped into the open.

"Ah, Ms. Watkins. This is our visitor, Corporal Reggie Daniels."

She said hello but the man barely acknowledged her.

"Shakayla, can I see you in the kitchen for a moment?"

Sergeant Major Bilkins walked away without waiting for a response. Of course, she followed, not wanting to be left alone with the stranger.

Once they were both in the kitchen, Bilkins sat down, sighed heavily, and removed his hat.

"Ma'am, the only way to put this is that I have some concerns about Corporal Daniels."

"Concerns? You don't mean—"

"Hear me out, please. When I went outside, he wasn't out front. I did a complete circuit of the building. I was about to come back in when I heard something in the woods just west of here. The rain's still coming down in buckets, so I couldn't figure out what I would have heard over the downpour. But it came again, kind of an animal sound. So I wandered over to the edge of the trees and waited for it to come again."

"And did it?"

"Yes, it did. It was Daniels. He was out there with his head thrown back, howling up at the moon. He turned and saw me watching and it was like someone flipped a switch. He smiled nice and bright and walked straight to me with a hand extended. I shook it and we made our way back here."

"Why would you let him in if you have real doubts? I mean, assuming he might be the thing from your experiments was one thing, but actual suspicion ..."

"Well, you convinced me we want to be sure about this. I think I can give him a test of sorts. Then we'll know."

"And if he flunks?"

"Then I coax him back outside."

"Holy shit. What kind of test?"

"I need to get him to write something down. If he's AO1, he won't be able to write anything but squiggles. Some kind of cognitive slippage with the process of transforming. Can't read or write. I don't suppose you have anything to write with?"

"No, but I know where to find something. I saw a legal pad and some pens in one of the back offices when I was wandering around."

"Would you mind? I don't want to leave Daniels alone too long."

Shakayla headed out of the kitchen but stopped when Bilkins said her name.

"Yeah?" She turned her head in his direction.

"Where's that boy of yours?"

"Oh, he's around. I told him to wander, keep his mind off things."

He stared but said nothing more. Then he headed back to the training room. A chill rose up on Shakayla's arms as she left to retrieve the writing supplies.

She'd almost forgotten about the smashed-open locker in the office until she switched on the lights and saw the one door hanging open. She never had found out what was inside, so she went to the cabinet now and pulled both doors wide open.

A neatly racked display of military rifles greeted her from the right side, but it took her a moment to remember why there was something wrong about that. The other side boasted a row of metal drawers. Sliding one open she saw that it was packed with ammunition.

No weapons on site, Bilkins had said. No weapons and no ammo. Her blood thinned to wine in her veins. What the goddamn hell was going on here?

Needing time to think, and not wanting to arouse suspicion, she gathered up the yellow legal pad she'd noticed earlier and a ballpoint pen from a container, then headed back to the kitchen and deposited both items on the table.

"Sergeant Major Bilkins?" she said, making her way to the training room. "I found some paper and a pen."

Both men were standing when she rounded the corner.

"Fine, thanks. I was just telling Corporal Daniels how we should all write our contact information down, in case anything happens. That way we'll all have each other's details."

"Good idea," Shakayla said. "The paper's in the kitchen."

They all filed in and took a seat around the table. Without waiting for further instruction, the distressed Corporal Daniels drew the legal pad toward him and picked up the pen. After scribbling what looked like a short sentence he pushed the tablet toward Shakayla, who glanced at Bilkins before looking down at the page. The sergeant major wore a curious, anticipatory smile that she found off-putting, considering the situation.

But then what Daniels had written claimed her attention entirely: *It feeds on fear—will kill me if I speak to you.*

A suspicion that had been growing in her mind since discovering the arsenal now went into full bloom. Could it be that Sergeant Major Bilkins, not Corporal Daniels, was the product of a military experiment gone wrong?

She slid the pad in Bilkins' direction, playing on her hunch. "You want to put your deets under his?"

"I don't think that'll be necessary."

He stood up and began unbuttoning the jacket of his uniform. Once he'd slithered out of it he tossed it to the floor, then went to work on his shirt. Breasts began to swell from his chest as Shakayla watched in fascinated horror, and as he undid the buttons of his shirt, dark skin could be seen beneath. Once topless he dropped his hat on the table. His previous mane of brown hair, neatly parted on one side, was gone. From his bald scalp a black afro sprouted and crept outward until it covered his entire head. By the time he went to work on his pants Shakayla knew what she would see: black, feminine legs. He removed everything, including his briefs and dress shoes. There he stood before Shakayla and Corporal Daniels. Only he was no longer *him*. He was *her*. Shakayla stared at her exact replica, except that she never could have leered so serenely, or with such obvious intent.

Her doppelgänger stared back at her but reached with one hand for the corporal's throat. The young man was too stunned to resist until it was too late. As the creature crushed his windpipe, Daniels clamped both hands around the thing's arm. This seemed to anger his attacker, who hauled him into a standing position before forcing him into the wall behind him without letting go. It pulled back and slammed the head again. Shakayla heard a horrible cracking sound. The next blow was softer, wetter. The fourth ended the man's life. She knew this even before the thing let go of his throat and he slid down the wall, leaving a bloody question-mark trail with no dot to end it.

Shakayla's hand went to the scissors blades as the Bilkins-thing crouched down and began gnawing at the man's face. It must have grown fangs, because the ripping and gurgling were intense. Its head made jerking movements as it feasted as well. She wouldn't have a better opportunity. Rising from her seat, the scissors poised to strike, she crept up behind it.

It heard her at last and spun its head around. The face was a gruesomely masked mirror image of Shakayla's. Growling, it showed the fangs she had expected.

Now or never! her brain screamed, and the scissors came down fast and vicious. She was going for its eye but missed badly. Maybe it had shuddered to one side, realizing her intention. Whatever the case, the coupled blades sank deep into the creature's neck. Barely aware she was doing it, she pried the scissors handles apart by hooking her thumb through one of them and a forefinger through the other. The blades responded by opening an awful cut in the thing's flesh.

That might have been enough to disable a man, but AO1 clearly had abilities that went beyond shapeshifting. Her blow only angered it and she knew she was doomed.

Leaving the corporal to bleed, the Bilkins-thing sprang for Shakayla and latched onto her with all four limbs, like some kind of parasitic lower mammal. Its tongue came for her first, dabbing at her lips, nose, cheeks, and forehead before probing both eyes. She tried to recoil but it seemed to anticipate every movement. She was powerless, but she refused to go down, taking small backward steps to keep her balance. Like dancing.

Then came the fangs, puncturing her face in what seemed like a dozen locations. The pressure of each bite was worse than the last, and by the time she tipped over backwards she could hear the cracking of bones in her cheeks. As she lay supine, the thing still attached, its powerful jaws went to work on her skull, as if it wanted what was inside. Maybe that was how it would claim her personality, by literally eating the contents of her brain.

All she had for comfort was the certainty that she was close to death and soon this would be over. *Please, God,* she thought, *save and protect my precious boy.*

* * *

Dom woke with a fluttery feeling in his chest, unsure where he was for several moments. "Ma!" he called out, which was when he remembered the situation he was in.

Red lights in wire cages dotted the cylindrical hallway. He was glad he could see a little, but the light was eerie. He wasn't sure how long he'd been out, but it felt like maybe quite a while. Pulling his phone out of a pocket in his jacket he saw that it was 4:42 a.m.

No noise from above made it down into the tunnel, so he

had no way of knowing what was going on up there. That gave him a goal. He would sneak up to the main area and see how things looked. Picking up a few things from the fridge might not be a bad idea, either.

Now that he knew where the tunnel led, he wasn't even as afraid as he had been at first. Still, he hoped that everything was okay up top, so he wouldn't have to climb back down. The tunnel looked like it dead-ended in both directions, but actually it turned ninety degrees at each end. He was nearest the turnoff for the ladder leading to the small chamber where he'd said goodbye to his mom. He made short work of the climb and eased open the door to the main floor.

No sound, other than air moving through ducts in the ceiling. That scared him a little. Made him cautious. He'd expected to hear voices.

As he passed by the kitchen, a smell came to him, hot and coppery, but the lights were off and he kept moving. Sneaking a look around the corner into the front room, he saw his mom sitting in one of the chairs, her back to him. He almost ran to her, but something wasn't right. It wasn't only that her clothes were streaked with blood. It was wrong how she sat perfectly still, staring at the front door.

Still, he took a step toward her. It was his mom, after all. He opened his mouth to speak, took another step. Then he noticed that she was trembling slightly, and a quiet rumble sounded in her chest, as if she was talking to herself at low volume. Something told him that now was not the time to engage.

Instead he retreated as quietly as possible. Maybe he would see if he could find Sergeant Major Bilkins or the other fellow. But first, it was time to load up on provisions from the kitchen. He knew there was a six-pack of Sprite in the fridge, and crackers in one of the cupboards. That would be a start.

❋ ❋ ❋

AO1 stared at the door, shaking a little in its seat, its head lolling slowly from side to side. There was something it couldn't make sense of in the air. Was it a lingering remnant of the delicious fear it had gorged on in the kitchen, or was it something else?

Had there been another one? *No, I'd remember that.* There *is* another. *Impossible. I'd know.* How much do you really remember from Bilkins? It's fading. *Shut the fuck up! I'm not going to take your shit anymore. I'm going to take the boy and ...*

Boy? What boy?

The answer didn't want to come. There was something there, but it was ... protected.

It leaped to its feet, picked up the chair it had been sitting on, and flung it against the front door while letting loose a roar that was irritatingly restrained by its current vocal chords. This angered it enough to throw a second chair at the door, with only a grunt this time. Somewhat calmed, it sat down in the only chair still upright and resumed its staring.

❋ ❋ ❋

Domenick's mind raced for an escape from what he'd seen in the kitchen. He didn't know how it could be possible that his mom lay dead on the floor—blood pooling around her, the sergeant major's uniform draped on top of her—while also sitting motionless on a chair by the building's entrance. But he knew the real one was gone. He felt it deep inside. Whatever sat watch by the door was not his mom.

Domenick's body was also eager to make an escape, which meant climbing back down into the tunnel. He couldn't have explained to anyone how he'd managed to avoid screaming his lungs out when he walked into that kitchen, but doing so had bought him a chance. He felt sure of it. Now he had to take that chance.

He opened the door to the ladder, and that's when he

heard the thing start hollering and throwing chairs around. The door swung shut on its own as he descended the ladder until both feet were firmly planted on the floor of the lower level. Then he ran like hell to the far end of the tunnel.

Spinning into the left turn at the end, he banged his shoulder into the wall and did his best to ignore the pain. Here was another metal ladder, identical to the other one. He had climbed it before and knew there was a hatch with a wheel lock at the top. What he didn't know for sure was whether he'd have the strength to open it.

But what if the thing in the chair had followed him? The thought took hold of him like a vise. He had to know, had to brave a look around the corner and see if the thing that looked like his mom was dragging itself along the tunnel to get him.

He looked, one eye barely peeking around the corner. His relief when he saw nothing but an empty, red-tinted tunnel turned to tears, the first he'd shed for his mom. There would be many more, he figured, but right now he needed to get up that ladder and see if he was right about what the hatch opened onto.

The wheel wouldn't budge at first and that gave him a touch of panic. He kept at it, though, taking short breaks between attempts. After the fourth or fifth go he felt it slip. Maybe only an inch. Maybe less. But it had moved. That was all the encouragement he needed to press on. After several more small, hard-earned movements, the wheel gave up most of its resistance. Turning it the rest of the way was no problem.

When he could turn the wheel no more, he set about pressing his shoulder—not the injured one—into the underside of the hatch. It was awkward work, but the hatch proved lighter than he'd feared. He eased it back into place and used his hands instead. Soon the hatch was all the way open, resting on hinges the size of his fists.

The sky was dark but the rain had stopped. Climbing all the way out of the hole, he saw that it opened onto a field between the building and a forest of trees, which made sense to Dom. The tunnel was too long to have connected two rooms in the same building. He figured it had something to do with the training that took place on the premises.

Now that he was out, he wondered about his plan. His mom had let him drive the pickup once or twice, so he knew he could get it running. Keeping it on the road was another thing. To reach the pedals he'd need to slide so far down in the seat that he'd lose most of his view of what lay ahead. But if there was a better way out of this mess, he didn't know what it was, and there was no one left to ask. Not even the stranger in the kitchen with his mom.

Walking to where the pickup was parked, he became aware of a blade of light at the far horizon. Sunrise was close. That would help with the driving, put more traffic on the roads, too, which meant he might find someone to help him.

The magnetic key holder was inside the front driver's side wheel well, just like always. Without that spare key he didn't know what he would have done. He hoped it was the first in a string of lucky breaks.

He unlocked the door and slid in behind the wheel. Taking a deep breath, he inserted the key into the ignition and closed the door. About to turn over the engine, he saw the front door of the building swing open and bang against a support post. His mom, but not really his mom, staggered out. She looked at him and gave a terrible smile before walking in purposeful strides toward him and the pickup.

The gun. Was it still in the glove compartment? This his mom had never let him touch, but he'd gone out shooting at beer cans with his dad. Maybe the old man's lessons from those outings would prove useful and give some purpose to the role he'd played in the lives of Domenick and his mother.

But could he really shoot what looked exactly like his mom? He'd have to decide soon. She—*it*—was halfway to the truck.

He popped open the glove compartment and there it was, the 9mm heater, as his dad called it. He snatched it up and got back out of the vehicle.

"Mom, don't take another step." He stood beside the pickup, legs apart, gun drawn. He even steadied his firing arm with his other hand, just like he'd been taught.

The thing did stop, too. "Son, you aren't going to shoot your own mama. Now give me the gun."

"No, I want you to walk over to where that hatch is open in the ground over there."

It looked over its shoulder. There was enough light to see by now. It seemed to get the message.

"I don't think so, son."

"Go over there! And get in and close the hatch."

It started walking toward him again, still grinning. "You know, I almost forgot you were here."

That shattered the illusion for him. Not in a million years would his real mom have forgotten about him, not even for a minute.

He pulled the trigger, and there was still enough dimness to the morning that he could see the flash that sent a bullet roaring into the thing's head. He'd been aiming for the chest, but he wasn't about to fault himself.

Its body dropped to its knees, remaining that way for a second or two before collapsing face first onto the paved lot.

There was much he didn't understand about the world, but he felt the need to get away from that place, before he could catch its troubles. There'd be time for confusion and pain and terror—for more folks than him when they got to investigating this scene—but right now those things would only prevent him from putting miles between himself and this nightmare.

Trying his best to look away from the fallen creature, he crawled back into the cab of the pickup, tossed the gun onto the passenger seat, and brought the engine to life. He gave the thing on the pavement a wide berth as he drove himself through the gate to the highway and beyond. And even though his feet could barely touch the pedals, he felt as though he had taken a giant step into adulthood in the course of a single night. He didn't like it worth a damn.

THE PRIVATE AMBITIONS OF ARTHUR HEMMING

I arrived in Teufelsgarten a weary, depressed, and hopeless wreck. My bags had been stolen by highwaymen not five miles from the edge of town; the baying of wolves had kept me from catching so much as a wink of sleep on the interminable journey from Welchenberg; and the weather upon my arrival was as welcoming as a cliff's edge to a blind adventurer. But as I stepped from the coach and paid the driver for his troubles—thank God the brigands had left me the coins in my pockets!—a brilliant flash of lightning momentarily illuminated the rain-lashed village, and the castle that loomed above it from its perch higher up the mountain. My spirits were restored instantly, for I knew that in that castle dwelt a man who might hold the answers to questions that most men feared to ask.

Teufelsgarten would have felt more like a graveyard than a town had the coachman deposited me anywhere other than at the steps of the Hook and Dagger. A gaslight streetlamp showed enough of the sign that swung on two creaking chains above the entrance to reveal the name of the establishment, as well as part of a criss-cross blade-and-baling-hook engraving beneath the words. Thunder pealed overhead, and a chill passed through me. In Munich I would have pulled my cloak tighter against the wind and rain as I moved on in search of a more inviting inn, but in the mountain villages, one took what one could find.

I pushed open the door and acquainted myself with the

barkeep straightaway, dashing my waterlogged hat against my knee before setting it on the bar. The barkeep's round, warm face, though unsmiling, was a comfort, and I very purposely avoided eye contact with anyone else, though the place was clearly doing a brisk trade. More laughter and chatter filled the room than any reasonable soul could have guessed possible from outside. I ordered a mug of whatever courage flowed from the Hook and Dagger's tap, then turned around to face the madding crowd. They would, after all, have questions for me, and I wasn't without my own curiosities.

The room was split into two levels. The upper level, where the bar was located, gave way to a kind of sunken fire pit. The latter is where most of the activity was centered, as people there enjoyed the warmth of a happily glowing hearth, in addition to whatever was in their steins or in their bellies. Some of the laughter was clearly the result of jokes told at my expense. To be expected from people as cut off from the world as these. I took it all in good humour. Besides, of far more interest to me than the drunken louts in the fire pit was the voluptuous young woman clearing off one of the nearby tables.

Taking my tankard of ale with me, I approached and stood across from her, not *because* of the enhanced view it afforded me of her already impressive décolletage, but not unaware of her considerable charms, either.

"Excuse me, miss," I said. "Do you know the way to Castle Lebenmort?"

She finished making a circle with a wet cloth on the tabletop and then held it in place, her entire body suddenly motionless. In the same instant, a hush fell over the room, as if she had conducted the revelers into silence with the circular gesture of her delicate hand. At length she ventured a slight movement of the head, which allowed her to look me dead in the eye. But before she could speak, a man's voice boomed across the room from the pit.

"Who is it wants to know the way to Castle Doom?"

"The name is Hemming," I said to the broad-shouldered

villager who emerged from the sunken area by the fire. "May I ask who it is that *I* address?"

"*Now* you get around to it. Maybe you should have aimed your question at the men folk to begin with, instead of putting the red-hot irons to Miss Geldhaber here." The man's voice was as large as the rest of him. Had to be a farmer from the back slopes.

"Oh, Günther," the buxom wench replied, sweeping a lock of yellow hair behind one ear. "Leave him alone. He only asked a simple question."

"You want to visit the castle?" Günther asked me. "I'll take you there myself."

"Don't be a fool!" cried Miss Geldhaber.

"Silence, Katharina! He must have business with the doctor, and he sure as hell won't find him on his own. Hemming, I cordially invite you." He gave a mocking bow. "Follow me to Castle Doom, if you can keep up. And if you dare."

Turning to a nearby table, he hoisted someone's half-drained tankard.

"To the doctor!" He finished the borrowed ale in one and slammed the tankard back down. Foam leapt into the air and fell to the table in emphatic puddles.

I didn't bother mentioning that I was a doctor myself. He might have been toasting *me*.

The pretty barmaid and I watched him remove a burning torch from a wall sconce and stride purposefully out the door, into the cold, dark streets of Teufelsgarten. Half smiling, I wondered if Günther the Loud would hike all the way to the castle before noticing that I hadn't budged from my place at Katharina Geldhaber's side. I imagined him huffing and puffing his way up a particularly steep piece of the climb, while I made time with the beautiful woman who was obviously the apple of his eye. But in the end I had no choice but to follow, for it was likely to be my only chance at finding someone brave enough to guide me to the castle. I had hoped for more rest before resuming my journey, but again, this wasn't Munich. If I wanted to reach Dr. Lebenmort in his mountain retreat, I would take what guidance and help I could find, regardless of its source or motivation.

Outside, the wind and wet had softened to a thick mist that floated at the level of the streetlamps flickering here and there. As I struggled to keep pace with my athletic guide, I grew disoriented by an illusion whereby the houses and shops seemed to be approaching *me* out of the veiling mist, rather than the other way around. The optical trick had a vertiginous effect on me that I was happy to leave behind when Günther led me past the town's boundary and into the deep of the woods beyond.

We weren't far from the outskirts of Teufelsgarten, however, when we found our way obstructed by a rather disquieting scene. A small carriage appeared to have struck a tree root that arced up out of the rough trail we were on, for the conveyance lay crosswise on its side just ahead of the root. The whole tableau was odd, though, for no body was present, and there were no horses. Only a carpet bag near the trail's edge.

On the one hand, it was good to have caught up to Günther, and to catch my breath, but the flesh at the nape of my neck crawled. Something wasn't right. Still, I didn't stop my guide when he headed in the direction of the bag, or when he squatted down to pry it open and examine its contents. And by the time he realized it was empty and stood up again, it was too late. A small, wiry man darted out of the woods at him, armed with a thick wooden cudgel. Did the quick little man really leap into the air as he swung the weapon against Günther's head? It seems unlikely, but I swear it was so. Ach, who can trust his own memory in times of sudden violence? It was all over terribly fast, and now the accident scene had its body. Günther's body.

The wiry fellow stood over his bloody handiwork, breathing heavily, the cudgel swinging lazily at his side. We were above the mist now. The moon was high and mostly full, and while it spared me the horror of complete darkness, now that Günther's torch lay doused in the mud, it also lent Günther's attacker an eldritch cast. I don't remember seeing him turn away from Günther's body, but I remember that suddenly his wide eyes were on me, his drawn features pallid in the soft light of the moon.

"What have I done?" he asked, his voice ragged and hoarse.

"What have you *done*?" I repeated, stunned by the simple naïveté of the question. "I should think that was fairly obvious. You've killed a man in cold blood, you blackguard!"

"Have I?" He leaned down and touched the corpse's neck. "Oh, dear. Not another one." He stood up again. "I was only supposed to knock him out."

"At whose request?"

"The doctor's, that's who! Oh, I've made a mess of things. He'll have my skin for this."

"You're not making any sense, sir. What's going on?" I asked the question, though I had my suspicions.

"What's it to you, eh? Maybe you'd like to meet the same fate as your friend here."

I elected not to respond, hoping he might calm himself, or at least change the topic. Instead he heaved the cudgel into the very woods he'd sprung from only moments before.

"Now *there's* a thing," he said.

"What do you mean?" I asked.

"The weapon. Who do you suppose tossed it into them bushes?"

"What do you mean, who? You did. I watched you."

"Did you? I say maybe you're the one who tossed it and I'm the one did the watching. And if you're the one who disposed of the weapon, by God, maybe you're the villain who laid this man out with it."

"Me? A murderer? You must be mad. Besides, I have no motive." But as soon as the words were out of my mouth, I knew them to be untrue, for jealousy was the oldest motive of them all. It would be a simple matter to convince the regulars at the Hook and Dagger that I was the guilty party in this crime. Maybe Katharina herself would suspect the worst of me, a complete stranger to these parts.

That was before I got to know her. I could almost laugh at the notion of her disloyalty now.

The man before me saw the dawning of truth on my face, and he smiled like the very devil.

"Well, what have *you* got to be so proud of?" I pressed. "It doesn't sound as though your hand in this would be a hard tablet for someone to swallow … This doctor you mentioned, for instance."

The smile fell from his face.

"It isn't Dr. Lebenmort, by chance, is it? He and I have enjoyed a lengthy correspondence, you know. In fact, he's what brings me to this dreary mountain. He and his work."

"What do you know of the doctor's work?"

"You tell *me* what you were hoping to accomplish out here tonight when you inadvertently dispatched my companion, and maybe I can satisfy *your* curiosity on a point or two. Perhaps we can even have the bulk of this conversation on our way to Castle Lebenmort. You do have another carriage secreted away in these woods, don't you?"

He did, as it happened. In fact, when he wasn't needed at the castle, he hid himself away in a ramshackle hut less than a mile from the trail where Günther had breathed his last. In an attached lean-to, he kept a pair of horses that were as wiry as their owner, probably living off the same rough food as he did most of the time. And out back there stood his horse-drawn conveyance.

"The name is Kreutz," he had informed me as I followed him along a narrow path through the trees to his humble domicile.

"Hemming," I said. "Dr. Arthur Hemming."

"I don't mean to give insult, but the doctor hasn't mentioned you that I recall."

"Does he confide in you when it comes to matters of personal business? You are merely his servant, are you not?"

Not another word was spoken until he had hitched up his team to the rickety wagon and we were once again on the move.

When he turned from one trail onto a somewhat more punishing one, I asked, "Will there be many more turnoffs? It seems a rather circuitous business getting to your master's castle."

"Nah, that was the last one. This road here will take us straight to the main gate."

Hardly straight, I thought as I reached into my waistcoat pocket and felt for what was concealed there—a little precaution against tomfoolery that I was very glad I had taken. *I doubt there's a single straight road in the entire Black Forest.* But I was relieved to know that the time had come to act.

I've often marvelled at how odd it is that the most momentous turning points in life can be among the simplest to execute. That's what it was like as I withdrew the small metal case from my pocket and flipped open the lid. If the metallic sound it made caught Kreutz's attention he didn't let on. I slid a syringe from its cylindrical chamber, along with an adjacent ampule filled with a viscous green fluid. Unscrewing the cap from the ampule, I deftly drew a quantity of the solution up into the syringe and, without any fanfare, pushed the needle deep into my driver's neck and depressed the plunger.

He looked over at me suddenly, like a hurt child. His eyes filled with tears. Of shock? Pain? I didn't have time to quiz him, for he quickly slumped in his seat, his eyes closed in a state of semi-consciousness. I screwed the cap back onto the ampule and returned it and the syringe to the case, which I pocketed before taking up the reins and issuing a loud, hopeful, "Giddup!" to the horses.

They obeyed, whether out of a misplaced sense of loyalty or blind fear, and soon I was racing along the ledge of a dizzying drop-off, en route to Castle Lebenmort. Its window eyes and battlement brow watched over my approach, as a father would who expected his young gentleman son to arrive at any moment for a visit, or his young daughter's suitor.

In due course I arrived at my destination.

After urging the team through the open gate of the castle

wall, I pulled them to a stop not far from the interior entrance and disembarked. Kreutz was surprisingly heavy for his size, but I managed to drape him over my shoulder and carry him to the castle entrance. There I deposited him unceremoniously and slammed a brass knocker—an angel with its head thrown back and its eyes closed—against one of the twin oaken doors. Only then did I allow my gaze to wander up past the huge arched doorway and scale the great gray walls to assess the enormousness of the castle itself. It was everywhere, its own mountain atop a mountain. Higher still, a thin strip of cloud sliced the moon in half. I nearly jumped out of my boots when one of the doors lurched inward with the screech of heavy wood scraping across stone.

The figure who stood before me in the entryway was close to seven feet tall. His brown hair curled at the shoulders, hints of white glinting in it here and there. A mustache, similarly salted, ran down each side of his mouth. His dress was plain but tidy.

"Yes?" He asked in a sonorous baritone, glancing at Kreutz's limp body.

"Dr. Lebenmort, I presume?"

He only stared more intently.

"My name is Arthur Hemming, sir. *Dr.* Arthur Hemming. You'll remember our correspondence concerning—"

"What is this? Why have you come? And what's the matter with him?" Stiff-backed, he shook a long, bony finger in Kreutz's direction.

"He'll be fine. I can explain everything, I assure you. I wish our introduction could have been more dignified, but if you'll just let me in …"

"And Kreutz?"

"Him too. I'll carry him."

"Very well." His posture slackened somewhat. "I suppose I can't leave my henchman and my fondest admirer on the doorstep to catch their death, now can I?"

I might have laughed, but the doctor beat me to it, and if there's a soul alive who could have returned his joyless, guttural laughter, I like to think I've never met the lunatic. It was the laughter of a man very unused to the activity.

* * *

Dinner was cold sausages and thin soup, elevated some by the Italian vino with which we washed it down. Kreutz lay sprawled across a sofa to one side of the dining hall, while the doctor and I dined across from each other, a candelabra blazing between us on a long table.

"I'm afraid you've caught me unprepared for company," Dr. Lebenmort said. "With a little notice I could have readied a room for you and—"

"Nonsense, doctor. I require very little. In fact, I offer my assistance, and if it isn't wanted, you need not put up with me for an hour longer."

He silently stirred his soup, so I went on.

"Your man there, Kreutz, has killed someone in the woods." I took a nonchalant spoonful of soup. "He was deeply concerned about what your reaction might be, as you had only wanted him to knock the man unconscious."

Again I gave my host a chance to have his say, but he only stared into his bowl and continued to stir, happy to give me plenty of rope with which to hang myself. I obliged, as is my nature.

"Might I suppose that this violence has something to do with your ... metaphysical experiments?"

Now he set his spoon down and looked me in the eye. I likewise returned my spoon to the table.

"You understand a great deal," said the doctor, "but you don't see the whole picture. You have no idea how far I've come since my last correspondence with you. Bungling of this nature could ruin everything at this late date. I should rip the scoundrel's throat out while he sleeps!"

"But then he'd be of no use to you," I quickly put in.

"Oh, there are other servants to be had. He's not indispensable."

"I don't mean as a manservant. I mean as a conduit."

"Eh? Oh! You mean ... Well ..."

"Think about it, Dr. Lebenmort. It's perfect. I may need to be brought up to speed on the progress of your experiments, but I can't imagine that the crux of your intentions has changed. You wish to follow someone—a *dying* someone—into the next reality. But that someone has to die at just the right time and at just the right pace. You can't leave that kind of precision to the fumblings of a man like Kreutz. And unless you've made significant progress on ascertaining whether a man's soul is destined for heaven or hell, he's as good a conduit for your purposes as any man on earth."

After a thoughtful pause, Dr. Lebenmort replied, "You've not only studied the letters I sent you; you've laid your hands on some of my published papers. Papers I regret ever *having* published, by and large. I have not made much headway in discerning the fate of a man's soul, you're right. But it's the only variable that still causes me concern, and I can't wait around forever for an answer that may never come. I've decided to take my chances. I'll arrive, whether at the pearly gates or the vestibule of hell, as a visitor, a tourist. It will be a round trip, after all—and short lived. It's bound to work this time. I know it is."

"Then there's no reason to wait another instant," I said, standing excitedly. "Show me your laboratory, doctor."

"There remains the matter of timing the death, of course."

"Do you suppose I've come to you unprepared? How do you think Kreutz came to be in the state you see him in? An agent of my own making courses through his veins. It works similarly to morphine, but it's much stronger and more easily controlled. He's putty in my hands while under its influence. His moment of expiration is utterly bound to my will. With access to your laboratory, I can easily make more of the stuff."

"By God, maybe you're right, Hemming. Perhaps it *is* time

at last." Dr. Lebenmort also stood, ostensibly gazing upward at the high ceiling of the castle dining room, but he was clearly looking with his mind's eye at some distant, hopeful point of revelation and discovery. He wore an agitated look of bewildered delight. It was a look of madness, in fact, but even as I recognized it for what it was, my enthusiasm for the venture grew. Such is the effect of the unknown on the heart of a scientist.

I felt honored to be in the presence of the great Dr. Lebenmort, so near to his hour of victory, but I was also proud that my own expertise in the field of psychiatry had brought me to such a promontory. It was an earned honor, in my estimation.

"There is the matter of this man who Kreutz killed in the woods," Lebenmort said, hell-bent on finding a loophole in all of this optimism. "That could give us some trouble."

"I don't think so. The wolves will take care of him by and by, and to give Kreutz his due, it wasn't a completely careless operation, aside from his overlooking my presence at first. He'd staged a bogus carriage accident as a trap. Could have saved himself the trouble with us, since we were already on foot, but that's beside the point. To anyone coming upon the scene, it will look as though Günther's wagon hit a tree root and he fell from the carriage, suffering a fatal blow to the head. The horses freed themselves and ran to safety."

"Günther, you say? The farmer? He'll be missed."

"Yes, and people know he was showing me the way to your castle, but lies can be told. What people see with their own eyes is almost impossible to overturn. Despite the illogic of it, they will contend that Günther suffered a terrible accident and I made it the rest of the way on my own. Maybe he and I hired the carriage. Maybe he found it after we'd parted company. You and I can work out the details and agree upon a story. The weapon is out there somewhere, too, but what of it? It's easily recovered and dealt with."

"You're a convincing speaker, Dr. Hemming. A very convincing speaker."

"What do you say?"

"I say … allow me to show you to my laboratory."

I grinned and lifted my glass in a silent toast before draining it. He returned the gesture, and I eagerly followed him out of the room.

We passed through an immense library with only the doctor's taper for a guiding light. On any other occasion I would have yearned for a tour of that room as well, but the situation being what it was, all my attention was focused on the matter of witnessing a successful trip to, and back from, the great unknown.

Beyond the library, a short study ended in a staircase, which we carefully descended. And then we stood in what at first I took to be the infamous doctor's laboratory, but as he crept about, lighting candle after candle, I soon realized that this must have been little more than a room used to conceal the truth of what really went on at Castle Lebenmort. I could use it to produce more of my injectant, perhaps, but surely it wasn't the space he used to conduct his experiments in metaphysics.

Lebenmort suddenly stopped lighting candles and spun around to face me.

"Kreutz!" he fairly shouted.

"He'll be out for a good while yet. Not to worry. Lead on, sir."

"Oh, very good. Yes, yes. Of course. Come along here."

He led me past the main scientific apparatus of the room to a row of shelves along the rear wall. Jars of things, mostly. Some arcane tomes lying on their sides. Tools, loose handwritten pages, shipping crates. He laid his hand on a large glass jar with a specimen of tissue floating within and slid it to one side. An entire section of shelves clicked free and he pulled it wide to reveal a passageway. He lit first one wall-mounted torch, then another, and continued in this fashion as I followed him ever deeper into the bowels of the castle.

At last we came to a door that only could have led to one place. It opened onto the most splendid sight my eyes have ever seen: the pulsating heart of Castle Doom.

The main laboratory was grand, both in scale and conception. Gaslight torches blazed from all corners as machinery hummed along throughout practically every inch of the place. Cables, hoses and tubes connected unlikely mechanisms to one another, and great iron pipes spanned the room near the vaulted ceiling. Some even ran vertically up *into* the ceiling, presumably expelling a kind of exhaust into the atmosphere without. Although we looked down into the main area from the landing we occupied, the space between us and the ceiling was greater still.

"Well," said the doctor, unable to conceal his pride, "what do you think?"

"Words defy me," I said, and my awe was genuine. "This ... Well, again, this is simply beyond words. I knew the work you were engaged in must require space and great mechanical achievement, but this ..."

"Come, let's have a closer look."

Much of what my gaze met with on our descent was beyond my immediate understanding, but there were two stations across the chamber whose purpose couldn't have been more obvious. Surely those two vertical glass tubes, with their wooden backs where they met the wall, were the encasements used for the actual experiments. A shudder snaked through me. Suddenly it all felt very real.

"There will be plenty of time to go over everything," Dr. Lebenmort went on as he conducted me through the maze of equipment, "but there are several key components to all this wizardry that you really should be made aware of straightaway, if you truly are committed to helping me with my research."

"Oh, I'm committed," I replied. "You may definitely rely on me."

"Very well. This," he said, gesturing toward a large metal drum that sat in a dark corner, "is the ionic transference inducer. It is the key to the entire operation. Without it, there is no contact made between my subject and me. And without that contact, I have no hope of piggybacking into the afterlife as my subject sheds his mortal coil."

"I understand."

"Yes, perhaps. Well, at any rate, this over here is the galvanic inhibitor."

This contraption—a low-profile metal cube with dials and switches all over its surface—sat on the opposite side of the tubular glass enclosures.

"Its primary function is to ensure that the transference does not exceed acceptable levels. See, an exact balance must be met. The current running between our subject and myself will be part electricity, part life force. It needs to be sufficient to allow my crossing over with the subject, yet not so strong as to bring about my actual demise. The inducer steadily ratchets up the current; the inhibitor keeps it in check. Now, both are controlled by the conversion switch."

"Conversion switch?"

"Ah, yes. In good time. Back this way, if you will. These glass tubes, of course, are the enclosures my subject and I step into for the procedure. After strapping us in and locking the enclosures, you will lower the head pieces into place."

Here he demonstrated by sliding a brass knob down the length of a faceplate in the stone wall. The dome-shaped metal head piece in the left tube descended to where a man's head would be. He slid an adjacent knob, and the head piece in the tube on the right was similarly lowered into place.

"Astonishing."

"Well, it's not advisable to handle the head pieces directly. They seem to retain a bit of residual charge. They're partially insulated on the inside, you see, so no current travels to the subject until it's forced through the gaps in the insulation. That's where the conversion switch comes in." He gestured to a long lever set into the floor between the tubes. "Once the headgear is in place, it's time to throw the switch. That begins the process. Now, the only other piece of equipment I'd like to make sure you're aware of right away is this panel over here." A flat metal sheet adorned with gauges, levers, and bulbs was set into the wall nearby. "This tells you what the inducer and the inhibitor are up to. When this bulb begins flashing red, you have exactly one minute to terminate our subject and cut the switch. Any longer than that and the galvanic inhibitor will grow increasingly unstable, putting me at risk for a permanent journey. Besides, once the subject is deceased, my own life force will drain much more rapidly. I do need *some* current, or life force, to ride back on, but not nearly as much as I do going out. So cut that switch as soon as Kreutz is dead! Now, if he were to die *before* the bulb begins to flash—"

"There wouldn't be enough current to effect the send-off in the first place."

"Precisely. And this bulb over here needs to be solid green from the time you throw the conversion switch. That tells you that the inhibitor is functioning properly and will give me that full minute from the time the red bulb begins to flash. If you see so much as a flicker of the green bulb before the red bulb starts up, the current needs to be switched off immediately."

"Why, it's as dangerous as it is elaborate. How do you power all of this?"

"With a very large battery cell that collects and stores energy from the lightning storms we see with such regularity in these parts. You'll see it in due course. Now, what about Kreutz? Surely he needs tending to by now."

"Yes, of course. Let's see to him."

* * *

Kreutz was in an almost constant state of torpor from that day forward, and when he wasn't, he yearned for an injection so badly that he was equally pliable. Not only was I able to reproduce my narcotic agent in the ante-laboratory that Dr. Lebenmort gave me unfettered access to, but I greatly refined it. During that time, Lebenmort had a number of calculations to perform, based on data from his last attempted journey, as well as mechanical maintenance to tend to. I helped him with some of his work, but we left each other alone a good deal.

I admired Lebenmort. It was impossible not to. He had an extraordinary mind in many ways, but I came to see that he limited his vision unnecessarily. Where he saw only the potential for one great step forward in mankind's understanding of what awaits us in death, I began to sense that it might be possible to *alter* the course of our travels after we pass on.

I was careful never to share this idea with the doctor, of course.

Weeks passed, owing to his irritating perfectionism, but at last the day arrived. Finally I would witness what I had imagined a thousand times, or at least a full-fledged attempt would be made.

"Now, you're sure you have the proper dosage in the syringe?" the doctor wanted to know.

I did. Of course I did. He had helped me run an intravenous line into the glass enclosure that Kreutz now occupied. I would be able to deliver the fatal injection within seconds of observing the flashing red bulb on the wall panel.

"What about you, doctor?" I asked in return. "Are you sure you're prepared for the possibility that Kreutz's soul is bound for the pit rather than paradise?"

I don't think I smiled as I said it, but I smile now. Surely Kreutz, the murdering lackey, was as damned as ever a man could be, and that meant the good doctor was in for one h—l of a ride.

"What choice do we have? We must focus on the scientific value of the endeavor, and that is the same regardless of his destination. I am prepared."

Maybe he was, but he certainly wasn't prepared for what awaited him upon his return.

Everything came together like a dream. I suppose some of the credit does have to go to Dr. Lebenmort and his obsessive attention to minutiae. He helped me prop Kreutz up against the board at the back of his glass tube and strap him in. I quickly connected the intravenous tubing at both ends as the doctor entered his own enclosure and began strapping himself in. I helped him finish when I was through with Kreutz and then closed the curved glass door on each encasement, locking them both tight. Down came the headgear, and we were ready to commence.

My only moment of hesitation came when my hand touched the lever of the conversion switch. I glanced over at the doctor, whose head was turned so he could also see me. The connection between us was stronger than I had realized. His trust in me was complete, though he *was* afraid. I could see it in his wide, unblinking eyes. He smiled faintly and turned his head away again. I stared at the lever for a few seconds, gritted my teeth, and gave it a tug with all my strength.

Sounds erupted all over the room, some small, others echoing in the cavernous laboratory. Lights began to blink. Dials whirred in response to the call of the energy driving the place.

Remembering the indicator panel, I rushed to the wall and kept watch over the steady glow of the green bulb. I have no idea how many minutes passed, but it felt like forever before the small red bulb took up its rhythmic pulse. My heart knocked against my chest as I rushed over to Kreutz and plunged the lethal dose of poison into his bloodstream. The enclosures had to remain closed during the process, but there was a small mirror attached to Kreutz's head piece, positioned directly in front of his mouth. By pressing my back against the wall I was able to peer over his shoulder and see whether his breath was fogging the mirror. For several seconds it was, at slowing intervals. Then, it was not. I waited a moment longer, wanting to be absolutely sure.

Kreutz was dead.

Just like Günther.

And that made me a murderer at last. For a moment it was as if the possibility of my own damnation hadn't crossed my mind until then—but of course it had, many times.

I reached for the conversion switch.

Jammed.

"No, damn it!"

Then I remembered the lock release on the handle. Lebenmort had reminded me repeatedly. I flipped it, and the lever slid easily back to the off position. The room quieted, except for the rapid singing of my pulse in my ears. It would have been easy enough to pass out if I wasn't careful.

But I had to keep moving. This wasn't over yet.

I unlocked Dr. Lebenmort's glass tube and threw open the door. He hadn't returned, but he would soon. His eyes wandered back and forth behind closed lids. His slack facial expression held no clue as to the nature of the experience he was having. Digging into my waistcoat pocket—the one opposite where I kept the metal syringe case—I produced another item I'd managed to keep hidden from the highwaymen outside of Teufelsgarten: a gold watch my father had given me as a gift before sending me off to medical school.

He would have demanded its return if he'd known what I was about to use it for.

Lebenmort's eyelids fluttered open, and the first thing his eyes locked onto was my watch as it swung before him at the end of its chain.

"You're very tired, Dr. Lebenmort," I said in the most soothing voice I could manage under the circumstances. "So very tired after your travels. All you want to do is sleep. You're falling backwards now. Falling ... falling."

His eyes never left the watch.

"You would have hit the ground by now, but there is no ground. You are floating in blackness, so you continue to fall. Spiraling. Tumbling. Down, down, down. Can you hear me?"

"I ... hear you."

"Good. You've been on a journey. When I count to three, I want you to wake from this trance and remember that journey in all of its particulars. But I also want you to be aware of something else. You have returned with an infestation. There are tiny, biting demons, hundreds of them, crawling throughout your body, just under your skin. They want out, Dr. Lebenmort, but they can't find the way. I can help you. I can make them retreat. Whenever you hear me say 'retreat,' you'll feel relief as the horde does in fact withdraw deeper inside of you, though you will know that they are only waiting for their next opportunity to dig and chew their way to the surface in search of an exit. I will be your only source of comfort whenever that happens.

"One. Two. Three."

His eyes flashed open and I quickly pocketed the watch.

"*Hemming!*"

I watched as he struggled against his restraints, hands balled into fists, chest heaving.

"Shall I undo the straps, doctor?"

"*Oh, my God!*" he screamed.

"Retreat!" I hollered back, and little by little his rigid body relaxed.

* * *

And as easy as that, the castle became mine. It was a sad business, the doctor going out of his mind as he did. The villagers of Teufelsgarten pretended to mourn the passing of his quiet rule over the mountain, but in truth, they were—to a man, woman, and child—elated that Castle Doom had a new master.

That is, until whispers concerning my own mad experiments began to circulate ... and the odd traveler to Teufelsgarten started vanishing into the mountain mists, never long after arriving. The fewer attachments that are allowed to take hold, after all, the better. The practice of relying on visitors for my experimentation has had the added benefit of lulling the locals into a feeling of relative safety from harm, which has kept me in their good graces, more or less. Perhaps it is only fear.

Now, however, even *my* reign at Castle Lebenmort has

reached the end of its rope, for I am prepared at last to engage in one final experiment. I'm afraid that Dr. Lebenmort will have to pay the ultimate price, but if he were still of sound mind I'm sure he'd throw his full support behind my attempt to guide my posthumous destiny to a place in the clouds rather than to the lake of fire. Besides, he'll have good company: my own. For my experiment requires the death of not just one participant, but both. I expect my soul to ricochet, if you like, off the doctor's departing spirit, sending him in one direction and me in another. The operating of the laboratory equipment will be left to Katharina, who has been an extraordinary helpmate these long, arduous months of research and dry runs, each of which has necessitated the sacrificing of a single subject. Thanks to those trials, and the numerous papers left behind by the doctor, I feel confident in my conclusions now. I've also spent countless hours interviewing Dr. Lebenmort about his brief experience on the other side. Some of those interviews have been conducted under hypnosis. Many have not. All have been revelatory.

So, call this my confession if you like. No one will ever read the words I've laid down here as long as I still draw breath. Presently I will lock these pages away in a chest, along with my copious notes and diagrams. I vow to carry the key to that chest about my neck until the end of my days—an end that creeps ever nearer. But then, isn't that true for us all? Katharina will likely discover the chest before long, and then she'll know why I wear this key.

What began as an insane quest to conquer the afterlife and claim the castle as my own has continued out of love and admiration for Katharina. If I can know that she and I will share the same eternal fate, every strain on my living soul will have been worth it. *Her* place among the angels is guaranteed, of course. If someone is reading this now, I hope that I've won the same prize for myself.

Please don't be in any hurry to join me, Katharina. Live a full, rich life. We'll have all the time we could possibly hope for when you arrive in my arms again.

A DREAM COME TRUE

"No, I said they *were* showing me dreams I'd already had." Jimmy pushed up the sleeves of his sweatshirt, the drawstrings for the hood coiled on his chest like serpents. Cool Pacific air tousled his hair as he watched Seattle recede from the upper deck of the ferry. "That's all changed now, which is why I wanted to meet."

"Why not before?" Benjamin asked. They both gripped the green-painted handrail and gazed across the glimmering bay, avoiding eye contact.

"It was different when the videos were of past dreams. Creepy as hell at first, but I started getting used to it, you know? I got to thinking maybe I should keep to myself, figure out a way to work an advantage from it."

"Like what, getting it to work for other people?"

"Yeah, maybe. I don't know. I didn't get that far …"

"Before the videos started showing you what you're *about* to dream instead of what you *have* dreamed."

"Exactly, and it's got me spooked." He turned to Benjamin. "Like *seriously* spooked. I wake up in the morning and there's a new video on my phone, as if I took it myself, or the damn thing was trading signals with my brain while I slept."

"And whatever's in the video—"

"Is what I dream that night."

"You said you'd show me one of these masterpieces."

Jimmy nodded. "But not here. That's why we're spending the weekend on Bainbridge Island, away from prying eyes."

"And here I thought we were finally going to consummate

our relationship," Benjamin said with a smile.

Jimmy laughed. "I thought I didn't have to be gay to be your friend."

"Don't flatter yourself. You're not my type."

"Not even a little?" Jimmy put on a hurt expression.

"Too hairy and not enough meat on your bones, sorry."

Jimmy fell silent and Benjamin let him have the moment. "I think they're getting weirder," he said at last.

"What are?" Benjamin asked.

"The videos." A pause. "The dreams."

* * *

The cabin Jimmy had rented lay hidden in a dense copse of evergreens, with barely enough of a clearing at the front for Benjamin to park his Acura. Jimmy had wanted privacy and he'd found it.

"You sure you're not trying to get into my pants?" Benjamin joked as he stepped out of the car and shouldered his pack. "It's awfully romantic."

"I just want us to be able to find the headspace to think this through. You probably think I'm playing you, or not thinking rationally, but wait until you see."

"That brings us close to the problem, don't you think?"

"I don't follow." Jimmy climbed the steps to the front door of the cabin and fished the key out of his pocket.

"These videos. They're showing you the future, yeah? How am I supposed to verify that you're actually dreaming what's in them?"

"You'll have complete control of my phone." He tossed it to Benjamin and led the way inside. "You'll have to take me at my word about tonight's dream, but tomorrow morning only you will see the next video. I'll tell you what I dream tomorrow night. Then you'll know. There's also the quality of the videos. We're talking works of cinematic production value here. They couldn't possibly be shot raw. Like I said, you'll see."

* * *

They threw together a supper of canned chicken-noodle soup and sourdough toast, then Jimmy went off to bed, hoping he would dream better if he was well rested. But you already know what you're going to dream, Benjamin had challenged. Maybe there's a way to trick fate, Jimmy had countered.

Left to the six pack of Sam Adams he'd brought along for companionship, Benjamin made a nest of blankets for himself on a rustic couch and began flipping through the videos on Jimmy's phone. Jimmy used a lock-screen code, but he'd given Benjamin the sequence of numbers. The thumbnails alone claimed Benjamin's attention. He could see what Jimmy had meant about production value. One from a week-and-a-half ago showed a gorgeous woman holding a sword of flame as doves swooped and dived all around her. "Heteros," he muttered with a roll of his eyes.

He wasn't sure when the videos had changed from descriptive to predictive, but he assumed it had been recent. Scrolling past thumbnails of bizarre facial expressions, alien landscapes, and indistinct chaos, he landed on one with a thumbnail image that was solid white.

He tapped play.

The white began to ripple. Cloth in the wind, hanging to dry? No, as the camera zoomed out, it became apparent that the cloth was lying over something and he was being given an aerial view. The zoom stopped, and so did the ripples. With a shriek of synthesizer chords played in quick succession, a face pressed upward from the center of the cloth, its mouth a scream, its eyes sunken, its cheeks gaunt. Fabric clung wetly to the features, hugging every line and depression. There could be no mistaking Jimmy's exaggerated countenance.

As the camera resumed its slow outward zoom, Benjamin

could see an end to the cloth at last. A continuous edge soon framed the white, which was rippling once again. Eventually, patio furniture gave away the scene: a swimming pool. But that meant the version of Jimmy that was pressing against the fabric was enormous, his facial impression taking up most of the pool's surface area. Jimmy's right hand shot up to press against the cloth (a single chord on the synthesizer), then his left (an arpeggio like shattering glass).

Jimmy was trapped, drowning under a massive cloth that perfectly covered the water of the pool and nothing else.

But drowning was not in the cards for Benjamin's friend. Five large men wearing trunks in an assortment of bright colors rushed to the poolside and quickly peeled the cloth away from Jimmy's trapped form. They balled it up in a corner of the pool area and ran back in the direction they'd come from.

Jimmy, now of normal size, paddled his way to the edge and looked after his saviors. "Come back!" he pleaded. "I didn't get to thank you."

Not a gay bone in his body is how Jimmy had described himself on more than one occasion. Maybe with him it was in the muscles, then. Benjamin smirked at the thought.

Still, pretty scary dream. Had Jimmy said they were getting worse? Not a hopeful scenario.

Two beers in, Benjamin let himself collapse on the sofa and drift off to sleep.

❊ ❊ ❊

He woke at four-fourteen a.m., according to his phone when he pulled it from his pants pocket because it was pressing into his leg. As he reached out to set it next to Jimmy's phone, notification of a new video appeared. He didn't remember turning on notifications for that. He thumb-printed himself into his phone, quickly tapped his way to the videos folder, and sat up. The last video he had taken was a narrated point-of-view clip of him on a hike through Seward Park, but now the thumbnail showing the russet trunk of a madrone no longer occupied the last slot. From a thumbnail in the space after it, Benjamin was greeted by a single staring eyeball.

He got up to fix himself a cup of instant coffee, which he took back with him to the sofa. His phone seemed to call out to him from where it lay on the coffee table, almost like a holy relic he was afraid of disturbing but knew he had to.

This already felt like proof that something inexplicable was afoot, and it tightened his stomach. The final verdict was within his power to extract, of course. All he had to do was watch the video. It probably had nothing to do with Jimmy's situation. Only a coincidence. Someone had sent him a video. Somehow.

He tapped the video open and settled back to see what he had.

* * *

It didn't begin with the close-up of the eye in the thumbnail. A woman in a scarlet evening gown descended a cliff in high heels, facing forward as if navigating a simple staircase. It was all Benjamin needed to see. He flung the phone down, and, though it continued to play, he had no need to watch it through. He knew the woman would make it halfway down the cliff before leaping into the dusky air, her gown transforming into diaphanous wings that would carry her out over a large body of tumultuous water. Knew that he would meet up with her in mid-flight and take her hand in his as the salt scent of the water reached him. Knew also that when she turned to him with a warm smile he would recognize her as the mother who had left him when he was seven years old.

He knew these things because he had dreamed them the night before.

"I'm sorry," Jimmy said from behind the couch.

Benjamin twirled his head around, startled.

"What the hell's going on?" he asked.

Jimmy stepped around to face him. "I couldn't take it anymore. The dreams … They were getting—so bad. Horrible things. I did such horrible things in some of them."

"I don't understand. Is it over now? My dream from last night is on my phone."

Jimmy sat down beside him.

"I started to learn from some of the recent dreams, how to transfer this burden to someone else."

"What? And you chose me?"

"Not to hurt you. Please believe that. It needed to be someone I have a strong connection with. Besides, I thought maybe we can pass it back and forth when it gets to be too much. Just until we figure out how to make it end for good."

"I don't fucking believe this."

"Well, it's true. So much is true. You'll learn the truth now, too. Our dreams … They matter, as much as reality, maybe more. They're no less real, actually. In order to pass this on, my dreams had to connect up with so-called reality. You know, intersect. Part of making sure that happened was bringing you here."

"Do you realize how—"

"I can't explain it all. You wouldn't understand even if I could. The knowledge you crave is in the dreams, and understanding requires patience."

"This is some weird shit, Jimmy."

"Yup, scary, too. That's another reason we're in the middle of nowhere. Out here you can be as afraid as you want. Scream your soul to ribbons. Go out back and chop wood until you run out of sweat. But I'll be here to talk you through the early stages. You'll have a much better idea of what to expect than I did."

"So I'm supposed to go to sleep tonight as if all is right with the world? I won't be able to sleep for a week."

"You'll sleep fine, and you're many nights from the change …"

"Some comfort."

"Things will look better in the morning. It's not a death sentence."

"You should have seen your face on the ferry ride over. Looked like death would have been a relief."

❋ ❋ ❋

Jimmy had wanted to tell Benjamin that it would eventually feel as though death was the only escape from the nightmares, but it would have been unnecessarily cruel. There was no reason to leave his friend in a panic. Besides, it was easier to effect his own escape from the island with Benjamin sleeping soundly in the cabin, now that he had finally drifted off again.

Piloting his uncle's motorboat toward the northern edge of the Seattle waterfront, Jimmy regretted having lied. There had been some truth in his vague description of how his dreams had shown a way to be free of the curse, but the transference of the bizarre phenomenon had never been meant as a temporary thing that could be passed back and forth at will. Jimmy had intended to be free of the freaky videos—and dreams —permanently. Besides, there were intimations that there was another stage to the process, when the dreams would start breaking through into reality, and Jimmy wanted no part of that shit.

The most important thing was to distance himself from Benjamin. His friend would rise in a rage in a few hours, when he discovered that Jimmy had taken a powder. He would focus that rage on laying the curse back on its rightful owner, which would be harder to do the more miles there were between them.

As a secondary precaution Jimmy would be forcing himself to go through life without the aid of smartphones and tablet computers, at a minimum. He still wasn't sure how magic had found its way into the digital veins of such devices, but he suspected it would make hay with the speed afforded by their manmade capillaries and robotically engineered neurons.

Whatever the case, he was done providing the biological Wi-Fi. He proved it to himself by letting his phone slip noiselessly from his hand into the dark blade of water that lay all around.

He fully intended to research what had happened to him, whether or not any meaningful findings were to come in time to save Benjamin from madness. Maybe this was a virus he could wipe from the map of human experience, now that he had liberated himself from its clutches, but he would have to make do with lower technology than what was found in the pockets of countless unsuspecting users the world over.

As for Benjamin's chances of ridding himself of the dream-plague by passing it on to yet another conduit ... Well, good luck to him. Jimmy wouldn't have laid money on it. It had taken every inch of knowledge he could put his hands on to develop the meditative skills necessary for accomplishing the transfer. Benjamin had many endearing qualities, but patience and mindfulness were not among them. Maybe he'd be better off giving up *his* phone cold turkey, but that might prove to be no easier in the end. Jimmy had never known anyone more glued to a device than Benjamin was to his phone.

Out of earshot, he throttled up the outboard motor and closed the remaining distance from shore.

HIS BLADE SO KEEN

Few stars were shining by the time Reichert reached Elliott Square Park, which was more of a plaza in ruins than what people long ago would have called a park. A strip of deepest blue shrank from the eastern skyline—what he could see of it through the clutter of business and residential towers—leaving a wake of honest-to-God morning sunlight. The city was a depressing pit, dead in more ways than he could count, and moribund wherever its heart still beat at all. But it hadn't eclipsed nature yet, despite its constant efforts. The sun still rose, to the pleasure of those few like him, if there *were* any like him anymore. And now his favorite tree in the city inched into view. It was the last specimen of flora he would encounter before arriving home, and close to being the last tree in the entire downtown area. It was almost possible to look upon all of this decay as if he hadn't brought it on himself.

He shifted a brown paper bag and its contents from one hand to the other and stopped to consider the magnificent Lombardy poplar's beauty. A light midwinter wind stirred its many leafless boughs, which in turn struck a note of warning, the way they brushed at the sky. As if to punctuate the message, a murder of crows erupted from their nighttime roost, putting them on a course that led directly between Reichert and the tree. They cackled to each other as they flew. "Look at the foolish man," was his translation of one bird's scolding. "I wonder if he's the goddamn sonofabitch who set the end of the world in motion," sang another, as he imagined it. "Should have dropped a shit on him if he is," cawed yet another. "At least he looks suitably recalcitrant," chimed the vociferous bringer up of the rear.

The best part of his walk, he knew, was over. The rest of the way he would see nothing but uniformly neglected storefronts and workers with vapid grins going through the motions of make-believe purpose. He would see conveyances, all the same muted brown color, driven by professionals with no greater ambition. But he would hear no hollering voices, no cat calls or arguments. There would be no sirens, even if emergent care was required in the vicinity. Such alarming measures had been ruled unnecessary some time ago.

All because of a discovery he himself had made, almost singlehandedly, when he was a biomech professor at Northern. It didn't merely seem like a lifetime ago; it seemed like someone else's life altogether.

Thank the gods for twenty-four-hour liquor dens, he thought. Surely their days were numbered.

The tower he lived in approached out of the urban gloom. Almost no sky was allowed admittance into this region of packed-together steel and concrete. A darkness hung there at all hours of the day, no matter how high and bright the sun, and a perpetual wind snaked its way through the architectural canyon.

The lobby was tidy and neat but devoid of ornament. Aesthetics was one of the first human values to fall away in the age of the Tantalus implant. No one gave a single God damn how things looked anymore. It wasn't the most egregious loss the world had suffered, but it was a ubiquitous reminder of the state of things.

His elevator crawled to the fifty-seventh floor, where it dislodged him like a bit of indigestible beef. He was always glad to be out of the contraption. If the last worker to have performed maintenance on the car or any part of the shaft had been recently juiced, a sense of urgency and ethics may have been supplanted by a feeling that however poor the job, the earth would go on spinning. A dumb smile was almost sure to follow.

Reichert made a sound of disgust and shook his head as he unlocked the door to his unit. A small mirror greeted him from the entryway wall. He paused to take in his wizened features, only partially hidden by a gray beard and untamed locks. The man who stared back at him was almost used up. If he were to pass him on the street he'd give him six months to live, and wouldn't be surprised if the cause of death turned out to be suicide. But Reichert wasn't ready to go quite yet. While there was a chance of undoing some of the damage he had done, he would take it. As long as there was hope, no matter how tattered and evasive, he would pursue it. When that ran out … Well, who could predict the future?

After depositing his parcel on a scrap of available countertop and setting a kettle of water to boil in the tiny kitchenette, he hung his overcoat in the closet and took a seat in his favorite chair. He retrieved the book he was reading from a basket on the floor: *A Brief History of the New United States of America*. He didn't know the author—one Edna H. Gaugin, Ph.D.—but she seemed to have her facts in place. The writing was even pretty good, approaching passionate in places. Very unusual in a book written within the last thirty years. The index cited seventeen instances of his name, several of them page ranges. He was almost halfway through the book but had only reached two references in the actual text. Surely there were many unpleasant reminders in coming chapters of his role in the world's decline. It was a little like watching a man come up behind someone with an axe. On the one hand, you didn't want to watch and do nothing while a stranger suffered an act of horrible violence, but on the other, you didn't want to be deprived of the spectacle, either. In Reichert's case, he was the potential victim, and it was part of his penance to keep his eyes trained on the viciousness to come.

Besides, it was amazing that books existed at all anymore. Beggars couldn't be choosers.

Two sounds claimed his attention simultaneously before he could dive into the next chapter. The kettle whistled its preparedness from the stove and the door buzzer squawked to announce a visitor. They were both warnings, Reichert realized, hauling himself out of the chair to tend to his tea before answering the buzzer. The kettle's desperate note warned of heat, the buzzer of the unpredictability of strangers, and how some paths led into the woods but not back out again. Suddenly the Lombardy poplar filled his mind's eye, its branches reaching, bending, scratching at the sky.

Omens everywhere, he thought. *Omens furtive and omens bold.*

Leaving his tea to steep in a tin mug he'd rescued from a park bench years ago, he went to the door and pressed the intercom button.

"Reichert," he said with a rusty voice, then let go so he could hear the response.

"Ah, hello," came a scratchy reply through the dozens of feet of old wiring that led from the main entrance to where Reichert stood. "Dr. Lander, at your service, sir."

"Come." Reichert held a small switch in place long enough to allow the man time to enter the building.

He made sure the door to his unit was unlocked before retrieving his tea from the kitchenette and retiring to the chair once more. The tea was brackish and pungent, flavor being another casualty in the war on discomfort. Still, he always left the bag in, since he sipped the warm liquid mostly for the caffeine, which almost no one had an appetite for anymore.

A triplet of raps came at the door.

"Enter."

In walked a narrow, bald man not many years Reichert's junior. Even from across the room Reichert could see that he wore spectacles with incredibly thick lenses, perfectly round. He was attired all in black.

"So, I meet the famous Professor Reichert at last," Dr. Lander said.

"*Infamous* is more like it." Reichert stood and approached the man. "Please, come in."

They shook hands and Reichert hung Lander's coat next to his in the closet.

"Have a seat." He gestured to a stiff green chair across from his more padded recliner. "Can I get you something to drink?"

"No, sir. I'm okay. Thank you." Lander took a seat and brushed some creases out of his slacks.

"Your prerogative. I think I'm ready for something a little stronger myself." Reichert picked up his tin cup and walked it to the kitchenette, where he emptied it into the sink and removed a bottle of golden liquid from the paper bag on the counter. When he returned he carried the bottle in one hand and his soon-to-be repurposed mug in the other. Setting them both down on a small table next to his chair, he sat with his guest at last.

"I'm afraid it's a little unclear why you sent for me, Dr. Reichert."

"My apologies for being vague. It's just that there's so much I want to discuss. I wouldn't have known where to begin in a note or over the phone."

"What's on your mind, then?"

Reichert opened the bottle, poured himself a good two-and-a-half fingers, and took a belt before responding.

"Science is a funny thing, Lander. We're like dogs on the scent, in a lot of ways. We'll dumbly chase any damn thing we set our sights on, no matter what field of weeds it leads us into. By the time we realize we're off course it's often too late. Then we try to come up with solutions to the problems we've created, or at least contributed to. The world becomes dependent on our work to an extent that goes beyond all reason."

"You shouldn't let such things bother you. Have you had your dosage checked recently? You know, you can do that at any center." Lander gestured toward the bottle. "You'll find you won't need that poison anymore, either. And you certainly don't have to take such elaborate measures to set up a house call."

"This isn't a house call, for God's sake."

"What, then?"

"I used to think that when I got old, maybe beautiful

women would smile at me more readily. I wasn't the type of young man who women smiled at much, you understand. Something about my constant focus on the work, I think. It gave me an unwelcoming look. Well, I've got them smiling now, and I wish I could erase every last goddamn grin. When everyone smiles, almost without pause, it loses all meaning. You're doing it now. Do you even realize?"

"Sir, you really need to be seen. Your levels must be out of whack."

"You're not getting it, are you? You're a doctor, for Christ's sake. I don't *have* a fucking implant. Has it become so rare? Surely there are others like me."

"No Tantalus implant? Who removed it for you?"

"I never had one put in."

"Why not?"

"Why? Because I like being human. I enjoy being motivated by a constant state of want, even when it hurts or creates challenges. With the implant, I designed a tool for numbing us to everything that makes life worth living."

"But your efforts have improved things enormously for humankind. Stress, depression, anxiety ... even pain. These are largely phenomena of a bygone era. You've brought calm to the entire world. Dr. Reichert, you've played a central role in bringing about world peace. The Tantalus implant has all but put an end to war. Surely you don't regret that."

"Ah, but there's still *some* suffering, isn't there. Isn't it true that you can remotely increase the surge of endorphins to the point of overdose? Aren't we essentially euthanizing our populace prematurely, instead of treating them?"

"It's true that we have seen a decline in the average lifespan. People are willing to put up with less suffering than they used to. It stands to reason. When they start to hurt, many get scared and want out. If anxiety and pain reach a certain level, it's beyond the capability of the implant to rectify the situation without ending the life of the patient."

"You asked me who removed my implant." Reichert took

another drink. "Is that done?"

"Oh yes. Some implants go bad and need replacing. And some people do change their minds, or want to go without one for a spell, though this is becoming less common as reliability improves. It's a simple procedure. I use the same tool as when I put them in, in fact."

"I assume it's some kind of painless injection by now …"

"I'm afraid not. It's still a bit primitive, actually, but we need to make sure the implant is deep and precisely situated. Someday I'm sure they'll be able to do it with monitors and pneumatic glide injectors, as is already the case with certain other procedures, but we're not there yet."

Reichert stood and went to the window. The view was claustrophobic and depressing, so he turned back to face the doctor.

"I want you to do something for me, Lander. Do you have the implement on you?"

"I do, of course. We all carry our blades with us, in case of an emergency of some kind."

"Good. This *is* an emergency of some kind. May I see it?"

"I suppose, but you really should schedule an appointment at the nearest implant center. There's no need—"

"Just let me see the damn thing."

Lander reached a long, bony hand into his sport coat and pulled out a slender wooden box. It opened on hinges along one side, and within, the implant blade rested on a molded felt bed. Reichert reached out a hand. Lander hesitated but finally gave up the case, still open. It was a beautiful instrument, gleaming even in the dingy light from Reichert's overhead fixture. The blade itself was at least as long as the brushed handle, with a slight curve, ending in a deadly point. It reminded Reichert of a miniature scythe. It didn't look like a tool of precision. There must have been much training involved in putting it to its proper use.

But today it had a less precise purpose, one that required no special training. Only fortitude and resolve. His unadulterated brain housed plenty of both. Yanking the knife from its indentation, he flung the case aside and took a step toward Lander, who rose immediately, and whose smile dimmed.

"What's this?" Lander asked.

"This is justice," Reichert replied.

And he slashed the blade across Lander's neck from left to right. Before the man could get a hand up to stanch the red flow, Reichert swept the blade back across in the other direction. So much blood, but he continued to slice. Cries issued from Lander's gaping mouth, but they grew indistinct as he fell to the carpet. Soon they were little more than wet gurgles. And still Reichert put the blade to its new purpose. Finally he stepped away and beheld the crimson fountain he'd created.

Blood and gore all over the floor, and me without a spoon, he thought, recalling a nonsense rhyme his mother used to say in her odder moments.

Feeling his gorge begin to rise, he went to the sink to clean his weapon. No, tool. He was no simple killer of men. He was a redeemer. A righter of wrongs. He had no idea how many Tantalus-certified surgeons there were in the world, but he already had a list of almost one hundred fifty of them. A daunting number for one man, but he would take out as many as he could get to. The message his work was about to send was as important as the work itself, and the complacency he'd helped to instill in the world would work in his favor as he toiled. Law enforcement was in a kind of semi-dormancy ever since the rise of the implant. In a world where would-be criminals could be dissuaded from doing harm with a remotely controlled adjustment of endorphin levels, and victims and prosecutors could be assuaged in the same manner, police work was quickly becoming an encyclopedia entry.

He smiled as he searched for the box he'd thrown so carelessly aside in his haste to begin his new calling, all but ignoring the seeping corpse that lay sprawling and limp on his living room floor.

The future was now, and it held terrific promise.

THE THING IN THE ROAD

"It was two beers," he said, tightening his grip on the steering wheel, "maybe three."

Kimberly had to know this was bullshit. Dale must have drained the better part of a sixer, not to mention the shot she'd watched him down, and those she hadn't witnessed.

It was almost completely dark now. The wind blew fall's rain-muted colors across the winding two-lane road as a shower began to graffiti the windshield. They were both done smoking for the night, but the stale odor coming off the Coke can they'd been using for an ashtray was enough to make him feel a little sick.

"Why did I get in a vehicle with you?" Kimberly asked. "I thought *I* was too drunk to drive, but shit, you—"

"Will you shut up and let me concentrate? This road's narrow as shit."

"Wide enough for two lanes, but I guess you need them both in your condition, huh?"

He looked over at her. "I swear to God—"

She pointed ahead, her arm springing out like a mechanical clown arm at a haunted house. "Watch it—shit!"

His gaze swung drowsily back to the road, but it was too late. Whatever she'd seen was soon passing under their wheels with two jarring thumps. Dale slammed on the brakes and skidded the Accord to an angled stop on the shoulder.

There they sat, not with their lives flickering before them, but as though time had slowed almost to a standstill. They stared into the darkness beyond the headlights, not at each other, and certainly not behind them.

Dale threw the car into park. "What do you think that was?"

"I—how the hell should I know?"

"Well, was it already on the road? Did it jump in front of us? What?"

"I don't know! I think I might have seen movement. I'm not sure. Only three things it could've been."

He turned to her and could tell from her expression that he must have looked about as well as he felt.

"Could have been a tree branch," she continued. "I like that possibility. Then again, maybe it was an animal."

"But you don't think so."

"Pretty unlikely that a deer gets hit by a car and stays on the road, don't you think?"

"I guess. You usually see them on the side of the road."

"Sure. They come storming out of a thicket on one side and *WHAM-O!*, they've got momentum in two different directions."

"But if it was some other kind of animal, just sort of wandering ..."

"It's possible."

"And we both know what's behind door number three."

"Yeah, but you know what? In this weather, a tree branch isn't out of the question. You going to find out or what?"

He slowly raised his eyes to the level of the rearview mirror and breathed a sigh of relief when he saw that the roadway was too dark behind them to make out more than an outline of a shape. But then he thought of the brake lights.

"Anything?" Kimberly asked.

Dale shook his head but kept his eyes on the mirror. "Going to use the brakes to see if they give off enough light to ..."

The red glow thrown across the object from the Honda's brake lights only made matters worse. It was like being shown an image recorded in hell. The night air was even cool enough to make infernal fog of the car's exhaust. The obstacle he'd struck or driven over might have been a large branch or a wild animal or a human being. He still had no idea which, and the otherworldly lighting brought still more possibilities to mind: lycanthrope, chupacabra, Mothman? Hell, why not?

His legs began to tremble. "I guess I'll have to get out and check."

"Well now, wait a minute. Let's think this through. We've both been drinking. Have you been on your phone tonight? Tweeting or anything?"

"No, what are you—"

"Good, me neither. I mean, sure, we can be connected to Ted's party, but we're hardly alone in that. Plus there's about five different routes back to town from his place."

"And this *is* a public road." He was cottoning to the plan taking shape.

"Now you're talking." She gave his leg a playful slap. "I say we head home, maybe stop off somewhere to check for damage, clean off the front end of the car if need be. Then we're home free."

"Okay, I'm in. But promise me something. This has to be a bond between us, forever. Okay?"

"Don't be so dramatic. We'll know in a day or two if it was a person."

"Forever," he repeated, staring her down with a fierceness he'd never felt before.

"Okay, okay. Forever. Jesus."

Shifting the car into drive, Dale pulled back onto the road and hightailed it for home.

* * *

As he and Kimberly disappeared over the crest of a hill, the object they were leaving behind remained motionless under the pale light of a slender moon. The dark streak along its middle might have been forest bark, or a length of trench coat, or even the matted pelt of a woodland creature. Whatever it was, it lay still or stunned, inanimate or dead. It offered up no easy proof of its identity, no excuse for its existence, and no forgiveness toward those responsible for its condition.

THE DRAGON'S TOOTH

"**M**r. Lang?" the girl said as she opened his office door and took a step inside.

Though it was only a cheap western that he pored over from behind his desk, he pretended it was something from which he could not easily excuse himself. He stopped reading immediately but went on staring at the page. Could she make out the details of the cover from across the room—the rearing stallion mere inches from a deadly drop into a snaking ravine, its rider tugging at the reins with as much sheer will as brute force? He doubted it, but she would perhaps notice that it was a tattered paperback, unlikely to be of much lasting value. She was perceptive and he walked in constant danger of underestimating her. Ah, well. A director of his stature only had to go so far for the sake of illusion. Beyond that, let the hoi polloi think him a fraud if they must. For his work to remain serious, his leisure reading had to remain light. It was his way.

He set the book down at last and looked up into the girl's face. It was a pretty face, too, neatly framed by a slightly boyish haircut.

"Yes, Diane?"

"He's arrived, sir."

"Ah! Good, good. Well, send him in." He stood and straightened his tie, shifting from one foot to the other.

Diane nodded and retreated, leaving the door ajar. Mr. Lang remained motionless as a shadow filled his office doorway. That was the moment he realized it was actually happening. He was about to direct the most legendary German actor of the twentieth century.

"Fritz!" The man entered the room, arms wide, eclipsing all but a nimbus of light from the more brightly lit room beyond. "It is truly a great meeting, *ja*?"

Fritz Lang stepped out from behind his desk and extended a hand, which the other man firmly grasped. "*Herr* Emil Jannings. It is a pleasure, not just to meet you at last, but to know that we'll be working together on this picture."

"*Ja*, we make history with this, I think."

"And your travels from Austria, they were good?"

"Fine, fine. But now I am in Hollywood. There is much to see before we begin shooting. As you know, it has been many years since I've called this city home. I don't intend to spend all of my down time in a hotel room—or in your office."

"Yes, of course, but please have a seat. Let's talk before I send you back into the jungle."

"Very well." Jannings removed his hat and took a seat in a tan leather chair next to a bookcase.

Lang sat on the corner of his desk, one leg hanging off the edge. Neither man could stop smiling.

"This is a real opportunity for me," Emil said, his deep voice thickly accented. "I want you to know that I appreciate what it means. My reputation ..." He looked sheepishly at the floor. "It's not what it was. You know that. My misplaced sympathies with—"

"The war's been over for five years. The world needs to start moving on or maybe it never will. Instead it will freeze up and harden, then spin away like a cinder." Lang made little circles with his finger as he moved a hand through the air.

"Perhaps, but this film—*The Dragon's Tooth*—it's my chance to change who I am in the eyes of the world. Maybe that will help it move on, as you say."

"Well, I wish I could sit here and say I'm doing this all for you, but the truth is that I need a hit, Emil. My last picture was perceived as vapid. Oh, hell. It *was* vapid. If 1950 isn't my comeback year, I may be out of chances. What could give me a better shot than bringing the great Emil Jannings to America to shoot his first film since the war?"

"The script is very good, Fritz. Very good. Obviously it has a strong anti-Nazi message, which will appeal, but the story! Such an adventure. And the writer is a newcomer, you say?"

"First-time screenwriter, but a published novelist."

"Very talented. Let us agree that we both stand to gain from this undertaking."

"Fair enough, then. Do you have someone to show you around town? As you say, it's a few days before shooting begins."

"*Ja*, your lovely secretary put me in touch with a couple of people."

"*Sehr gut*. Well then, we shall meet again soon."

Jannings rose and took Lang's hand once more, this time clasping the forearm with his free hand as well. Smiling and donning his hat, he then took his leave.

"Diane," Fritz said quietly, his head poking out from his office, "who did you connect Mr. Jannings with? Only curious."

"Pardon?"

"He mentioned that you gave him the names of some people to take him around."

"No, sir."

"Hmm. A strange man."

"Yes, sir."

❊　❊　❊

The set was an elaborate mock-up of a Nazi officer's bedroom in one of the Reich's castle-like strongholds near Berlin. Eagle-themed candlesticks and red tapestries with black swastikas emblazoned on them adorned the chamber.

"May I have a word, Fritz?" Emil scratched his cheek and looked at his shoes, clearly a little embarrassed by whatever he had to say.

"Of course. What's on your mind?"

"This is the script's one trouble spot. I don't understand Otto's motivation here. He's followed Gretchen upstairs to the master bedroom. He barges in and catches her attempting to steal the brooch."

"The Dragon's Tooth, yes."

"That's just it. *She* knows it's the priceless Dragon's Tooth, Officer Lehmann's prize possession. That's why she's taking it, so she can use it to finance the French Resistance. But Otto?"

"Well, he's British Resistance, yes? He suspects he might have an ally in anyone scrambling around Lehmann's mansion the night of such an important gathering as what's going on downstairs."

"And he trusts her based on this hunch? Even resistance fighters squabbled among their various factions."

"How can he hope to bring down the Nazi elite, or even escape with his life, without a bit of good fortune? You have to trust someone when you're surrounded by cutthroats."

Emil's belly hitched. Then he chortled, and eventually it grew into a rich laugh as he placed a hand on Fritz's shoulder.

"Ah, see? You should have co-written the script, Fritz. That line should be in the movie."

"Does that clear things up for you, then?"

"*Ja*, I think I'm ready to try again."

"Terrific." Lang took a step toward the set. "Places, everyone! Let's get another take."

* * *

The daily workprints that Fritz Lang was getting back for review were extraordinary. Not only was he making his best picture in years, but Jannings was delivering the performance of a lifetime. Not even his bellhop in *The Last Laugh* or his fallen general in *The Last Command* could compare. The world was sure to take notice.

He blew cigarette smoke at the monitor in the small

viewing booth and played the film forward a bit more.

Not a bad piece of filmmaking for a half-blind Austrian, he thought. *Not bad at all.*

On the small screen, Emil Jannings as Otto the cook took the diamond- and ruby-encrusted brooch from the delicate fingers of Gretchen, played by the alluring Mary Cornish. The Dragon's Tooth had taken its name from the fact that it was shaped as though it could have been the tooth of an enormous creature, as well as for the association between dragons and jewels. An exquisite treasure.

Otto turned it in his hand, holding it aloft for maximum brilliance. "This beauty could fund the resistance for a thousand years, if that's how long the Reich truly persists."

"It won't," Gretchen said in a soft but firm tone. "It will not survive the decade."

"Of course, the dragon has more than one tooth. His maw is lined with them. He also has claws, and a fire in his belly."

"What's your point?"

"Only that it is a many-headed beast we fight, not to be underestimated."

"How can you underestimate an adversary with no morals or compunction about doing evil? My estimation of the Nazis can go no lower. It has hit bottom."

"Then let me take this away for you. Tongues might start wagging about the pretty little stranger who roams the castle freely, but they're suspicion won't be as quick to fall on the cook, especially since my food is delicious. Get yourself away from here. I'll follow before dawn."

The scene was wonderful, perfect in all but one respect. After Gretchen agreed to let Otto abscond with the Dragon's Tooth, he looked directly into the camera and pulled an almost rakish grin before exiting the bedchamber. It wasn't in the script, and Lang sure as hell hadn't told Jannings to do it. Yet there it was, executed so close to the last spoken line that it was as if the great actor knew it would be impossible to cut it out plausibly if the rest of the take was acceptable.

Well, it was more than acceptable. If it had been merely good, Lang might have settled for the implausibility of a jarring cut. Otto's exit from the room could have been reshot easily, after all. But the take was perfection, and maybe Jannings knew that, too. Was it an error, or a bold artistic flourish? Maybe it wasn't important. Lang had missed it in the moment, and now it was destined to remain a part of the film, for better or worse. Grist for the critics, perhaps. Something that might get talked about at cocktail parties. The thought eased his concerns about the unscripted shot. Immortality was immortality, after all.

* * *

The booth was fine for watching dailies, but the studio had a special projection theater for screening rough cuts. The room could accommodate an audience of a couple dozen, but Lang only ever allowed two others to join him for these initial private screenings. One was his producer, which, in the case of *The Dragon's Tooth*, was Howard Welsch. The other was Diane, his indispensable secretary. She had a good head for the grammar of film, and he trusted her judgment more than just about anyone else's. As for Welsch? Well, it was pretty hard to deny the film's producer a seat at the table.

Diane was first to notice that something wasn't right.

"Wait a second," she said. "Shouldn't Mr. Jannings have entered the scene by now? This is where he finds Donovan in the bookstore and strikes up a conversation about joining the British Resistance."

Howard snickered. "I'm sure it'll become clear in a moment, sweetheart. This isn't Fritz's first rodeo."

"No, she's right." Lang leaned forward, an index finger resting on his lips. "I may only have one good eye since the Great War, but I can tell when a scene isn't right. Where the hell is Jannings?"

"I can find out for you." Welsch started to stand.

"Not where is he in Los Angeles. Where is he in the film?"

"Listen," Diane said, still looking intently at the screen.

"Hey, buzz off, huh?" It was dialogue from the film, Donovan sitting on a low stool at the base of a towering stack of old books. "I ain't got no beef with the krauts. Live and let live, huh?"

There was a strange pause, during which Donovan looked up as if startled, but there was nothing there. "You know how it is. Lookin' for new opportunities. Girls, I s'pose. Birds, they call 'em over here."

The line was supposed to be in response to a question from Otto: "What brings an American civilian to London in wartime?" But where was the question? More to the point, where was the questioner? Lang remembered shooting the scene as if it had been yesterday, and he'd watched the workprint. There were no takes without Emil. They didn't even need a stand-in for coverage during over-the-shoulder business—often Jannings' preference due to exhaustion—because there was no such business. The whole sequence had been shot wide on purpose. The director wanted to emphasize how insignificant good men could seem in a world of proliferating evil.

Lang pressed a circular white button on the armrest of his seat.

"Yes, sir?" came the voice of the projectionist.

"Show the next reel, please."

"Yes, sir."

Frame after frame flickered before their eyes. Reel after reel. The great Emil Jannings was nowhere to be seen. The audience of three watched in mute disbelief, as if witnessing a horrible accident in slow motion. Finally they arrived at the dramatic confrontation between Otto and Gretchen. The bedroom door swung open ... No Jannings. Mid-scene, however, when Gretchen handed over the Dragon's Tooth to Otto, the camera cut to him, and there he stood to receive the treasure. Holding it in his hand he said his lines and looked into the camera with the unscripted grin—then vanished as the brooch fell to the floor.

"*What has been done to my film!?*" Fritz roared.

The projectionist buzzed him. "Sir?"

"What is it?"

"Someone wanting to see you. I told her to wait outside your office."

Fritz glanced at Diane, who rose immediately and exited the theater.

"I don't know what to say," Welsch said.

"No. Nor do I. I'd better see what this woman wants."

"It's not possible." Welsch seemed to be talking to himself this time.

Fritz stopped with one hand on the door. "No," he said again without turning and left the man to himself.

❋ ❋ ❋

"What do you mean, dead?" Lang was seated behind his desk.

"Just that, I'm afraid." The woman, a Miss Meiers, sat across from him. "I found a letter from you among his things. A job offer, it seemed. He would have been touched. He dreamed of working again."

"But he *did*—"

He cut himself short. Did he really plan to tell this stranger that he'd been working with Emil Jannings for months on what might have been the greatest film of either of their careers— when she knew the man to be dead and buried in Austria? He could show her the single scene that had retained Emil's image. It was proof of something, but what? That Jannings had been to Hollywood and worked on a film while his people back home mistakenly thought him dead? Or that the actor he had been working with all this time was not Emil Jannings at all, or any man, but rather a cipher?

No, it wouldn't do. Besides, he hadn't made up his mind

about what to do with the inexplicable footage. Maybe he'd hold onto it, so at least he'd know where it was. But could he live with such a haunted thing in his possession? *Maybe it should be destroyed*, he mused.

"Well, my condolences, Miss Meiers. You really didn't have to come all this way."

"Oh, I wouldn't have, but I thought I might make a holiday of it. I may never have a better chance to visit Hollywood. He always spoke so highly of it."

"I'm sorry to hear that cinema has lost one of its giants. Truly I am, but you'll have to excuse me. I have quite a lot of work to do today."

"I understand. And thank you again for thinking of my uncle. He would have made you proud."

"I have no doubt."

Who was I corresponding with before his ostensible arrival in the U.S.? Fritz wondered. *And where are the other items I sent to him? Like the script, for Christ's sake!*

He sat in silence for a time after the woman left. Jannings had provided a different address for Lang to use for all correspondence after that first letter. Why? To avoid detection by his niece? Again, why? It was a lot to try to make sense of. He wondered if it might be possible to lose his mind trying. Eventually he engaged the intercom and asked Diane to step in for a moment.

"Yes, Mr. Lang?" she said upon entering his office.

"The rough cut, the dailies, all of it. I want it burned."

"Sir?"

"Destroyed. Not a trace. I want *The Dragon's Tooth* to vanish from the face of the earth."

"Very well."

That was that. He could rely on Diane to take care of things, as he had on so many occasions over the past few years. Good. He felt better. Maybe Jannings' image would eventually fade from the filmstock that retained it, but it wasn't something he was about to leave to chance.

Even if he wasn't destined to be haunted by the celluloid spirit of Emil Jannings, though, he wondered if he might end up being haunted to the grave by the question of whether the actor, in ghostly form, had been trying to make amends for his Nazi affiliations by making an anti-fascist movie for the ages, or simply committing one last act of mean-spirited subterfuge. It shouldn't have mattered to Fritz, but it did—more than the incredible nature of how the man had accomplished whatever he had, in fact, accomplished. He doubted he would ever have answers, just as he doubted he would ever again set eyes on the enigma that called itself Emil Jannings.

* * *

She would miss working for Mr. Lang. He had been good to her. But life grows dull for the young, especially after experiencing an impossibility. On the one hand, Diane took hope from the events surrounding the *Dragon's Tooth* production. It meant there were wonders in the world. True wonders. But it also meant that Hollywood had probably coughed up as much as it had to offer her. It was time to move on.

Opening the trunk of her green Chevrolet she flung her suitcase inside, followed by several canisters of film. Then she closed the trunk and got behind the wheel, feeling sure she had the makings of a nest egg in the back of the automobile but not having any idea how to make it so.

Maybe the road would take her someplace with answers. If not, wonders would have to do.

THE CHANCE OF
A LIFETIME

C aptain E. Waverly stood swaying in the wings, waiting for his cue to reenter the farcical drama playing out on the stage of the Adelphi Theatre. In part he swayed from the claret he'd swilled three quarters of an hour earlier, and in part from the affliction he attempted to treat with drink. He had yet to announce the condition to anyone, but it was clear that he was suffering from aristocrat's disease. In short, he'd come down with the gout, which meant spending as little time as possible on the affected foot and trying to look natural while doing so.

Beyond the usual nervous excitement of opening night, there was a particular thrill in the air this evening. In addition to the audience's warmth toward the comical business of the actors, the material was nothing less than an adaptation of the Bardell versus Pickwick trial from Dickens's *The Pickwick Papers*. It was the kind of thing upon which great careers were built if one did well—and upon which promising careers blinked out of existence if one did poorly. Thus there had been more than one reason for the wine, even though Captain Waverly never needed an excuse to imbibe, whether before, during, or after a performance.

His was the role of Mr. Pickwick, whose innocent words had, by this time in the evening's performance, been misconstrued by Mrs. Bardell as a promise of marriage. The ensuing trial for breach of that promise was underway, and so it was into the fray of jurists, witnesses, and onlookers that Waverly now stepped, with all the affable boldness and rotundity he could affect. The theatregoers roared their approval. Deep down he suspected that they cheered at least as much for Dickens's creation as they did for his own modest celebrity, but their enthusiasm fueled his performance nonetheless.

Gout, however, is a fickle complaint, and it turned against the good captain—who had never truly earned that or any other title—with a vengeance, before he could utter his first line of the scene. Down came the gout-ridden foot upon the boards, and up shot a vicious flame of agony. He collapsed on the spot and managed only a "Damn!" before the curtains closed so the crowd could be assuaged and the understudy located.

"I beg you to understand," Captain Waverly pleaded with Mr. Brissle, the house manager, the next afternoon in the man's office. "This is not a permanent condition. I mean, it *is*, but it is inconstant. The pain comes and goes. I can master it, I promise you."

"Ha!" said Brissle. "And that, I suppose, has as much validity as Pickwick's promise to Mrs. Bardell. You're finished, Waverly. Gout's a bad business and you have my sympathies, but you're not the first to lose a career to it, acting or otherwise."

Captain Waverly stood and replaced his hat upon his head before laying both hands on the other man's desk. "Be forewarned, Mr. Brissle, that if you allow me to walk out that door under the terms you've laid out, the next time you see me might be as I gut you like a hog from navel to throat."

"If you think I'll beg you to stay because of an idle threat like that, you're as stupid as you are mad, sir. Now if you'll kindly leave me to finish calculating last night's receipts ..."

Brissle was correct about the threat being an empty one. Waverly may have wanted to do mischief against the manager, but Newgate Prison held no allure for him. And so he left the office without another word, assuring himself it had been worth a try.

A mouldy dusk lay upon the city of London by the time
he reached the clutch of houses in which his humble garret hid.
So long did it take him to navigate the labyrinth of cowering
buildings that it was practically dark by the time he let himself
in and climbed the uneven staircase to his room.

He had tied the rope to an exposed beam in the ceiling the
night before, upon returning from the Adelphi. All that was left
to do was move his reading chair into place beneath the noose
and kick it out from under him—once he'd fitted the loop around
his neck, that is.

These things he did, and soon he swung like a sack of
onions from the rafter, his last sight in this world a sliver of
moon through the room's only window. Eventually his vision
went dark and the rope ceased its creaking where it rubbed
against the wood.

The room was as quiet and still as a churchyard for many
minutes, until Captain Waverly dropped to the floor. Well, it
couldn't have been Captain Waverly, exactly, for he looked up
and saw himself still hanging from the rafter. But he wasn't
greatly diminished in this new form, either. Examining his
hands, he was gratified to see that they had real substance. His
hat had fallen from his head when he came to the end of his rope,
he noticed, so without a moment's hesitation he stooped down
to pick it up and placed it on his new, bare head.

He was a bit worried how long this new condition might
persist, but he also saw that it presented certain possibilities.
Perhaps, as he had read concerning situations like this, he
merely needed to complete a piece of unfinished business before
he would be allowed to move on.

Further testing his relationship to the corporeal world,
he walked across the room, without a twinge of discomfort, to
where an ancient chest of drawers stood. He was able to coax the
top drawer open with ease.

Good, he thought, a moon-tinted smile spreading across
his face. That meant he would also be able to retrieve the knife
that lay hidden within, and do such bitter business as the day

would quake to look on.

CAUGHT IN A TRAP

She lay face down on the procedure table, staring through the doughnut-shaped headrest at the tiled floor below. It was the last place she would have expected to find herself two weeks ago, but a phone call to a friend had changed all that, and here she was at the witch doctor's, waiting for the man with the needles to return and work his ancient magic.

Acupuncture had one thing going for it: it wasn't likely to make matters worse, even if it didn't end up alleviating her anxiety. That had been her initial pep talk to herself. Eventually she required more convincing. She couldn't swallow the idea that a practice dating back many hundreds of years had accidentally turned out to have valid physiological underpinnings that would stand up to the rigors of modern medical science. Her way out of that puzzle was to concede that maybe acupuncture tapped into neural signals to the brain, augmenting its own power to heal from within. She wasn't about to call it *Qi*, but she knew she was in that ballpark.

That's when she decided to reconnect with Jan and, after apologizing for a previous lunch date that had involved a certain amount of condescension toward Jan's reliance on acupuncture for a number of ailments, ask for her acupuncturist's contact information.

Dr. Joseph Zhou: Whole Health Acupuncture and Herbs.

As if in response to her reminiscence, there came a soft knock at the door of the procedure room, followed by an accented, "Ms. Evans? May I come in?"

"Yes, come in, please." Her voice was somewhat muffled

because of her position. "And call me Susan."

"Oh, Susan. Okay." He stepped into the room. "You have acupuncture before?"

"No, this is a first."

"Very relaxing. No pain. I've been doing it almost thirty years." She felt him lift her stocking feet and place a pillow of some kind under them. "I was medical doctor in China before coming to Seattle."

She wasn't sure that was a credential she'd wave around like a flag if the roles were reversed, but she wasn't there to be operated on, or even diagnosed. It was a perfectly safe procedure. Perhaps it would even help her.

"You here for anxiety, yes?"

"I am. It gets so bad sometimes I get headaches. Backaches, too. Maybe it's not all related, but it seems that way to me."

There was something about being in the small, dimly lit room, and hearing the soothing timbre of Dr. Zhou's voice, that almost made her admit she'd been having more spells of mental hyper-acuity lately as well, but she refrained. That was her secret for now, and she intended to keep it that way, even if it was connected to some of her other issues. The knack for guessing at things with uncanny accuracy and knowing what people were going to say before they said them had been with her since a roll-over accident she was involved in shortly after she and her husband moved to Seattle seven years ago. She didn't feel like explaining why she'd waited all that time to tell anyone about it, partly because she wasn't sure herself. At any rate, Dr. Zhou wasn't going to be the first to hear of it.

"Okay, sound good," the doctor said. "I need to pull down your sweats just a bit. That okay?"

"Yeah, that's fine."

And by the way, doc, sometimes I hear things that people are thinking. Take you, for instance. You'd like to do more than pull down my sweats, wouldn't you? A whole lot more. But you're not that kind of man. You love your wife, and you wouldn't dream of jeopardizing your marriage or your career. The lust is just a passing reaction. I can live with that.

After pulling the waistband of her sweatpants down several inches, Dr. Zhou proceeded to lift the back of her shirt almost to bra level. Interesting that he didn't feel the need to check in with her before performing *that* little maneuver. She tried to connect with his thoughts again, but the door to his mind was closed.

"The needles are very sharp and won't go in far, but I'll be placing twenty today. Most along your back. Some in your neck and legs."

After sliding the elastic cuffs of her sweatpants up several inches and scrunching the tops of her socks down a little, he dabbed at spots along her calves, back, and neck with what felt like a moist wad of cotton. Alcohol, she assumed. At least he believed in sterilization.

Then the tapping of needles began. Her flesh quivered at each prick. He'd been telling the truth. They didn't hurt, exactly. But he was so unceremonious about it. One moment he was talking to her. The next he was puncturing her skin with needles. By the time she began to wonder whether there was a state or local agency that inspected places like this, he was done.

"Feel good?" he asked.

"It does," she answered truthfully, a little surprised at how relaxed she felt already.

He swung a heat lamp into position over the middle of her back and switched off the overhead light.

"I'll be back in twenty minutes," he added as he left her to her thoughts, closing the door behind him.

Immediately she felt a little silly. She taught fifth grade, for Christ's sake. What business did she have coming to an acupuncturist for stress? She wasn't a corporate CEO or a tech drone. She wasn't a commercial airline pilot or emergency-room doctor. They were the ones who ought to be coming to Dr. Zhou, not her.

But then she remembered walking down the long hall from the herb shop and front counter to the back area of the clinic, where the procedure rooms were located. Almost all the doors had been wide open, revealing dark, empty chambers. And there was another hallway of rooms off the main one. Dr. Zhou didn't exactly seem to be enjoying a booming trade. If the capitalist psychos and world-changing altruists wanted a little help with their anxiety, Susan was pretty sure Dr. Zhou could find a way to squeeze them in.

Her sense of relaxation deepened. Every muscle in her body felt slack and comfortable. Her eyes threatened to close. She could barely keep a thought in front of her as images and ideas floated in and out of her consciousness. It reminded her of the Buddhist meditation she used to do in college, but it always took forever to reach this level of disconnectedness back then. Here it was sudden and unbidden. How could she attribute it to anything other than the acupuncture? Soon she would have to fight off sleep, she realized with a slow blink.

The need to fight did indeed come, though she wasn't sure why she viewed it that way. What was wrong with a little shut-eye? It would make the time pass more quickly and possibly relax her even further. Yet she resisted for as long as she could. At last, sleep claimed her, thin but comforting.

She awoke to a flutter in her chest. It happened sometimes when she woke suddenly from a short nap. She used to think it was her heart, but a check of the pulse was all it took to disprove that. Her heart rate never matched the speed of the fluttering. *Weird.*

How long had she been out? Surely not more than five minutes. Maybe she should conk out again. Where was the harm? With a revised attitude, she closed her eyes and welcomed sleep.

When she woke up a second time, she knew that more time had passed. Considerably more. Her mouth was gummy, her hair matted with sweat to the tissue paper that lined the procedure table. And the heat lamp burned intensely at her back. Her sense of relaxation vanished, replaced by a keen awareness that something wasn't right.

Yet so strong are social customs and norms that she felt powerless to call out. How foolish she would have felt if Dr. Zhou were to come running to her aid, only to learn that she had misjudged the time, or if he felt pressured into apologizing for some minor delay that had been outside of his control.

At the same time, however, her unease continued to grow. She didn't dare stand up with all the needles piercing her back. For all she knew there was a special technique for removing them that had to be followed to the letter to prevent infection or nerve damage. But what if something had happened to Dr. Zhou? He had been the only person manning the shop, and as far as she knew there wasn't another patient in the whole damn building.

In the end it was the heat lamp that prompted her to act. The steadily intensifying heat coming off of it was the strongest evidence that something was amiss. Surely with his decades of experience Dr. Zhou wouldn't make such an obvious mistake as letting a patient lie for too long under the burn of a lamp.

She pushed herself up with both hands and rolled into a sitting position, pushing aside the adjustable arm of the heat lamp in the process. The sudden movement dizzied her some, but she didn't think much of it. Rising too quickly, especially from a prostrate position, often had that effect on her. It would pass.

"Dr. Zhou?" she called out, not too loudly. Just enough to get herself used to the sound of her voice in the small, dark room. He wouldn't have heard it from the front of the clinic.

She dropped down to her feet and recognized her mistake immediately. The room spun as the flow of her blood adjusted to the sudden change in position. As her dizziness intensified, she wheeled her arms around, trying in vain to find purchase of some kind. Her legs refused to move, even at the knees, and the floor began to loom. There was no help for it. Down she went, as if in slow motion, twisting as she fell.

But when she landed on her back and the needles plunged deeper into her flesh, time returned to its normal rhythm, and pain erupted throughout the warm patch on her back. It quickly spread to her shoulders and neck. Her head began to throb. Fear took hold. What had she done? If acupuncture was capable of healing, could it also cause harm? If the needles were meant to go in only so deep, what was possible when they exceeded that depth?

Dear God, to go from incredulity to adamant certainty of the efficacy of this absurd practice! Was she losing her mind?

"Dr. Zhou!" This time she meant to be heard.

But her cry met with silence.

Standing seemed an insurmountable task, but she knew that the longer she hesitated the more frightened she'd become, and the less likely to act. Placing one hand on the edge of a linen organizer she was able to haul herself to her knees, but the flimsy pressboard unit wouldn't take her full weight, or at least she couldn't be sure that it would. And there was no way she was going to invite a repeat of the pain that had exploded through her back when she fell—pain that still throbbed there to an alarming extent. It was time to call upon gumption and the brute strength of her quads.

One foot slid forward in an awkward sweep. She wobbled some on the other knee and never let her hand fall away from the organizer, but soon she was able to swing her other leg into place. Once on her feet she continued to push herself up to a standing position.

Her top was still bunched up above the needles in her back, and the thought of it sliding down, possibly breaking needles off in her skin, prompted her to clutch a knot of the fabric under her breasts and hold it where it was.

Turning the handle, she pushed open the door and stepped into the hall, realizing that between her bunched up shirt and oddly revealing sweats, she probably made quite the picture of crazy.

Good, she thought, and filed away the notion that maybe, just maybe, there'd be something about this experience that she'd be able to look back on and laugh about.

But before she could start counting any chickens, she

needed to find out what the hell had happened to Dr. Zhou.

She didn't bother calling out as she negotiated the dim hallway leading back to the front room. The silence that was sure to answer would only do more to unravel her nerves.

The herb shop was empty, so she shuffled through aisles of home remedies, still in her stocking feet, to the main counter and stood on her tiptoes to peer over the top.

Oh, my God! she wanted to scream as she peered down into the narrow space between the counter and a back wall that housed row after row of small jars filled with mysterious herbs. There lay Dr. Zhou like a dropped puppet, a look of eternal pain on his motionless face.

Her phone still in her purse back in the procedure room, she got the clunky old desk phone turned around and dialed 911, never letting go of her death grip on the knot of sweatshirt at her abdomen. The call made, she hung up and had to resist the urge to slide down the glass-fronted counter to rest on the floor until help came. She had remembered the needles in her back just in time and stood completely still, staring with a vacancy of cognition. She was in the same position fifteen minutes later when the paramedics arrived.

For Susan it was a simple matter of removing the needles from her flesh, which a young woman wearing purple pseudo-latex gloves did right there in the herb shop before treating her puncture wounds and sending her on her way. Dr. Zhou, on the other hand, was beyond help. Myocardial infarction, they deemed it. His ticker had given out on him, just like that. It occurred to Susan as she stepped through the front door and into a surprisingly sunny afternoon that we spend an awful lot of time worrying about unimportant bullshit, considering the solemnity of the finish line we're all rushing toward. Then she chided herself as she would one of her students for using soap talk, and she could almost hear Reed Watkins respond: *What, we can't talk about soap?*, when he knew damn well what she really meant.

Sliding behind the wheel of her tan Toyota Camry she

pulled out of the small lot and merged into traffic, homeward bound.

* * *

There are places in the world so empty that they would drive most men mad. The cold, dark, rat-infested cell of a Russian prison. The barren, scorching sands of the Australian outback, where only the most cruel and cunning animals survive. The belly of a bustling Indian city, so crowded over with impoverished humanity that it becomes a kind of perverse emptiness unto itself. Such locales, and others like them, would eat at the minds of most men over time. But there are those who seek out the emptiness, so they can fill it up with their own brand of pollution. There are, in short, men like Jacob Kettering of Indianapolis.

Jacob, who sits before his laptop computer, aglow in its digital emanations. Jacob, who ignores the chewing and scratching sounds inside the walls, the beetles and cockroaches that trace intricate zig-zags across his floor and countertops. Jacob, who has never known a single reason to smile, but who smiles anyway. Jacob, who stares not at a website or e-mail window but into a void, seeking a connection in the vast nothingness of cyberspace. His hands hang at his sides, for he does not need to type to connect. He needs only to make himself ... empty—though he would never admit it to another soul.

* * *

The house was quiet upon her return. In most households, she supposed, that would mean no one else was home. There were no such guarantees in the life of Susan Evans. Her husband might be out, or he might be in the downstairs den, deep in the throes of an art project that he'd never finish. Or he might be napping, tired after a long day of contemplating the work it would require to make any one of his pipe dreams real. Probably he was at a coffeehouse, watching movies on Netflix as research for the novel he swore was in him. Across the courtyard from probability was the remote chance he was even fumbling his way through some kind of affair. She doubted it, but she wouldn't fall over from shock if it proved to be the case.

The sad truth was that she really didn't care all that much. Certainly not enough to ask him about it. The last thing she needed was another reason not to respect him. That tower of Jenga blocks was very near its toppling point as it was. It didn't need her pulling at its beams.

Suddenly she was very tired. Her favorite chair—a chair most people found to be more pleasing to the eye than to the posterior—seemed to draw her into it. Without having made a conscious decision about what to do with the rest of her afternoon, she wrapped one leg underneath her as she flipped open the case of her tablet computer and settled in for a lazy session of e-mail, YouTube videos, mindless games and maybe a chapter or two from one of the e-books she had going. She hated reading on a screen, but it was so much easier to make sure she had only one item in her hands when she fell into her chair or boarded a train or visited a park. Technology had led to progress in some areas, but it had a lot of explaining to do in terms of what it was doing to the human soul, as far as she was concerned. And yet she was just as susceptible as everyone else. If she wasn't on her tablet, she damn sure had to know that her phone was within easy reach. She did a pretty good job of keeping most technology out of the classroom unless it served a specific purpose, but in her private life she was just another digital junkie. Her tablet was the high-tech equivalent of a big-box store: one-stop shopping and all the diversions you could hope for.

Had she typed something into a search engine while her thoughts played out in their tired, aimless fashion? Surfing had become so goddamn automatic it was hard to tell. She didn't remember tapping or typing anything, but her screen had changed. She was in some kind of application that took up all the real estate on her tablet. Was an image forming in the center? And another smaller image in the top right corner? She'd never seen a modern device behave like this. It was the same lack of comportment that had marked a bygone analog era. The stuff of console television sets that could break a mover's back. The result of a poorly positioned antenna or a bad vacuum tube. Or the visual equivalent of listening to the ghostly static–chatter between radio stations that were close neighbors on the dial.

It gave her the creeps, whatever it was, especially when both images began to take on the vague outline of human faces. What the hell was going on? Part of her didn't want to know, wanted to switch off the hand-held computer and slip it into a drawer somewhere. But some other part of her must have been more curious than that, because not only did she leave the tablet on, but she stared intently at the screen, eager to know what the blurred forms in front of her were becoming. Yes, the progress was slow, but there was clarity at work in the circuitry of the machine. It steadily gained a stronger foothold. Soon she would have some kind of clue, even if it turned out to be something as banal as a pop-up ad. At least she would know.

But she felt certain it was more than an ad.

An ad ... An-ad-iapolis ... Andiapolis ... Indianapolis?

* * *

At 111 South Meridian Street, in Indianapolis, Indiana, a computer screen flickers and blinks off. The man in front of it thinks there may be a technical problem at first, but it comes back to life before his fingers can reach the keyboard to begin troubleshooting. A face obscured by the kind of grainy black-and-white snow that used to plague old television sets materializes before him. He's made contact before, but never with this much detail, or preceded by such a dramatic surge of power to the monitor. He is excited that it is a woman. He was hoping for a woman.

He winks at the built-in webcam above the screen, and its cobalt beam swells on, bringing his own face to life in a small corner of the monitor. His smile broadens. He has gotten very good at all of this. In the beginning it was only reading the thoughts of others. Then he started planting ideas in people's minds. Now he can turn things on and off, sometimes even move them. He suspects he is becoming a god, but he hasn't shared his secret yet. When the teeming masses of the world begin to realize that Jacob Kettering is the antidote to the emptiness of their lives, his godhood will be plain enough. That's the trouble with people nowadays. They've lost their faith.

He will restore it.

The woman's features are quite clear now. She's pretty but not beautiful. Her blond hair is thick and piled about her head in an attractive fashion. Kindness and intelligence flow from her eyes. Here is a woman who might just be bright enough to receive his truths, and recognize them. His ever-present smile stretches wide.

If she turns out to be just another mindless vessel, despite appearances, there will of course be consequences. For as with all aspiring gods, the benevolence of Jacob's message is tempered by an angry, wrathful distaste for insubordination.

His smile returns to its usual low grade.

❋ ❋ ❋

The images on her device were very sharp now, and it was clear what was going on, though not why it was happening. Someone had hacked into her tablet and opened a video chat session. Presumably it had been the unwashed young man occupying the largest portion of the screen. Her face occupied the small video square in the top right corner. Instinct screamed at her now to close the tablet, but this time it was more than curiosity that kept her from doing so. She was being held by his will.

His eyes were black pits in the grainy sockets of his face. Strings of greasy black hair cradled each cheek, and an unnerving smile shifted its tilt continually. Left corner up, right corner down. Right corner up, left corner down. An odd nervous tick.

His name is Jacob.

"My name is Jacob," he said, a slight delay between the sound of his words and the movement of his lips. It was a reedy, ugly voice.

Her leg had fallen asleep, so she uncurled it from beneath her and sat forward in the chair.

"Susan," the man continued. "That's a dependable name. Are you a dependable person, Susan? Do you live up to your name?"

Her head shook slowly back and forth. "How … Who are … How do you know my name?"

"You're not the only one with gifts, you know. In fact, there are many of us. I'm in contact with dozens."

"Gifts?" She refused to assume anything. He would have to spell this out.

"Ah, dependable *and* cautious. Both commendable traits." A certain wryness stole into his tone. "But don't play dumb. It's rude, it's irritating, and it's ineffective. Yes, I can read your thoughts. That's what you're wondering. And you caught hold of *my* name, didn't you? That was impressive. Your abilities are fairly strong."

She almost asked why he was bothering her all the way from Indiana. Didn't they have psychics and misfits enough in the heartland? But before the thought could form completely, she crumpled it up and rolled it down an imaginary bowling lane, hoping she was quick enough to keep it from this man's feelers. He'd get it eventually, she supposed, but he'd have to go fishing.

"What do you want with me?"

"You're one of the strong. I want you to join our ranks."

"What, you mean like a club?

"An organization. I won't lie to you, socializing isn't a prominent attribute among our tribe. Our talents often keep us at the boundaries of societal norms, but that doesn't mean we have less need for social interaction than others. It just means we might not be as good at it as we are at ... other things."

"And just like that you expect me to join up? Is there a membership fee?" She didn't bother to keep a little laugh from escaping. But although she found the whole proposition somewhat cracked, she was already reminding herself that it *was* summertime, and she had no real obligations for almost two months. The timing could have been worse for a convention of mental adepts.

"No fee as of yet," he assured her, "though you will be responsible for your own airfare and hotel ... should you decide to come."

"This is crazy. You really went to the trouble of contacting me to invite me to Indianapolis for a meeting of the minds?"

"An apt way of putting it. Consider, Susan, that you are in a very elite group. Only the strongest of the strong are capable of picking up a signal of this nature. And the fact that you've been able to keep it live for this long is astonishing. I haven't been in contact with anyone as gifted as you in quite some time."

The incident at the acupuncturist's. Could it have had something to do with this? Could it have influenced her ability to connect mentally with people? Augmented it? Another thought worth keeping hidden for the time being. She balled it up and rolled it down the lane: a perfect strike.

"How many of you are there. How many will be convening, I mean."

"How many of *us* are there. And I expect at least a couple dozen so far. There might be some last-minute RSVPs."

Silence bothered her. It seemed more likely that he'd be able to pick up on her thoughts if she didn't keep talking. This was the case with her own powers of mental assessment. But she was at a loss for words. She didn't want to leap into a commitment, but she also didn't want to linger like an open gate through which Jacob could send a Trojan horse at any moment. It already felt as though he was pulling her to him with his mind.

"Can we connect about this again soon?" she asked. "This is a lot to take in. I need time to think it over."

"Think away," Jacob answered. "I'll be waiting. There's no pressure, of course, but I think you'd find comfort in the gathering. And I know that you'd have much to contribute. Please consider it carefully and thoughtfully. We may have a role in this world that has yet to be determined. Why shouldn't we actively shape that role? Surely we can do more as a group than we can individually."

She shuddered at the realization that he hadn't spoken any of these last words. His entire response had been sent telepathically, almost hypnotically. *Dear God.*

"One request, though," he added. "Don't mention this to anyone. One of the items up for discussion when we meet up is the matter of how much we wish to reveal about ourselves, and to whom we wish to reveal it."

Jacob's image blinked out of existence on Susan's screen and she was left staring at herself, as if into a tiny mirror. Then her image also shrank to a pinprick before leaving the screen completely dark. She set the tablet on the edge of a nearby end table without looking. It fell to the floor, which barely registered with her. A swirl of fear, exhilaration, and wonder had her in its dizzying ebb and flow. Each wave was like a new torsion on her faith in reality.

It hadn't been a lie, her claiming to need some time. But she didn't need it to make up her mind. That was already made up, whether completely of her own volition or not. How could she resist an opportunity to meet others like her? Even before the ill-fated appointment with Dr. Zhou, Susan's mental sensitivities were a source of frequent distress. If she now belonged to an even rarer group of people, she would need the comfort and guidance of those similarly burdened souls. What she needed straightaway, however, was time to hone the use of her abilities. Jacob was clearly an adversary of sorts, even if he preached the gospel of inclusion. She would need to be as prepared as possible before reaching out to him again, would need to develop confidence in the recent heightening of her extra-sensory awareness.

Yes, she would need time. But not much. Jacob would be hearing from her again soon. Susan was overdue for a change of scenery. Maybe it *was* partly his influence at work, but not entirely.

* * *

She was pretty sure it was Roseanne Barr who had joked that the reason women lie to men is that it takes too long to explain the truth. Sometimes comedy wasn't much of an exaggeration. It had been so much simpler to tell her husband that she'd joined a women's group that was meeting in Indianapolis than any conceivable version of the truth. It had been Jan's idea, she told him, knowing he'd never check in with her best friend. The two of them could barely stand to be in the same room. No, dearest Paul would barely know that Susan was gone. He'd probably already forgotten where she told him she was going.

The airplane hit a bumpy patch of air, rousing her from her reflections. The bald, heavy man beside her shifted in his sleep. Heat radiated from him; sweat slicked his hirsute arms. She didn't really mind. They were twenty minutes from touchdown. There were more important things to be worrying about than the sweat of a stranger.

Her sanity, for instance. What the hell had she been thinking, traveling all this way to meet up with a complete stranger, or close to it? They'd gotten to know each other somewhat through the strange communications that continued after their initial meeting, but that was largely a game of hide-

and-seek. She and Jacob were both holding a good deal back from one another. Especially Jacob. A child would understand the danger she was rushing into, yet here she was, twenty-two hundred miles from home, about to step into the dark unknown, if she hadn't already.

So be it. Maybe the dark unknown would prove more interesting than the bleak sameness of the connubial misfire that was her marriage. There had been a time when she wouldn't have exchanged her career for all the doubloons in El Dorado, but even the shine of her calling was beginning to dull. It was salvageable, she felt certain, but a change was in order.

Neither of these was the main reason she was about to land at Indianapolis International Airport for a risky assignation, however. The plain and simple truth was that her psychic acuity scared her—more than ever since her fall at Dr. Zhou's—and left her feeling very alone in the universe. Jacob Kettering (his last name had come to her in a dream) was one person with similar abilities who she was actually able to meet. If he wasn't a complete nutjob, she might actually learn something from him. And if he was sincere about introducing her to a whole conglomerate of special folks, all the better.

A half hour later she was gathering her bags from the United carousel. She tried to link up with Jacob's thoughts, more to see if she could pick up his whereabouts than anything, but there was nothing. They'd had a couple of sessions that were unfettered by technology, but apparently he was blocking himself. A tattooed girl with dyed black hair was selling coffee drinks at a nearby stand. Susan decided to roll her luggage in that direction, grateful that the appetite for decent coffee had spread well beyond the boundaries of the Pacific Northwest.

The milk steamer hissed, startling her. The barista took notice and smiled.

"What can I get started for you?"

Susan must have answered, because the young woman immediately began tamping finely ground espresso for a fresh drink.

She parked herself in a reasonably comfortable chair to finish her latte, took one more futile stab at connecting with Jacob, and went in search of a cab. If her host was still offline by the time she checked into her hotel, she'd trim two nights off her reservation and do her best to find a flight back to Seattle the following day.

Anger thrummed somewhere in her midsection as it grew increasingly apparent that Jacob was a no-show. There was also a sense of relief, she couldn't help admitting to herself, but definitely anger at the fact that he had convinced her to invest her time and money in this excursion, and now it was all for nothing. What kind of game was he playing? She knew that she should accept defeat and give up on Jacob Kettering and his society of freaks, but the upset in her belly, mixed with the wonder of her condition and the answers Jacob might be able to provide, drove her to think it unlikely that they wouldn't meet eventually.

The cab driver, a bearded old Sikh with a meticulously maintained turban, took her luggage as she slid into the backseat.

"The Airport Marriott," she said once the driver was behind the wheel.

He eyed her in the rearview mirror and gave a quick nod before pulling into traffic.

❊ ❊ ❊

She is at the airport, Jacob thinks, deeply disappointed in himself as he stares at the familiar water stains of his ceiling. He sees shapes in them, seldom the same. One day they might form an army of soldiers on horseback, riding into some unknown battle. The next, maybe the misshapen head of a giant. Today the stains are a brownish roiling cloud with a portal of white near the center. The portal beckons to him.

He should be at the airport, greeting her, showing her to

his car, driving her to his apartment and …

She isn't empty like the others: devoid of intellect, bereft of curiosity. Susan Evans has things to offer him. Maybe she can even pour some of her essence into his vessel, fill it to the top. It would diminish her in the end, but it would bring him one step closer to the divine state he now sees as his birthright. What he really needs from her is …

Courage.

No, not courage. What a stupid thought. He needs her ability to operate among the empty masses. She can teach him how to better fit in, or pretend to.

He rises from his little cot and steps into the pale light trickling in through an east-facing window. The Sailors' and Soldiers' Monument isn't quite visible from his apartment, which looks down onto Meridian Street. He lives on the third and top floor of what appears to be a very small turn-of-the-century brick building to passersby, though it actually extends back away from the street almost to the next block. On the ground floor is a shop that sells Catholic supplies to area churches and religious fanatics. The owners use much of the space in the back as storage, and they occupy the second-floor rooms themselves.

It's a shitty apartment in a shitty neighborhood of a shitty town. He ought to be living in a mansion overlooking some vast acreage, ruling from on high.

"Patience," he whispers to himself. "Your time will come."

❋ ❋ ❋

The only reason she'd been able to get any sleep was that she focused on shutting down her internal signal processor, a kind of meditation that she'd been getting better at with practice. The initial analogy to meditation had come from Jacob. She was pretty sure he was still unaware that she'd gone scavenging in his psyche for help with the process of locking up her thoughts. It was something he was frighteningly adept at, and she'd needed to lessen his edge. She wasn't yet his equal, but she'd closed the gap considerably. Enough to get a good night's sleep, at any rate, without worrying about a middle-of-the-night intrusion from her mentor. Maybe he could find a way in, a back door of some kind. She'd managed it with him, after all. But she was gaining confidence in the integrity of the walls she put up from time to time.

Now the morning sun stole into her hotel room and beckoned her back to Seattle. She pinched her nipples through her cotton pajama top as she stretched and yawned, almost laughing out loud at what an odd, unintentional action it was. Her mornings were often filled with such involuntary business: rote matters of dressing and cleaning herself, coupled with the small random actions and digressions of a sleepy consciousness.

She was pleased to be in good spirits. She'd need them when she arrived at the airport and put herself on the standby list for a flight home. It was the best the airline could do for her under the circumstances. At least they didn't charge a fee for the privilege, like they did for checked luggage and extra leg room.

More than three hours after she'd showered, dressed, and checked out of the Marriott, Susan was finally cleared to board a plane. Another hour and some change to Chicago, then about four-and-a-half for the final leg. It was what the old-timers used to call a full day.

Much soap talk had run like a soundtrack through her mind as she soared high above the heartland that afternoon, and she wouldn't have taken back a single *fuck* or *shit*. Later, with the approach of evening, home had never felt more welcoming. She was almost eager to see Paul when she waved the Uber away and unlocked the front door. He walked past her on his way to the basement staircase, pausing to give her a peck on the cheek.

"You have a good trip?" he asked, completely ignorant of the fact that she was home sooner than planned.

That pretty much rolled up the welcome mat.

"Peachy," she replied and dropped her bags in a corner to deal with later. By the time she added, "Just fucking peachy," he was out of hearing range, though she did pick up a wisp of his mental gymnastics as he headed for the den: *What if they break into the workhouse just as one of the boys is smashing the jug full of coins at the feet of the prostitute ... Brilliant!* God only knew what he was dreaming up this time. Whatever it was, Susan wouldn't start spending his advance for it quite yet.

❊ ❊ ❊

Jacob's first night on the road is spent in a Motel 6 in Fergus Falls, Minnesota, northwest of the Twin Cities by a stretch. Near the North Dakota border. After twelve hours of driving he is in desperate need of sleep. But it will not come. He is unaccustomed to the cleanliness of his surroundings, the comfort of the mattress he lies on as he stares at the Stucco ceiling of his room, the lack of sirens and drunken shouting. What most would consider a recipe of sorts for restful slumber, Jacob views as a barricade. He does not know what to make of this room, devoid as it is of filth, familiarity, and decrepitude. And it's a strain to find patterns or shapes in the tiny, faint shadows of the bumps on the ceiling.

Then it hits him like a stone fist to the solar plexus: he cannot sleep because he is afraid of the room's emptiness.

But how can that be? He has been called upon to eradicate emptiness wherever he finds it, to pour his true version of reality into that emptiness whenever it threatens to leave a place cracked and decimated. If he is able to fear the void, what does that say about his prospects for becoming a divinity?

Despite a meandering trail of similar thoughts, he drops into a fitful sleep at last.

But he awakens trembling. A quick glance at the clock on the nightstand tells him he had roughly two-and-a-half hours of sleep. It is time to move on. Another long day of driving. He intends to reach western Montana before nightfall, though he will be lucky to make it half that distance without veering off the road, the way he feels.

Coffee and cigarettes, then. That will be his fuel. For the red Dodge Monaco he drives, gasoline will have to do.

His smile shifts.

Left corner up, right corner down. Right corner up, left corner down. When did he become so aware of that habit?

He is ready to fill the Dodge with gas, his belly with doughnuts and coffee, the burgeoning day with his wandering presence. In short, he is ready to ride.

Tonight he will try to connect with Susan Evans. Tonight he will not let fatigue get the better of him. And by tomorrow night, Ms. Evans will have a visitor. These things he promises himself as he carries his laptop and suitcase outside, where the bright morning sun reflects fiercely off the roof of his car.

* * *

A pleasant evening breeze stirred the cedars, firs, poplars, and dogwoods of Volunteer Park as Susan made her way along the meandering paved path, hands jammed into her pants pockets. Her stride was comfortable, her posture confident. She assumed that the people who occasionally passed by took her for an average woman enjoying a routine constitutional. Some nodded and smiled. A few even said, or thought, hello. But no two people ever have the same day, and just because the sun is shining doesn't mean it's cherries all around. Some folks suffered in the warmth of summer. Others prospered in the chill of winter. Come the change of seasons, their roles might reverse right along with their fortunes. Life was like that: full of confusion and mystery, asymmetry and false hope.

If anyone knew that, it was Susan Evans. She'd been back in Seattle for two days now, and still no signal from Jacob Kettering. She didn't like it. It made her buggy. He'd made such a fuss about having found her, and she had bought into the idea of meeting others with her abilities. The silence didn't fit the situation, and it didn't fit what she knew of Jacob's character. He wouldn't have cut off communications permanently. So what was he up to? What was he plotting?

"Susan." It was Jan, calling to her from a nearby bench.

Susan gave a brief wave and crossed over to her. Crows and pigeons argued and scrapped in the area, and a couple of seagulls cavorted in the higher currents above the treetops. It really did want to be a fine end to a fine day. Something in it wanted to prove universally irresistible, but such cajoling brought out the cynic in her. Let the general mood of the world stoop down to her level. She wasn't about to budge.

"How's my favorite schoolmarm on this beautiful summer evening?" Jan asked, smiling, her brown hair pulled back in a ponytail. "The only clouds in the sky are made of cotton. How often can you say that in this wet, dreary town?"

"You know me," Susan said. "I love a nice overcast."

"Oh, how do they let you teach fifth-graders with an attitude like that?"

Susan sat down beside Jan and gazed out across the park at the looming Space Needle and, beyond it, a narrow rectangle of Elliott Bay. The meeting had been her idea. She'd even considered letting her friend in on some of what had been going on with her. It seemed ridiculous now that the opportunity was at hand. As ridiculous as confession had always seemed when she was a good little Catholic girl. Those days were long gone. So were the days of her running to Jan with every little problem and trusting her to offer the perfect solution.

Still, she was glad she'd called her. It was good to feel her friendly presence beside her. She looked over at her and smiled. For a moment she thought she might cry, but she reeled herself back in.

"You okay, Suse?"

"I think so, yeah. Summers are always a little jarring, you know? I put so much into the teaching, and then at the end of the school year it's all yanked away, like a carpet from under my feet. I guess I'm floundering a bit more than usual this year. I feel so damn untethered."

"How are things with Paul?"

Oh, she had a knack for getting to the heart of things, this one. Only this time Paul wasn't at the heart of things. Not even close. This whole situation with Dr. Zhou and Jacob Kettering was well out of his league. *Leagues* out of his league. But he suddenly seemed like a handy scapegoat for her obvious strain.

"Never great, to be honest. He lives in a different world than you and me. I don't know what's running through his mind half the time." Which might have been true, but she was getting a clearer sense of what occupied his thoughts the other half of the time than she ever would have before Dr. Zhou's little needles went in a bit too deep. It turned out the truth wasn't any better than what she used to have to imagine was creeping around in her husband's brain. It was a miracle that he ever managed to turn a profit from his hair-brained ideas. Of course it was never the writing or art projects that brought in any cash. It was quixotic real estate deals and complicated business transactions that occasionally hit pay dirt. In Susan's view he was lucky to have a handful of intelligent, if unscrupulous, friends.

"How long has it been since he was laid off at Boeing?"

"Almost a year-and-a-half."

Jan only shook her head, but it spoke volumes about the disgust she felt toward Paul. The feeling had always been there, since long before the layoff. It had taken Susan much longer to draw some of the same conclusions as Jan about the man she'd married. The marriage itself had been a mistake, she supposed, but she didn't have the wherewithal to confront that particular problem yet. If their marriage was doomed, then maybe it would continue to unravel until there was nothing left to do or say. If so, it would be an easy job to make the split final, and legal.

Jan Pullman.

Susan heard the thought in Jacob's voice. The faintest smell of residual cigarette stink came to her. He was back.

"Susan?" Jan checked in, clearly alarmed by a change in Susan's manner or posture or facial expression.

Shit, she had to put up a wall, and fast, but that took concentration. She couldn't do it while carrying on a conversation with Jan. And yet how could she reasonably excuse herself? Better to embarrass herself a little than let the increasingly unsavory Jacob Kettering collect any more personal details than he already had, she decided. Hell, she was practically giving them away. Jan would understand, eventually.

"I'm not feeling so hot," she replied, running the back of a hand across her forehead. "I get these spells once in a while. Too much stress and not enough sleep. I'll be okay, but I should probably get back home."

"You should find another acupuncturist," Jan said. "You barely had a chance—"

"I know. But I don't think I'm so good for *their* health."

Jan smiled, but it was awkward, forced. She was uncomfortable with black humor.

Paul Manning. You didn't even take his name.

"God damn it! You little fucker. What is it you want from me?" She only thought this, but it had been close. Little Reed Watkins would have shit himself a four-pound brick if he'd heard some of the words coursing through her mind just then.

"I'll give you a call, Jan, okay?"

She didn't give Jan a chance to answer, simply made a beeline for the parking lot. She knew she wouldn't have to make the call. Jan would be texting her within five minutes and ringing her within the hour. It was good to have a close friend nearby, but right now she needed to rely on her own resolve—maybe more so than ever before. She fished her phone out of her purse and turned it off. Not only would it keep the world at bay while she built defenses against the wolf at her door, but it would give that wolf one less conduit to her.

❋ ❋ ❋

Livingston, Montana, proves not to be much different

than Fergus Falls to the eyes of a drifter like Jacob Kettering. He holes up in a Super 8 instead of a Motel 6, noting the emptiness between the two numbers (why no chain of 7th Heaven Inns?). A sign, perhaps.

He is too impatient after checking into his Spartan room, can't resist the urge to reconnect with his new friend. It is a mistake. His intrusion into her thoughts startles her, and she quickly retreats and begins efforts to block him. He should have used his phone, might have been able to do some quiet spying through hers that way. Something he's been practicing.

Still, he has gathered a couple of juicy nuggets. He is no longer afraid of the husband, for instance. That has been a thorn in his ambitions, but a little mental dredging plucked it out like child's play. Paul Manning is a modern-day roustabout. Jacob imagines him to be simpering and shy, weak of color and build. Not even empty, but rather full of shit. Shit thoughts, shit dreams, shit regrets. Shit piled on shit piled on shit.

This Jan Pullman, on the other hand, seems an extraordinarily empty vessel, practically longing to be filled. He has to remember that his impressions of the woman—and the husband, for that matter—are being filtered through the perceptions of Susan Evans, but there are possibilities there.

First, however ... Susan. Without question he will fill her first, but if that goes well and she is receptive, he might just extend his stay in Seattle.

If he ever fucking gets there. The road beneath his wheels is taking a toll. It is an emptier of men, and though he should be immune to its gravity, he is not, entirely. The road has weakened him, but there is only one more day of travel.

Not counting the return trip to Indianapolis.

He will survive this test.

Must survive this test.

That may not prove true for everyone.

❊ ❊ ❊

She knew Paul had entered the room, though it was difficult to pinpoint what had tipped her off. The sound of his muted steps on the carpet? Unlikely. A whiff of his cologne, maybe? A vaporous shadow passing across the pages of her book as he stepped into the doorway, blocking the low-wattage entry-hall light? Why couldn't he just stride into a room and announce his presence like a normal person?

Christ, her college self would be screaming in horror at her middle-aged self as it pined for normality. Well, maybe she wouldn't be pining if the odd and quirky had manifested itself in a more appealing way in Paul, she told herself. But she wondered if that was entirely true. It couldn't all be his fault. Maybe she lacked self-awareness, as well as the courage to send her man packing. Probably shouldn't have married him in the first place. Now the bother of a divorce barely seemed worth the effort. A separation, perhaps …

"Hon," Paul said, still behind her as she sat on the couch, her book upside down on one knee, "can we talk for a bit?"

Suddenly the floor lamp beside her didn't give off nearly enough light. This was not his place, to catch her unawares with something heavy. If anyone was going to initiate a heart-to-heart, it was damn sure going to be her, not him. Her heart jackhammered in her chest. Jesus, she was fucking *scared* of this!

"Can it wait?" she asked, turning her head a little in a token show of attentiveness. "I was just going to finish up this chapter and then meet up with Jan for an evening coffee."

"Well, can we set a time, then? It's important."

"Sure." She set her book beside her on the couch and managed to stand and face him with a smile she hoped didn't look as fake as it felt in the subdued light. "Can we do that tomorrow?"

"What, set a time or actually meet?"

"Set a time."

They stared at each other. She couldn't read his expression perfectly, but he seemed perplexed, unsure how to proceed. Maybe a little stymied. His head dropped, and he turned and left her alone in the room.

The meeting with Jan had been a lie, but now it felt like a good idea. She picked up her phone from an end table and roused it to life so she could text her friend, but the image on her lock screen stopped her cold. Within the small glowing rectangle of her phone was the leering face of Jacob Kettering in close-up. As a still image it was unnerving enough, but when it suddenly came to life and his head began to bob up and down with laughter, she actually dropped the phone. When she picked it up again, the image had gone back to being the picture she had taken of the front of Pierce Elementary that spring. It was like looking at a photograph that someone else had taken in a city she'd never visited. She could barely imagine returning there to work in the fall.

Quickly swiping the image away, she texted Jan. Jacob might still be lingering in the circuitry, but so be it. Chances were his appearance had only been a reminder of his presence in her life, which was bad enough. He already knew about Jan, anyway. Still, she was careful to refer to their usual coffeehouse as the "regular place," not the Bumpin' Grind, in her message to Jan. She was done feeding freebies to Jacob.

In seconds, Jan had responded in the affirmative and Susan was out the door. She felt like a bit of a shit. It was unfair, the way she'd treated Paul, but he'd caught her off guard. Blindsided her, truthfully. That was no excuse for her childish behavior, but it might get her through the night. Maybe Jan would have some additional suggestions. It would be a sign of end times if she didn't.

The place was close to empty when she walked in, so Jan would have been easy to spot even if she hadn't been sitting in their usual corner.

"You okay, love?" Jan greeted her.

Susan had decided on the way over to let Jan in on some of what was going on. She couldn't scatter all the beans, of course, but she was scared enough to want someone to know she was scared. Besides, anything was better than talking about Paul.

Maybe they could work their way to that kettle of carp, but it wasn't going to be the opening salvo.

"I'm all right," she said, taking a seat across the small table from Jan. "Tired, I guess. I haven't been getting enough sleep."

"You mentioned that yesterday at the park. Anything in particular keeping you up?"

She placed her head in her hands momentarily, then said, "I think I'm being stalked."

"What? Jesus, that's a hell of a bombshell. What do you mean, you *think* you're being stalked? By who?"

"Whom," Susan corrected, but Jan's steady gaze told her it was no time for grammatical policing, and she let it drop. "Sorry. Look, I really don't have the energy to go into all the details tonight, but I want you to know that I'm ... concerned."

"Well, shit yes. So am I. Good God, stalked ..." Jan shook her head in disbelief. "Have you talked to the police?"

"No, not yet. I haven't even brought it up with Paul."

"Don't you think you ought to?"

"I suppose. I don't know. It's complicated."

"Do you know the creep? Are you safe at home?"

"He's an acquaintance. I'm safe for the time being. He's not in Seattle right now. He's not even in Washington."

"Well, that's a relief. Listen, you can come to me with anything. You know that, right? Anything. Any time."

Susan nodded, surprised to find herself a little choked up by the quick sincerity of Jan's concern.

"Are you going to have anything?" Jan asked, taking a sip from her cup.

"I guess I could handle a decaf," she said, trying to smile. "It's too late for the real thing. Be right back."

In a few moments she returned with her low-octane coffee. They both slipped into mundane conversation, as if agreeing telepathically that they'd had enough of the heavy stuff for one night. But there was nothing telepathic about it. For one thing, Susan had vowed not to pry into the mind of her best friend. That was one Pandora's box she had no intention of opening. When her mother had died Susan read her journals. It remained one of her deepest regrets. She wasn't about to make the same mistake on a far more intrusive level. The temptation was there, of course, but wasn't it always? Like a figure in the smoke, beckoning with the repeating curl of its forefinger …

❉ ❉ ❉

He watches her leave the coffee shop with the ridiculous name. It is a name empty of meaning, and he loathes the intentional avoidance of meaning. All things in the coming age will be filled with meaning. *His* meaning.

Susan Evans is on foot, and it is nighttime. Good. Contact will be easy. Real physical contact at last.

He follows her into the next block. There is less light, less activity. He increases his pace, closes the gap. She stops dead and turns her head slightly. He also stops, sensing that she is aware of both his presence and identity.

"Face me," he says. In his mind it was an implacable command, but it comes out soft and timid.

Nonetheless she complies.

"I guess I knew we'd meet eventually, even though you stood me up in Indianapolis," she says.

"You weren't ready. I thought you were, but you weren't."

"I see."

❉ ❉ ❉

What she really saw was that he was lying through his crooked teeth. He was the one who hadn't been ready, or capable, in Indiana. The question was, Ready or capable of what?

"And what is it I'm now ready for?" she asked, playing his game for the time being.

"To be filled up."

She didn't like the sound of that.

"What do you mean?"

"I want you to be my acolyte. I wish to fill you with knowledge and wisdom, make you my disciple."

Jesus.

"How do you see that happening? I don't feel like I need … filling up."

"Oh, but you do. They all do, but you're special. I plan to fill you in another way as well."

"Jacob, no."

"Oh, yes, Susan. You are to be my bride. I will fill you with my seed, and then you will be fertile for my message."

Fight or flight? It was an actual conscious question, not a mere evolutionary reaction. She felt the need to make a choice, and it was flight. But not before she could get off a barb.

"You goddamn empty-headed little pervert."

As she peeled off in the direction of a nearby alley, his voice thundered after her. No longer timid, it bellowed and resonated. Was he sending his response mentally as well? Hard to tell, but it was loud and fearsome:

"You'll pay for that, you insolent bitch!"

So much for her vague hope that a remonstrance might cool him off.

His boot heels clacked on the pavement as he began his pursuit. He was blocking his thoughts from her, which was good. It was harder to reach into the minds of others when you were busy guarding your own. Her defenses were also up, which gave her additional protection. He already had the advantage of surprise and strength. She wasn't about to welcome him into her head as well.

Block after block rolled away beneath her feet and his footsteps neared. She tripped on a bit of uneven sidewalk but didn't go down. Still, she was tiring, and he sounded very close.

"Do you think you can actually win against me?" His voice was choppy from heavy breathing. He was tired, too.

She didn't bother to respond, but the conservation of her energies was for naught. A hand clamped onto her shoulder and gave her a spin, as if she were a top. The motion sent her stumbling into a parking strip and banging face-first into the trunk of a vine maple. Stunned, she stared at the tree and struggled to remain upright, knowing that falling would spell defeat. In the end it didn't matter. Jacob was upon her before she could collapse. Defeat had come.

❊ ❊ ❊

"Where are you taking me," she wants to know.

"You'll see," Jacob responds.

She doesn't scream. He will kill her right here in the middle of the street if she screams, but it is not the way he wants this to end. He has held a contingency plan in his mind's back pocket since an epiphany halfway between Livingston and Seattle. Like everything in his life, what he knows of Susan Evans has been stolen. That includes the location of the school where she teaches fifth-grade students how to be productive members of society. He wonders if she is unwittingly producing another potential god like him as well. If so, he may have competition in the future.

His smile shifts from one side of his mouth to the other as he pushes her through an open gate in the chain link fence that runs the perimeter of the schoolyard.

"Do you know what people yearn for most, Susan? What they lack more than anything?"

She shakes her head nervously.

"An unbelievable story," he continues. "A story that shocks and bewilders but is absolutely true, to all appearances. That's exactly what we're going to give them."

They arrive at a rear entrance to the old brick schoolhouse, and she looks at him with wonder.

"The key, please," he says. "And don't bullshit me. I know that it never leaves your purse."

Her struggle to find a believable lie is obvious. She quickly resigns herself to the futility of it and hands over the requested key, which he uses to let them in.

"Now, take me to your classroom. Then we'll talk."

Once inside room twenty-three, he takes a seat on top of one of the undersized desks and motions for Susan to do the same. She declines. He shrugs and shifts his smile. Does she smirk at him briefly? He lets it go.

"I'll give you one more chance to be my willing bride. Rule with me in my new kingdom."

"I'll say this once," she replies, "then you do what you have to do. There is no pain exquisite enough, no longing deep enough, no fear debilitating enough to make me give myself to you in body, mind, or spirit. What I thought you had to offer turns out to be a complete falsehood, so I want you out of my life. How do I achieve that?"

"Easy," he says, standing quickly and pulling something out of his back pocket.

Before she can register his intent, he has her spun around and is cuffing her hands behind her. Real metal cuffs, too. They've been in his possession ever since he swiped them off a stolid cop who was hassling him and some fellow hooligans a number of years back. He still has the key somewhere, too, but no longer needs it. The lock is easily disengaged with a little concentrated thought.

"You've grown strong," he continues. "You are a citadel to me. What goes on in that head of yours, hmm?"

He doesn't wait for an answer. She is done talking and her thoughts are locked. He could break in, but he has other business to focus on, which is why he climbs onto the large desk at the front of the classroom and stands to his full height. Reaching almost to his limit he punches a ceiling panel upward. It lands askew on a flimsy metal framework. He is not satisfied and punches a second panel loose, and a third. *Ah, jackpot!* A thick water pipe runs above this last panel. He scoots the square of asbestos amalgam almost completely out of sight.

"Join me," he commands.

She turns her back to him and wiggles her fingers.

He jumps down and lifts her to a sitting position on the desk. After hauling himself back up, he is able to help her to her feet. If she expected him to undo the cuffs already, she was in for a great disappointment. She has worn a scarf out tonight. Good. He would have found something else—a cord from one of the window blinds, perhaps—but the scarf will make things much easier. Before she realizes what he's up to, he is knotting the crocheted garment around her throat, good and tight.

"Fuck, dammit!" she squawks.

With the same swiftness used to secure the one end of the scarf, he ties the other snugly around the pipe in the ceiling before looking intently into Susan's eyes to enjoy the dawning fear there. He doesn't see the kick to the groin coming, but it's weak and off center. He quickly jumps to the floor and squints fiercely. The handcuffs click free and fall to the desk. She aims for his head this time, but he manages to dodge the kick. He upends the desk in a cacophony of metal on tile flooring.

Susan drops to the end of the makeshift noose and twitches grotesquely, kicking one pump off in the process. Jacob watches her closely until her body goes limp and only swings gently back and forth. It is disgusting that things have had to end this way. He envisioned so much more for the woman. For both of them.

"You are now the story I referred to," he says to the strange pendulum. "People will devour your suicide. How could an elementary school teacher do such a thing? And why would she go to the trouble of doing it in her classroom after hours? In the summer months, no less! So many questions. So much symbolism. So much improbability. All of which will make it seem undeniably true. I wonder who will find you in the morning. Or will you hang there for days before a janitor bothers to check in on room twenty-three? Supposed to get pretty hot in the next few days. There is much to speculate about."

Retrieving the handcuffs, Jacob Kettering tosses Susan's school key to the floor and makes a hasty exit. He has never been more sickened, angry, or let down in his life, but he will not go forth like a lunatic. He will retreat as far as Livingston to gather his thoughts and prepare for the next campaign, but Jan Pullman will never be far from his thoughts. Maybe she will be the bride he hoped Susan would be, but he will not hold out any great hope. If she acquiesces, fine. If not ...

Well, if not, not.

* * *

She should have expected violence. Why else would he want to chase her down in the night and get her alone, away from prying eyes?

But why lead her to the very school building where she taught? It had puzzled her. Now, of course, she had an answer.

Stars filled the firmament of her mind's eye. Her neck throbbed with pain. If he'd used anything other than the scarf, she might not have been having these thoughts, might not have lived long enough to hear his bizarre logic in hanging her here. But he chose to lynch her with the scarf that Jan had crocheted for her the previous Christmas. It *could* have killed her, but a crocheted scarf has some give to it. In her case, that give had been enough to keep her neck from snapping when the desk had been yanked from beneath her. As a result, she now had a real chance.

Her weight shifted. Her thoughts had become a circuit, crawling up the yarn of the scarf to work loose the knot around the pipe before returning to their source to deliver a progress report and gather steam for a subsequent lap. Another slight bounce. It was working!

Two more laps of pure thought energy and she scarf broke free of the pipe, sending her crashing to the floor. She couldn't undo the knot about her neck quickly enough. Breath came in strained gasps as she rubbed her sore flesh. She had done it, actually used her mind to manipulate reality. Astonishing. And frightening, when she remembered that Jacob possessed similar abilities and was more skilled at using them. He was also still out there somewhere—barely out of the building, most likely.

She rose to her feet and immediately knew the movement had been too soon and too fast. The room began to rotate and tilt. She tried to focus on centering herself, but it was a lost cause. Her last thoughts this side of unconsciousness were of her experience at Dr. Zhou's acupuncture clinic. This was only a fall, she told herself. Worse than the one she'd experienced at Dr. Zhou's, perhaps, but not akin to the fall *he* had taken behind the counter while she rested in one of his procedure rooms. She would survive this, but right now her body needed quiescence.

And like that, it came.

❉   ❉   ❉

Night is the best time to drive. Some people think of the night as empty compared to the day, but it's an illusion caused by the blinding darkness. The world comes alive in the nighttime, claimed by a whole new race of creatures. The intentions of these night creatures are different than those of their daytime counterparts. And the darkness itself has a density that makes the daylight seem drained and withered by comparison. Empty.

He drives fast in the dark, unencumbered by the constant need to watch for danger, even though it still inhabits the world. Driving at night is like sliding down a tunnel: prescribed and inevitable. This particular tunnel will deposit Jacob in the womb of the Super 8 in Livingston. He can see this destination more clearly in his mind than he can see anything outside the windows of his Dodge in the impenetrable night. That's because the night shows you nothing but what you need to see. It will even show you the truth if you let it.

Jacob is very interested in truth tonight, but he's almost as interested in sleep. He spends so much time being tired these days, and there is no real rest in sight. But there is a Super 8 not too many miles up the road, and no shortage of ideas banging around in his head.

* * *

"Well, here it is," Paul said holding up the small clock radio she'd asked him to bring to the hospital. He placed it on a mobile tray set up for her use, plugged it into the nearest outlet, and set the clock. "I still don't understand why this couldn't have waited until after sunup, but I guess a brush with the beyond warrants an eccentric request or two."

She tried not to laugh but failed. "Sunup? Is that when you milk the chickens, Farmer Paul?"

He smiled warmly at her good-natured ribbing. It was odd how sudden adversity could wipe away years. She felt closer to her husband than she had when they moved into their first home. There was still the matter of what had been on his mind the night before, but it could wait. Maybe it could wait forever.

"I'm going to let you rest," he said. "I'll be back later in the morning. Do you need me to bring anything else?"

"No, and thanks."

He kissed her lightly and slipped out of the room. The holstered sidearm of a local police officer was framed in the doorway until the door swung shut again.

Susan reached over to switch on the radio. She tuned it to unadulterated static, set the volume so low it was practically silent, and then readjusted herself and closed her eyes.

Not that she was at all tired. This wasn't a sleep ritual. It was revenge.

* * *

His eyes flash open in sudden wakefulness. He was dreaming—a rich, complicated dream—but not a single detail is available to him now. Did he turn on the bedside radio before going to bed, or did he do it in his sleep? A song that he can almost name is playing, but it cuts off abruptly and is replaced with static.

He does not turn his head, only goes on staring at the ceiling, and listening.

The static fades to clarity.

"We have a request now, ladies and gentlemen," a female voice on the radio announces. "This one goes out from the Great Big Empty to one Jacob Kettering of Indianapolis, though I think I have him pinned down to a two-bit motel in western Montana at the moment. Folks, there is only one King, and we have him here for you right now, singing 'Suspicious Minds.' If you're out there, Jacob, I hope you enjoy this. I know you've been lonely, but you'll have company very soon. The kind of company that arrives with badges flashing and guns drawn. Good night for now ... and good morning."

It is her. Susan Evans. But how is that possible? Has she grown so strong that she can communicate even from beyond the grave, and along radio waves? The thought sends a chill through his body. He feels frightened and vulnerable. Worse, he feels empty. Empty of ideas, empty of will, empty of excuses. Empty except for fear and vulnerability. As if to punctuate the realization, his stomach growls with early morning hunger.

A pounding at the door.

"Jacob Kettering?" A man's voice, deep and ragged. "Police. Open up!"

It is like viewing his destiny through a funnel, his options narrowing as his gaze moves deeper into the cone. One thing he does not have to put up with for a minute longer, however, is the monotonous drone of Elvis Presley. He reaches across and slaps the radio off. The song continues for several seconds, which paralyzes him with terror, but eventually it fades to silence.

"I'm coming and I'm unarmed!" he calls out.

He will find a way out of this, locate his confidence again. But for now, compliance is the only way. They will regret hauling Jacob Kettering in on a murder charge. He will make them all pay for the emptiness of their decision to hunt him down like an animal. But he can play the role of the caged monster for a time, and he will take the lessons he learns back into the wilderness with him.

He pauses at the door. Someone is in his thoughts. No, not just someone. Her.

And in that instant he realizes that she is not dead after all. Somehow she has survived the hanging. And that means he is only up on charges of *attempted* murder.

His ever-present smile alternates its tilt. Back and forth. Forth and back.

"Here I come," he says as he opens the door of his motel room.

Here I come, he thinks, sending it across the miles to the puzzling woman with the gall to resist his will.

Her terror comes to him then, almost like a coppery smell, before she can lock him out of her thoughts. A small victory, but one that he relishes as they cuff him and squeeze him into the back of an awaiting patrol car.

Jacob Kettering has been had, but he just goes on shifting that smile of his all the way to the Livingston police station. He'll smile all the way to hell if he has to. For once in his miserable life he has something to smile *about*: he has met a worthy foe.

CHANDU'S BARGAIN WITH THE TOO-TALL MAN

The Vicinity of Bagdi-Kalera, a Small Fishing Village Near the Southwest Coast of India

2014

The village and its environs lie close to the great Arabian Sea. A dense coverage of trees and undergrowth protects it on all sides, but the Too-Tall Man has woven his way through worse. At eight feet tall he can reach branches most wouldn't give a second thought to, and use them to swing himself over patches of difficult terrain. With straw-like legs he can jump over fallen trees and treacherous ditches, always landing with insect precision. His brown skin keeps him hidden at night, and his wide, curious eyes—though yellowed with fever—see through the dark like a cat's.

Over each shoulder is slung a pouch dense with seed, and when the Too-Tall Man reaches his destination, he unburdens himself of one of the leather bags. He has chosen a grassy valley that lies to the northwest of Bagdi-Kalera, though not by much. Twenty minutes' walk for the average man is all. Less, if your legs are as tall and sinewy as the Too-Tall Man's. With a rictus that any onlooker would describe as sickly, or even pained, he begins to sprinkle handfuls of seed from the pouch he's removed from his right shoulder. He scatters the tiny black pellets in wide arcs, then winnows away what's left in his palm before reaching for another handful. Soon the clearing he has selected for the task is blanketed with seeds.

His work done, he shifts his way north, leaving the village far behind in no time at all. He has been called many things over the years, but what he truly is, more than anything, is patient. It is time once again to put that patience to the test.

* * *

2015

Chandu wandered farther beyond the outskirts of the village than he had for a long time. He knew it was farther than his grandfather would have liked, but adventure called to him now that the monsoon rains had lifted and given way to warm, bright days—the first in too many weeks.

He used to visit a small clearing to the northwest of the village, and he headed there now. It was as secluded as any of the places that were more popular with the other children of Bagdi-Kalera, and it had the added advantage of being relatively flat and free of the wild ground cover that dominated elsewhere. For that reason, he almost thought he'd misjudged his whereabouts when he parted the low-hanging leaves of a papaya plant, expecting to find his grassy hideaway but instead confronted by a dense cluster of plants—a variety he'd never seen before.

The layout of the area was unmistakable, however: round and wide where he stood, narrowing like a cashew fruit laid on its side as he gazed across to the point directly opposite. The strange new plant occupied every square inch of space. Leaning over, Chandu reached for one of the leaves that scrolled outward from a hearty stem. It was thick and pliant. Then he spotted a specimen farther in with a leaf that had snapped open, apparently from its own weight. The top side of the leaf was torn through, but the underside held and kept half of the leaf from falling to the ground. At the tear, something had oozed out. Chandu pushed his way through to the injured plant and touched the sap. It was sticky.

He stared at the smudge on the tip of his finger. His instinct was to roll the substance into a ball between his thumb and forefinger so he could flick it away, but a smell like rifle smoke and fresh sawdust drifted up and sent a thrill snaking through him. He couldn't resist bringing his finger slowly to his tongue. It wasn't much, just a dab, but it told Chandu that the nectar was sweet. He immediately ran the same finger along the seam of the leaf. This time it came back wet with the honey-like fluid. He pushed his finger halfway into his mouth and sucked every last bit of sap from it.

The sweetness intensified until it tightened his throat. He almost gagged, but then the sensation switched off without so much as an aftertaste. One moment his mouth was filled with the most cloying sweetness he'd ever known. The next it was as if he hadn't even tasted what flowed in the plant's veins.

Then he lost his vision, and nearly fell to his knees. He didn't lose his sight to darkness, but to a fantastic flash of white. This, too, intensified, and he squinted against the brightness in his mind. Still, he avoided panic by convincing himself that the strange effect would do as the sweet taste had done and be gone in a moment. It turned out he was right, and it happened just as suddenly.

Wanting to run home and tell his grandfather about the wonderful plant he'd discovered, he turned and took a step back toward the perimeter of the clearing. Then he stopped. A strange feeling worked its way up from his stomach to his throat, a cross between hunger and thirst, but stronger than either of those. He turned back to the plant he'd tasted from. It seemed to pulsate with a kind of blue radiance. Probably another after-effect, and one he did not attempt to resist. Taking the leaf in both hands, he tore half of it off at the seam and sank his teeth into the inviting flesh. So much sweet fluid gushed into his mouth that it couldn't all be contained. Some spilled out between his lips and dribbled from his chin to stain his shirt front. Most of it he swallowed.

Eventually he had his fill, and after his taste buds and

vision returned to normal once more, Chandu made his way back to the village—though he did not run. Something in the nectar had left him feeling sluggish and reduced. But also good. Oh yes, he felt very good indeed.

❊ ❊ ❊

2016

"Another set of twins?" Chandu's grandfather said to the boy's mother when she told him the news. "That's the fourth twin birth this year."

"I can't remember the last time there were twins in Bagdi-Kalera before this," she said.

"It's been seven or eight years, I think." The old man sat down on a mat and lit a bidi.

"Why now?" Chandu wanted to know.

"It must have something to do with the sweet-bright you discovered," his mother told him. "It can't be a coincidence."

"You know what I think?" said the grandfather. "I think it's a blessing from Allah. He's making our village strong, maybe preparing us for battle."

"Ach, battle," she said. "I swear, the frogs that hop around inside your skull. Besides, two of the recent births were Hindu."

"Maybe sometimes the gods collaborate."

"You shouldn't say such things, even as a joke."

"Why shouldn't he?" Chandu asked.

"He just shouldn't." She stormed out of the hut.

"Do you really believe what you said?" Chandu asked his grandfather once his mother was out of earshot.

"Sure I do. Why not? Ever since we started cooking with the sweet-bright nectar, stirring it into our curries and using it to flavor our sauces, our women have grown very fertile. It's a blessing, and we have you to thank."

"But I mean the part about the gods collaborating."

Chandu's grandfather smiled before blowing a cloud of smoke into the already hazy air. "What I say stays between us. You understand?"

Chandu nodded.

"Your mother thinks I go against our teachings when I talk about such things, but sometimes a man has to speak his mind, even an old man like me." He chuckled, which prompted Chandu to do the same. "To believe in and worship Allah is one thing, but to claim to understand precisely how He operates ... That seems like more of a sin to me than a little imaginative speculation here and there." He coughed and laughed at the same time.

Chandu thought his grandfather might have more to say, but another cough gave way to stony silence. With no further information forthcoming, and the smoke making Chandu a little lightheaded, he left the old man to his ruminations, and his cheap cigarette.

✹ ✹ ✹

2017

"Mama, come quick!" Chandu went down on his haunches to address his mother while she struggled with a bent wheel assembly on their wheelbarrow. "The woman across the square is going into labor."

"And what am I supposed to do about it?" She kept working, didn't look at him. "Not that your grandfather was much help while he was alive, but he's gone now, so there's even more to be done around here. And you, always fishing or swimming."

"But don't you want to know?"

"Know what?" She wiped sweat from her forehead and cheeks, then continued to tug at the axle.

"If it's triplets, like the last one. Some of the children are placing bets."

"I imagine we'll find out one way or the other, in due course."

Chandu thought he might burst, so he left his mother to the wheelbarrow and ran down to the little house across the square. The sounds coming out of it kept him at the doorstep, however. From inside came the wails and screams of a woman in agony.

Eventually a girl about Chandu's age stepped outside and greeted him.

"You want to know how many there are, I suppose," the girl said.

The crying of at least two infants could be heard now.

"It's triplets, isn't it?" he said.

The girl chewed on a leaf of sweet-bright. "One died coming out, but yes. It was going to be three. Looked like he might make it at first. I could see him gasping for air, his little eyes rolling around like he was looking for help, but there was none to be had. He gurgled a little, then his eyes rolled up and he was still."

Trying not to think about what they'd done with the dead one, Chandu snapped his fingers and slapped his leg. "I knew it! It's *that* stuff doing it, you know." He pointed at the succulent leaf in the girl's hand.

"Maybe so." She shrugged her shoulders and strolled away.

The scent of the syrup wafted to Chandu, and his mouth watered. Turning from the house, he made his way to the orchard, as he had come to think of the stand of sweet-bright plants, even though they didn't produce a fruit. He wouldn't be able to carry as many leaves as he would in the wheelbarrow, but maybe he could cheer his mother up a little with a small load.

First twins, now triplets. Had his grandfather been right about Bagdi-Kalera being chosen for greatness? Was the little village he loved marked for some kind of important change? "Choose your beliefs carefully," his grandfather had instructed. "Once they take hold, they aren't easily altered—and sometimes they lead to unpredictable consequences." He would dwell on this during evening prayer.

* * *

2018

Chandu sat at the prow of his fishing boat, violet clouds gathering in the western sky at his back, casting a long, jagged shadow from sea to shore. He would have to be satisfied with his meager catch for the day if he wanted to stay ahead of the storm: half a net of mangrove red snapper and a good-sized yellowspotted trevally. At least the red snapper would pay for the day's outing. After sweet-bright, it was the most popular food in the village.

Some of his customers worried about over-fishing, which he had to admit was becoming a problem. Company trawlers dotted the Arabian Sea these days, almost military in their formations. Chandu's mind was occupied by a different concern today, however. When the women of Bagdi-Kalera had been giving birth to twins, it represented maybe sixty percent of all births. The rate hadn't started that high, but that's about where it was by the time of the first triplet birth. Once the triplets started coming, all twin births ceased and the rate of triplets quickly surpassed the twin rate at its height. Now the village had moved on to quadruplets—no more twins *or* triplets—and the rate had climbed past ninety percent, in Chandu's estimation. Worse, though most of the children were surviving labor, more and more of the mothers were not.

His grandfather had taught him much of what he knew about the world, including mathematics, but he wondered if the old man had been wrong after all about the twin births being a blessing on the village. Now that the situation had evolved into quadruplet births, it felt more like a curse, or at least a serious problem. Where would it end?

Either way, it had to be connected to that damn plant.

Both his mother and grandfather had seen that as clearly as he did. As a boy he'd been proud to have discovered it. Now he wished he had decided not to go to his favorite clearing that day, or ever again—especially since trying to give up eating the leaves and the syrup they contained. That had been almost a year ago, and he hadn't tried to quit again since. It was hopeless to try to make it through life without the sweet-bright once you'd tried it. Impossible, maybe.

❋ ❋ ❋

Present Day

The Too-Tall Man waits for fear to settle into the hearts of the villagers, fear so strong that no woman of birthing age dares to take a lover. Pregnancy is now a death sentence in Bagdi-Kalera. Every fetus comes with seven siblings. No child or mother has survived this new plateau. It is a very pleasing development in the eyes of the Too-Tall Man. Where the villagers see despair, he sees opportunity. Of course, this has been his intention all along.

And so he wanders into the village to strike a bargain with the desperate people who live there. The first person he encounters is a healthy-looking young man. No doubt he'd be a father by now, or thinking about becoming one, if things were different.

"Chandu," The Too-Tall Man whispers from behind a tree, the name coming to him like smoke. "Come closer. I have a message for you."

The younger man is startled by the stranger's appearance —and that his name is known to him—but he warily approaches.

"Who are you? I've never seen you around here."

"I'm a farmer of sorts," says the Too-Tall Man, his voice like scorched butter. "A planter. You're familiar with one of my crops,

I think."

Chandu eyes the Too-Tall Man's leather pouches of seed before responding. "You planted the sweet-bright, didn't you?"

"Sweet-bright? Is that what you call it?" He smiles. "Yes, I can see why. It has gone by other names, but sweet-bright will do."

"I wish I'd never found the plants. They've made my village ill."

"Not ill, I think. Barren, yes?"

"Barren? Hardly. Our women are *too* fertile if anything."

"Have it your way. It amounts to the same thing."

"What have you done?"

"Nothing I can't undo if I so choose." The Too-Tall Man leans in close. "I can rip that crop from the soil and replace it with another."

Chandu takes a step back.

"Ah, that alarms you some. Fear not. The new crop will satisfy your cravings just as well."

"That's not why I—"

"Oh, I think it's exactly why. Perhaps you're also worried for the future of your little village, but your first thought was of the nectar, and how you don't want me to take it away."

"How would this new plant be different?" Chandu tries not to sound as curious as he is.

"Better flavor, stronger sensation, if that's what you mean."

"It's not what I mean, dammit!"

The Too-Tall man's features fall and darken. "Your women will go back to having twins."

"*Only* twins?"

"No more, no less. Such generosity on my part cannot go unrewarded, you understand."

"What's your price?"

"Nothing much, really."

"Name it, then."

"Such a small price, to be free of your current situation." A certain playfulness has crept into the Too-Tall Man's voice.

"If you're making an offer, I want to know the terms."

"Fine, fine. I'll lay them out plain, then. One twin from each set. That's my price."

"What? That's madness. What could you possibly want with them?"

The Too-Tall Man stretches to his full height. "The terms are not negotiable, and my reasons are none of your concern. You bring me a child from every birth, or I come for it myself." Then, almost in a whisper, "This latter option you do not wish to entertain. There are sometimes … additional consequences."

"What if I say no?"

"Then your pretty little village dies out, doesn't it?"

"Why didn't you just plant the new variety to begin with? Why bother with the sweet-bright at all?"

"That's not how it works." Frustration is beginning to show at the Too-Tall Man's temples. "The first sowing readies the soil. That's all you need to know."

"I'll have to talk it over with—"

"Oh, they don't need to know every detail at once. Why not let them sample the goods first, develop a taste for the new plant. In time you can assure them it's okay to begin copulating again. Shortly after," he says with a shallow bow and a spreading of the hands, "you can tell them the rest."

Chandu only nods and turns away from the Too-Tall Man, as if under a spell. The scatterer of seeds is satisfied that his message has landed on fertile soil. The young man will seek out the new crop, probably soon. It will be ready for him, too, for it grows like fire. And its nectar will shame the syrup of the so-called sweet-bright leaves. The village will be at the mercy of the Too-Tall Man before the passing of another moon, and soon he will have a family of his own. He has never learned the trick of taking a wife, but he will see his dream of a large family made true at last. The nature and purpose of that family is known only to him, and the people of Bagdi-Kalera are in for a horrifying surprise when the offspring begin to arrive. Some will come wearing horns, others fitted with fangs. Many will be born with skin like burned leather, a few covered in scales or fur from head to toe. Most will have deep-set eyes as black as coal. All will carry fury in their hearts and malice in their souls. The village women can keep their share of the children, as promised, but the Too-Tall Man suspects that most will choose to give up both twins, and hope never to give birth again. But they *will* give birth again, because there is a new addiction in the veins of the plant he intends to sow. A carnal addiction.

He slinks away toward the woods, eager to begin ripping the sagweed up by its roots. It will be pleasant work under a pale moon, and soon he will be pulling handfuls of seed from the pouch that hangs from his left shoulder and mantling the hungry ground with the grains that will grow into towering ferns of Iblis.

"May the villagers conjure an equally pretty nickname for you, my lovelies," he whispers, patting the heavy pouch as he walks in long, sweeping strides, "and may you sprout into a bumper crop! My family is counting on it."

THE WINTROSE CHRONICLES

The Desecration of Wintrose Abbey

He'd seen a terrible thing some nights previous, and after jotting down a handful of words, he realized he'd not be free of the image. He put it all down in ink nonetheless, hoping to cleanse his mind of the sight, hoping that writing about it would be a substitute for talking with someone, because that was no longer a possibility. He hadn't even spoken to himself since it happened, for fear of breaking the silence that ruled every crack and crevice in the decaying edifice. The quiet had been unsettling at first, but he'd grown accustomed to it and could no longer imagine what it would be like to shatter the stillness with a scream, or even a whisper. It would only remind him he was the last living inhabitant of Wintrose Abbey.

He hadn't always been such a fearful man. Seclusion had altered him. Seclusion and the thing he'd witnessed. Although it haunted his waking thoughts, as well as his dreams, to stare it down and describe it in words was a test of his abilities. He had become not only fearful but superstitious—the worst kind of cowardice. He began to worry that by calling attention to what he'd seen, he risked inviting a similar fate upon myself.

Seeing the man sway in the moonlight, like a cattail in a

spring breeze, had been a break in his monotonous existence. It was the lone monk he'd yearned to make contact with since arriving at the abbey, and the sight of him was a kind of glory to his tired old eyes at first, though it soon became obvious that something wasn't right. Still, the parched mind sometimes puts aside skepticism when faced with an oasis. Here was the man with whom he might finally discuss literature and philosophy. With whom he might joke and laugh, argue and reminisce. He wasn't eager to question such potential happiness. Here he was with the courage at last to confront the holy man, who for once wasn't slipping out of sight before he could reach him.

As he neared, however, it became clear the monk was in no condition to converse. His legs had been anchored to the earth with heavy iron contraptions that appeared to be screwed into his calves and shins at about a dozen different points. All around him, driven deep into the ground, was a circle of spikes angled in at him. If his body collapsed in any direction, he would meet the long, sharp points and jerk himself away. This is why the ascetic swayed so preternaturally in the windless cloister.

When our wanderer came around to greet the unlucky soul and offer what help he could, he found that the face had been peeled away, the tongue removed. But the eyes had life enough to see. The holy man's arms reached out, though the movement only caused him to fall backward onto a cluster of spikes, and to shoot forward once again. Had there ever been a thing as weary in the eyes as this man was? It was those eyes as much as anything that had forced Wintrose Abbey's newest visitor to slumber during the day, for sleep was an absolute impossibility in the incalculably dark mountain nights that enveloped him for twelve of every twenty-four hours.

He sensed it was only a matter of time before he'd be discovered by whoever had done this unholy work. He had no guess as to who it would be, or what the villain had against the poor man in the cloister. Out of pity, he'd opened the man's throat himself and put an end to his suffering, and that, too, haunted him. He prayed for the courage to end his own life before being found, but it wasn't likely. He was too much of a coward for that. But he would welcome death, in whatever form it adopted, if it brought an end to the images that refused to leave his brain and threatened to drive him mad.

His written account of the event didn't amount to much, but he sealed the document and hid it, hoping it might prove useful to some future soul—if nothing else, as evidence against whatever monster roamed those lonesome woods with blood on its mind.

❊ ❊ ❊

II

The Wintrose Crucible

"Do you think it's gone?" Brother Gabbin asked.

"I can't be sure," whispered Brother Drear.

Brother Wintrose only stared up through the cracks in the floor, flicking his eyes back and forth in an effort to catch a glimpse of the thing—or a sign of its departure.

The three monks had found the small house several months ago, and Wintrose immediately took it as a sign that he was on the right path, that he was one step closer to seeing his abbey built. Now he wondered why God would provide a shelter in which he and his brethren could begin their studies and plans in earnest, only to introduce such vile horrors into their lives as these beings that had been roaming the woods lately, and now infiltrating their dwelling. As a test of faith it seemed inordinately rigorous, but a divine test was a hopeful possibility, so he allowed it to become belief. If nothing else, it had given him something to tell Gabbin and Drear to ease their harried minds a bit.

Wintrose was about to suggest that he leave the crawlspace to investigate, when the clicking of nails on the floor above their heads resumed. He could imagine the long, ugly talons, four per foot, as they sounded on the wood from one corner of the room to another. The shins of these prowlers angled backward to meet knobbed knees. This one's long, flat head was likely to be swiveling now, searching at the end of its sinewy neck. Sniffing out meat. Its diaphanous wings would be drawn in to its sides while it was indoors. The monks couldn't hope to avoid capture forever. It was a miracle they hadn't been dispatched already. They had no good estimate of the numbers these creatures had achieved. More every day, at any rate. Or rather, every *night*, for they only began their hunting and seeking after sunset, which is partly why Brothers Gabbin, Drear, and Wintrose had managed to stay alive this long; the days allowed them to move around, fortify, and contemplate.

Drear had come up with the unsettling notion that the horrid beasts weren't just passing through, but were coming up from one of Hell's reeking vents to put down roots in the Rocky Forest. Maybe, he had suggested one night as the three of them passed around a jug of wine, the monsters weren't just after food as they scoured the countryside, snouts low to the ground. Perhaps they were looking for a place to start a kingdom, in much the way Wintrose hoped to realize his dream of a proper mountain hermitage, where the brotherhood could grow and flourish. The idea had an apocalyptic note Wintrose couldn't ignore—or claim to find wholly unappealing. In a way, it strengthened his resolve to raise battlements against the forces of evil. It wasn't impossible that Brother Drear had hit upon the very logic behind God's test, but Brother Wintrose knew to be cautious of convenient answers. Being overly eager to believe, he had learned long ago, was no better than rejecting intimations of the divine out of hand.

At length, the clicking trailed off. Presumably the horror had slunk out through the main door. Wintrose could tell the other two men were looking at him, though only a thin, washed-out facsimile of light trickled into the crawlspace. He stared back into their dimly lit faces but said nothing. The door to the house groaned on its heavy iron hinges and snapped shut. Dread crawled down Wintrose's back as he envisioned the thing pausing to close the door on its way out, no doubt with a toothy leer and one of the low grumbles they sometimes made when they were more or less content. At least this one hadn't done any of the hideous caterwauling they often exhibited— never a signal of contentment, only of sheer animal rage and frustration.

Wintrose pushed open the trapdoor and took a careful look around. The room was clear, so he hauled himself up and then helped his friends. The thing had left the dozen or so lit candles in the room unmolested, and he wondered if it had sensed holiness here—and feared it. He couldn't help seeing omens in almost everything these days.

Sleep didn't come easily to Wintrose. Not only was he shaken by their narrow avoidance of detection and capture, but the intruder had made child's play of the oaken bolt they'd used to lock the door. Tomorrow they would reassemble the mechanism, but nothing prevented the creature, or its deformed cousins, from returning in the night.

When sleep finally claimed him, it was deep and consuming.

In the morning, he was the last to wake, which was unusual. And how quickly daybreak chased away the flittering shades of nighttime's frights! Adjusting his appearance before a mirror, he attributed his sound sleep to a growing sense of being on the side of righteousness. All thoughts of being too scared to fall asleep in recent weeks were gone from his head, until he stepped away from the mirror and recognized his arrogance. Pride would be the topic of their next philosophical discussion, he decided.

"Brother Gabbin," Drear said, excitedly tapping his friend's forearm and struggling to swallow a mouthful of gruel, "do tell Brother Wintrose what you've just told me. You won't believe it."

He turned to Wintrose. "You simply won't believe it."

Wintrose joined them at the table but took no food, only clasped his hands before him in the manner of prayer.

"When I was out yesterday," Gabbin said, "I came upon a house along Bredloe Pass. I was trying to find the most accessible route up the ridge you've talked about as a possible site for the abbey, so I went deeper into the hills than we've yet been."

"This house," Wintrose said, trying to steer Gabbin back on course, "who lives there?"

"I watched it for some time and only saw a man come and go. Owns a couple of horses, he does. And a barn. He must live off his garden and whatever game comes his way. But I wonder if he might be of some help to us. Perhaps he knows something about these devils that have been sprouting up like tinderweed."

"Why have you said nothing of this before now, Brother Gabbin?"

"I only wanted to choose a time when you might hear the news with a glad heart."

"Not when I most needed a bit of cheering up, eh?"

"I'm sorry, Brother Wintrose."

"No need for that. I merely tease you, my loyal scout."

Gabbin looked at him with glistening eyes and pulled the hair back from his face, relieved to be in the abbot's good graces still.

Wintrose loved the two of them with all his heart. They put so much faith in his guidance, it was almost frightening. They devoted themselves to his cause—a cause he himself had trouble believing in without the occasional reservation—and asked nothing in return. If he could find more like them, his abbey would be a formidable bastion indeed. Gabbin, with his unruly, graying hair and awkward manners, was as true to God as any man Wintrose had known. And Drear's monastic black hair, cut short to frame his face, was the perfect cover for the exuberant wit and imagination of the man. Two very different men, in some ways, they wore the same muted gray cowl as Wintrose. He was their elder, and it was his vision they pursued, but all three men were equals as far as he was concerned. He felt blessed to be in their company.

Now they awaited his guidance.

"We shall travel to this house, you and I," he said to Brother Gabbin. "Brother Drear, would you stay here to mend our door and devise a better lock?"

"Of course, Brother Wintrose."

"It's settled, then. Both of you, finish breaking your fast. I'll take food with me on the road."

The day was clear and bright, with just a few fat clouds in the crisp blue sky. The high forest was seldom without its breeze, but today there was warmth behind it. The going was easy and time flew away from them as they walked and chatted.

"We've come a long way already, Brother Gabbin. If it's much farther we won't make it back to Brother Drear before nightfall. The sun drops quickly this time of year."

"Only a little farther, I assure you. Around that bend you see up ahead."

Wintrose stroked his beard and continued in silence.

Gabbin, of course, was as good as his word. As soon as they rounded the long curve through this part of the pass, the house and barn could be seen beyond a stand of towering conifers whose branches only began halfway up their trunks. A dramatic, rocky slope predominated the other side of the pass. Smoke drifted from a stone chimney as they approached the two-story house. The front door was wide open and revealed a woman in the main room. Her back was to them, but she appeared to be hunched over something.

"Must be the wife of the man you saw," Wintrose said when they were still some distance away.

"Yes, very likely."

Their sandals on the wooden porch steps alerted the woman to their presence, and she twirled around to reveal a man in a chair, his feet fastened to the legs with twine. Though a table prevented Wintrose from getting a clear view, the man's hands appeared to be similarly bound. A red handkerchief had been tied tightly around his head to gag him. His eyes looked wild—whether with terror or malice it was impossible to judge.

"Good evening, madam." Wintrose bowed slightly. "May we be of service to you in some way?"

"What do you want?" she snapped. "Away with you. I've got no alms for the poor."

"You misunderstand. I offer *our* help to *you*. There seems to be trouble here."

"Nothing I can't handle. Now off with you."

Gabbin gave Wintrose's sleeve a frightened tug, but Wintrose wasn't about to leave until he knew what was going on.

"I beg your pardon, but if you'll only take a moment to explain ..."

"Oh, very well. If you're not leaving, come in. Sit, sit."

Wintrose and Gabbin lowered the hoods of their cowls and sat across the table from the captive, who thumped up and down in his chair and muttered something urgent behind the cloth in his mouth.

The woman brought tea and sat next to the tied-up man. She pushed at her voluminous red hair in a couple of spots and tried to smile.

"The name's Meery Dagget. Apologies if I seem a little brusque this afternoon. Caught this one nosing around in the barn this morning. Been trying to figure out what to do with him."

"I'm Brother Wintrose, and this is Brother Gabbin. Is this man a thief, then?"

She seemed to search for an appropriate answer. "Let me be straight with you, Brother Wintrose. There have been some strange goings on in these woods of late. Very strange indeed."

Wintrose could feel Gabbin's gaze on him but continued to stare at the woman. He tapped Gabbin's knee a couple of times underneath the table in an effort to reassure him.

"Do you know what I speak of?" the woman asked.

A sound from upstairs claimed his attention

momentarily, but he tried not to let on. "Perhaps, madam. Do you refer to the creatures that swarm our hills when the sun goes down?"

Her smile widened and she cackled dryly. "I do! Would you believe, sir, that this little worm is working for the damned things? Helping them to establish dominion right here in the forest, he is."

Wintrose's flesh crawled. Perhaps Brother Drear was closer to the truth than any of them had dared imagine.

"That's a heavy accusation, Mrs. Dagget. Pray, untie the kerchief and let us hear it from his own lips."

"Never! He whines and howls in such a strange tongue— calling to his masters, no doubt. I'll not have them coming round here at his behest."

Something fell to the floor upstairs, followed by footsteps. The monks rose, apprehensive, as two pairs of boots could be heard clopping down the stairs. Suddenly a young man burst into the room, his face badly bruised, his shirt torn open.

"This isn't the man you saw around the place, is it?" Wintrose asked Gabbin, who only shook his head slowly back and forth.

"Free my brother, witch!" The young man shouted breathlessly, pointing at Meery.

"Ah, the cat's come out of the bag, I see. And has an urge to do some lashing, eh?" She turned to Brother Wintrose. "Their type never works alone. My husband took that one upstairs while I looked after this one."

A short, round man came around the corner at last, rubbing the side of his head. Meery glared at him but said nothing.

"That's him!" said Gabbin, with a poke of his elbow into Wintrose's side. "That's the man I saw."

"What lies has this viper been filling your ears with, holy man?" the young man asked Wintrose.

"No lies, boy," Meery interrupted. "Only the truth of how you and your friend here are agents of the very devil."

"Oh, she's a cunning one," the man said with a sharp laugh.

Mr. Dagget shrank into a shadowy corner and fingered his hat. He didn't appear to want much to do with the escalating tempers in the room.

"Enough!" shouted Wintrose. "Someone tell me what in Hell goes on here, or so help me, I'll make my own way to the bottom of it."

The young man jumped on the opportunity to have his say. "Sir, I'm Char, and this is my brother, Hyte. We recently learned some rather disturbing news about Mr. and Mrs. Dagget. We learned, in fact, that they—not us—have been in communication with the devils that keep us all indoors after dark these days. The last straw came when Hyte went spying and found these two cavorting with the demons in Hider's Glen. Naked, they were, and giving free rein to their basest urges. Isn't that so, Hyte?" His brother nodded enthusiastically. "We had to do something, so we came here to make them tell us all about the hellish monstrosities, see if the villains have a weakness we might exploit."

"They have a weakness, I assure you," said Wintrose. "They exist only to hate, and that is a profound weakness against the forces of goodness and justice. Humanity has the upper hand in this fight. Now, madam, what have you to say for yourself? Do you deny this man's charge?"

"Oh, what's the use?"

Mr. Dagget's eyes went wide at his wife's audacity, but he remained quiet.

"You've no prayer against us. They've given us a taste of their power. We'll share in that power as payment for helping them."

"You are beyond naïve, woman!" Brother Gabbin yelled.

"You see," Char continued, "these two were able to turn the tables on us. They took us hostage, but as you can tell, I've escaped." He looked back at Mr. Dagget. "This one whistles a different melody now than when I was in bondage, I assure you. There was no end to his threats and bullying then. Or his violence." He dabbed at a wound on his forehead and glanced at the blood that stuck to his finger.

"Madam," said Wintrose, "I want this man set free. You've no right to keep him here that I can discern."

Meery gazed into Wintrose's eyes a while before answering. "Very well. I thought he and his brother would make a nice gift for the horde, but we've gained their trust. We don't need these boys. Take them. I never want to see any of you again."

Char rushed to his brother's side and untied him.

"We'll wait outside," said Wintrose.

"Do you think Char is telling the truth?" Gabbin asked once they'd walked a short distance from the house and stopped in the shade of a willow tree.

"Char, yes. The question is whether Hyte told him the truth about what he's seen, and whether the Daggets are really as friendly with the demons as the woman intimates. There are mysteries in these woods, Brother Gabbin, to last a lifetime. And we're getting tangled up in them."

"Brothers," Char called as he and his brother hurried toward Gabbin and Wintrose, "thank you for waiting. The counsel of holy men would be most welcome in this matter. But first allow me to make a proper introduction of my brother. Say hello to Hyte."

Brother Gabbin bowed.

"Good to know you both," said Wintrose. "My friend goes by the name Gabbin, and I'm called Wintrose. Can you follow us back to our cottage? We can talk along the way."

"We'd be glad to. Wouldn't we, Hyte?"

"By all means. The sooner we devise a plan for dealing with the Daggets and those … things, the better."

"Agreed," said Gabbin with a hesitant smile.

The brothers reminded Wintrose of a traveling comedy team he'd seen as a boy. Char was fully a foot taller than Hyte, and much thinner. Nor was there any trace of kinship in their features.

As the four of them set off toward the monks' temporary home, clouds amassed overhead, bringing the illusion of early nightfall. Some minutes passed before anyone felt like uttering a word.

The Rocky Forest rains were legendary for their beauty, but not for any positive effect they had on the progress of travelers. By the time Wintrose and his party were within sight of the cottage, they were exhausted and drenched. And it was dark. Shadowy movement had been accompanying them along their path for several miles, but what could they do, other than slog on? Terror jabbed and mocked them, as though they were a menagerie exhibit, but the four men refused to give in to its ridicule. They knew, to a man, that opening the door on fear—out here in the dark, rainy woods, exposed—would be tantamount to tearing down a dike.

If it was the devilish creatures that crashed around in the underbrush as the men walked, they seemed content to observe. But there was no telling when that contentment might change to restlessness. Only when Brother Wintrose tried the door and found it locked tight did he allow himself any relief. Brother Drear had managed well without them, it appeared.

Wintrose pounded his fist against the heavy door, but there was no response. "Odd," he said under his breath.

The sound of pained coughing erupted somewhere.

"That came from behind the house," Gabbin said.

He was out of sight around the corner before any of the others had time to react. They quickly followed.

Sprawled in the wet grass was Brother Drear, glistening red wherever the rain hadn't sluiced away the blood of his wounds. Gabbin dropped to his side immediately and cradled his beaten head.

"What happened here, brother?"

Drear's body hitched as he coughed up a stringy clot of blood, but he seemed to nod toward the small house.

"Look there." Hyte pointed to a shattered window.

"Dear God," Wintrose said. "They must have dragged him out. It's a wonder they didn't kill him. What are the scoundrels after?"

"They revel in our suffering," Char said in an angry tone.

Before anyone could say or do anything more, an ear-splitting shriek came up out of the woods behind the cottage. Gabbin, Wintrose, Char, and Hyte stared in that direction.

"All of you, please, stay here and tend to Brother Drear," Wintrose said. "If I can catch these loathsome river maggots in the act of something, I must."

If the screaming didn't come again, he'd never be able to track the source, but he knew it would. One scream from an innocent victim wouldn't be enough for their diseased appetites. His instinct was good. The high-pitched cries came at regular intervals, making it easy to follow the sound deep into the trees. As he drew closer to it, he became less convinced it was a cry of pain and more certain it signaled abject terror.

He stepped into a moonlit clearing almost without noticing it, for it wasn't the clearing itself that was of interest but what was going on at its center. The devils must have been incredibly quick in their handiwork. Hanging by his ankles from a rope stretched high up between two elder-spruces was Mr. Dagget. In the grip of his hands were his wife's ankles. All that stood between her and a twenty-foot drop onto a cairn of sharp stones was her husband's strength, for as long as it held out.

A tittering noise worked its way around the edge of the clearing, but Brother Wintrose saw nothing of the creatures.

Meery Dagget started in on another shattering screech but cut it off when her eyes fell upon Wintrose.

"*You!*" she hollered, her voice hoarse. "Holy man, get us down from here. They've turned against us."

Wintrose took several steps toward her and examined the pile of rocks. "Not the way I'd choose to die." He shook his head. "If I had a choice, that is."

"Look, no one has to die if you'll just cut us down from here before my husband faints. He's been hanging here longer than I have."

From a distance he'd wondered why her skirts didn't hang down past her head. Now he saw that her arms and clothing were tightly bound to her body. Her fiery orange hair hung loose, however. Mr. Dagget, meanwhile, was putting his last reserves of energy into preventing his wife's head from colliding with those rocks. His face looked red, even in the dark and the wet. His lips pressed together in fierce determination.

"How could you?" Wintrose asked Meery Dagget. "How could you partner with such things as these? My friend lies, as we speak, at the very rim of Death's canyon. They broke into our home, dragged him out into the cold, rainy night and just about knocked the life out of him."

"Can we have this discussion after—"

"No, we'll have it now. It appears there are enemies in this world so monstrous even their friends are to be treated with the greatest suspicion and contempt."

"Is there no room for pitying the sinful in your doctrine? For God's sake, how rigid are the laws you choose to live by?"

"The sinful I can forgive, Mrs. Dagget. The unrepentant damned I cannot."

"You're taking a bold step if you walk away from us in this predicament, holy man!" But he was already retreating into the woods. "May your conscience be the—"

He shivered and closed his eyes briefly at the dull sound of the woman's skull cracking open on the sharp stones. He was glad to have been spared the sight. Then came the sobs of her unfortunate husband. Brother Wintrose pulled the hood of his cowl down over his eyes and returned through the rain to the cottage. The eerie laughter amid the trees had fallen to something like respectful silence, and he wondered if God was really the one testing him.

❋ ❋ ❋

III

The Pilgrimage of Brother Wintrose

The town of Lund lay nearly ten miles from the abbey, and Brother Wintrose was exhausted by the time he got there on foot. Lund's seaside shanties and various shops and homes all had a scalloped look to them, as though the whole town was submerged in salt water every high tide. A bracing, saline wind skittered inland, causing Wintrose to seek immediate shelter. The first establishment to present itself being a tavern, he ordered a mug of keg ale and sat near a fire that hissed and popped in its capacious hearth.

He was dimly aware of nodding off and trying to fight it when the door swung open and in walked Char and Hyte Fasserby, rubbing the chill out of their arms. It had been months since they'd seen each other, and though he'd written the brothers about meeting here, it was no sure thing that they'd actually turn up.

"Well, if it isn't the Rocky Forest abbot himself!" Char exclaimed, closing the door and joining Wintrose at his table. "Two more, Scap," he called to the barkeep, the same number of fingers raised.

"My friends," said Brother Wintrose. "It is good to see you both. Almost five years we've known each other, yet we meet so seldom. Thank you for agreeing to come."

Hyte had been warming himself before the fire but now sat down beside his brother.

"You're a long way from Scratch Mountain," Char said to Wintrose. "What brings you to the seashore?"

Wintrose tilted his mug and stared into it. "I need a boat, same as many a wanderer who's come before me to Lund, no doubt."

"A boat?" Hyte said. "Have you left the abbey for good,

Brother Wintrose?"

"No, no." Wintrose chuckled dryly and pulled at his beard. "I need to get to the Wizened Isle. A scholar there by the name of Donin has written me, requesting my presence."

"Has this to do with the scourge?" Char asked. Wintrose nodded. "Then we'll find you a boat, but it won't be here in Lund, not during high-trade season. And not with half the fleet here laid waste by the demons. We'll need to go half a day north to Briar. A fellow there by the name of Clurry owes me a favor or two."

"I can't ask you to—"

"You haven't asked us for anything. We're going with you and that's an end to it."

Wintrose's lips parted, but instead of speaking he hoisted and drained his mug. Soon the brothers Fasserby were done with their drinks as well, and the three men were out the door, heading north on foot.

The temperature dropped along with the sun, and when a cold mist drifted in from the sea, the travelers made camp. Char and Hyte set about building a fire under a span of broad-leafed boughs. No one had mentioned it, but they hadn't come this far without company. For the last several miles, strange laughter had been gathering on both sides of the path the men followed. And a rushing, tumbling movement could also be heard as the laughing things scurried to keep pace while remaining hidden from view. Now that the travelers had stopped for the night, the surrounding brush was quiet. Quiet but watchful, Wintrose presumed.

"Perhaps we should find a cave higher up, among the rocks," Wintrose said as Hyte stoked the fire into a good strong blaze.

"No," said Char. "I think we all know what's out there, following us. They'd love nothing more than to trap us in a cave, where they'd have only one exit to cover. I'd rather see them work a little harder than that if they're going to tear me limb from limb."

That settled it. Wintrose was in neither the mood nor the condition to argue. It seemed a cave might be a bit warmer, and there was sure to be one hidden in the rockier terrain, but if his weary body managed to find sleep here in the open, who was he to complain? Tomorrow would be a clean slate. He wouldn't be so quick to acquiesce after a night's sleep and a morning's breakfast.

As tired as he was, Hyte and Char were first to drift off—too many of Wintrose's fireside stories, apparently. The feeling of being watched kept Wintrose up, staring into the dwindling campfire, until long after the brothers had been reduced to snores. But fatigue won out in the end, and Wintrose slept until morning without interruption.

The far-off cawing of a predatory bird roused him. He rubbed his eyes against the dawn's glare as it reflected off the sea. He really did feel better as he reached for the small pack he'd carried with him on his journey. That's when he noticed that Char and Hyte were nowhere to be seen, the only remnant of their presence the crooked stick Hyte had used to cook a hare.

It was damned odd. He had no worries about reaching Briar. And Char had given him the name of his acquaintance there. But it wasn't like the brothers to pull a disappearing act like this. It didn't smell right.

The only thing to do was carry on. He pulled a dry hunk of bread from his pack and nibbled on it. His water was almost gone, but he couldn't resist a long draught. He stuffed what was left of his small loaf back into the pack, along with the remaining swig of water. Then, hoping that Briar would prove to be a community bursting at the seams with abundance and generosity, he hauled himself to his feet with the help of his crook—a somewhat new walking aid—and resumed his course.

Many morning sounds accompanied Brother Wintrose on his way. Early birds twittered gleefully from hidden perches. Dew squirted up from the grass in a susurrous drone as he stepped. And the pleasant buzz of reawakening insect life set the very air alive. But there was one sound missing from the scene: that of impish laughter and shuffling movement. The creatures seldom came out of hiding in the morning hours, but lately they enjoyed making their presence known in a thousand irritating ways, at all hours of the day and night. Wintrose didn't want to make the connection, but his thoughts were there before he could call them back. Char and Hyte's disappearance corresponded with the absence of the devils. Only two explanations seemed possible. Either Char and Hyte were in trouble, or they were in cahoots with the demons. Wintrose's thoughts vacillated between the two possibilities the entire way to Briar.

The town itself was bowl-like, as if its acreage had been scooped out to make the setting as unique as possible. Approaching from the far side may not have been as dramatic, because the bowl was shallower there—chipped. But coming at it from the south made it seem like something out of a fairy story.

Wintrose had no problem finding Clurry's hut. Char had indicated the location with the same casual precision Wintrose had long admired in the man. He cared about exactness. He cared, period. That's why it was so frustrating to think that he and his brother—toward whom Wintrose had always felt the same trust, if not intellectual admiration, he felt toward Char —might have given themselves up to the sinister cause that seemed to have limitless potential for spreading its poison.

"Yes?" said the golden-haired man who answered the door. "What is it?"

"I'm looking for Clurry." Wintrose pulled back the hood of his cowl.

"Not anymore you're not," the man said, his voice tired and short tempered. "What do you want?"

"We have a friend in common, Mr. Clurry. Char Fasserby. He said I might be able to count on you for a favor on his behalf."

"You know Char? Well, why didn't you say so? Come on in. Step lively, now. Let's have it out over a cup of tea, eh?"

"That sounds delightful. Thank you."

The place hadn't looked like much from outside, but

Clurry's eye for arrangement had cast a charming spell over the interior of the one-room hovel. Miniature framed art hung on the walls, and a cheery fire carried on in a hearth decorated with numerous tiles, each intricately carved as if part of a story.

They sat at a small, round table in the center of the room to drink their tea.

"It's a boat I seek," said Wintrose. "Passage to the Wizened Isle."

"The Wizened Isle? Why, there's nothing to the place anymore. Just Donin's Temple. Donin himself could have died fifty years ago and no one would know."

"He isn't dead. He wrote me. I must get to him, and soon."

"Then you shall. The day old Clurry can't figure out a way to put a man on a boat is the very day to start forging nails for his coffin."

"God be with you, Clurry. Your kindness will not go unfelt in the world if my hopes have any foundation in reality."

Wintrose might have reserved his blessing—or delivered it with less zeal—had he first laid eyes on the vessel Mr. Clurry was able to hire for him. It was smelly even for a fishing trawler, and the grease from a recent harvest had coated everything with a slick sheen. Wintrose's crook and sandals were all but useless in keeping him upright as he boarded, but with the help of two brawny stevedores he managed. It instantly became clear to him why Clurry had been so insistent about saying goodbye at the shipping manager's office. He must have known how humble Wintrose's accommodations were likely to be.

Of course, humility was nothing to be ashamed of. It was a virtue, and Brother Wintrose would have climbed a mountain of mackerel if it meant he stood a chance at ending the Rocky Forest plague. As it was, he only had to spend two-and-a-half hours breathing fish remnants before coming within view of the stony shore of the Wizened Isle.

The Isle took its name from the view it offered the eastbound traveler. Any seaman coming at the small island from the west, as Wintrose now did, was greeted by the dramatic profile of an extremely old man. It was merely the way the rocks that made up the island had tumbled out of the sea countless ages ago, but the resemblance to human features was startling. Wintrose could think of no better place to begin strategizing the next campaign in his war against the Rocky Forest devils than in the region of a naturally occurring stone tribute to humanity. He only hoped Donin had as much valuable information to offer as he had made it seem in his recent missive; the scholar's offhanded allusion to three holy relics had prompted Wintrose to leave his precious abbey temporarily without a head.

As soon as the stoical captain of the fishing vessel deposited Wintrose amid the sharp rocks and sandy loam of the Isle's jagged shoreline, he turned his boat around and headed straight back to Briar. There was much fishing to be done, and time was money, but the man promised to return in several hours. Before turning his attention to the climb that lay ahead, Wintrose watched the trawler grow smaller and smaller as it scudded toward the horizon.

He wouldn't have to go anywhere near the promontory of the island. Donin's Temple was famously nestled within a stand of western hemlock, roughly at the midway point of the island's anomalous rock formation. The climb was a test of his old bones, but he suspected they'd support him through worse before this was all over. It was steeper going than the hike between Wintrose Abbey and Briar but not nearly as long. Soon he was face to face with the arched blood-red doors that served as the temple's main entrance.

But how to proceed? There was no knocker, and the doors seemed too large and solid for knocking with bare hands. Noticing that one of them was slightly ajar, he opted for the direct approach by squeezing in unannounced. He stood in a small vestibule. Directly ahead an ornately carved door, much smaller than the main doors, blocked his way. On the other side of it was likely the temple proper, he reasoned. The small door popped inward with the slightest twist of a handle, the shriek of its hinges echoing around the circular room beyond.

"Brother Wintrose, is that you?"

He couldn't tell where the voice had originated, only that its reverberations sounded at every point along the perimeter of the room. A thick tree trunk rose from the center of the floor. His eyes followed it up about twenty feet to its midpoint. There heavy ropes were tied around the bole and extended across the high-domed room, anchored to the circular wall at four equidistant points. Something about the scene was very wrong, but Wintrose allowed his gaze to continue up the trunk to the top, which swayed gently despite the securing ropes. A wooden platform, maybe a foot square, had been affixed to the apex of the sawn-off trunk. On the tiny platform stood a heavy, trembling old man, his hands bound behind him. Wintrose marveled at the design of it all.

"I am Brother Wintrose. Tell me you are not Donin the Scholar."

"It is I. There's no time to lose. The demons were able to send a contingent to the Wizened Isle to do this to me. They must be growing stronger than I'd imagined."

"They are everywhere," Wintrose said.

"In the drawer of a small table in the vestibule you'll find a ring of keys. The black one opens the door to my chamber, behind me. The gold one unlocks a trapdoor set into the floor there. It opens onto a foot-deep cubby. In it you'll find a scroll and two small glass spheres. The scroll will describe in more detail the holy relics I mentioned in my letter—where to find them and what to do with them. The orbs are for your protection. They are filled with explosive powders and are capable of producing considerable fire when hurled at an object.

"I've managed to hold out for your arrival, Brother Wintrose, but I'm afraid my strength is at an end. Please, retrieve the items I've mentioned and be gone, so you won't have to witness anything unpleasant."

"But perhaps I could—"

"There's no time. *Go!*"

Wintrose hurried into the vestibule. Scanning the small

area, he soon found the table with the keys. As he slid open the drawer, a crash from inside the temple gave him a start. It sounded like a heavy vase dropping to the ground and shattering. His pace wasn't nearly as hurried when he retraced his steps into the temple, for he knew what he would find. Fatigue had taken its toll on Donin. The scholar lay prostrate on the floor, his head cloven and its contents spilling outward in an ugly pool of red and gray. Wintrose gave the mess a wide berth on his way to the man's chamber.

❁ ❁ ❁

IV

Brother Wintrose Collars the Devil

Iesvs Nazarenvs Rex Ivdaeorvm

He was far too old to be climbing up and down the mountain, but this had been an important quest. Pausing to wipe rainwater from his brow, Brother Wintrose pushed the hood of his cowl higher up on his head with his crook and eyed his mountaintop destination through wind-whipped rain and pale moonlight. The abbey loomed impossibly high. His body hitched in a kind of laugh. Maybe this was the end. Maybe he was to make it no farther than the rocky slopes that served as ramparts to his beloved abbey.

But the box he clutched against his side wasn't as easily put out of mind as his own well-being. It was the last of the three relics to be brought to the abbey. At least he hoped Brother Drear and Brother Gabbin had already returned with theirs. If not, something had gone wrong. Regardless, he had to deliver his, and if either of the other two boxes hadn't arrived yet, he would need to send more men out. Then he could die, if Death was so eager to have him. But not before.

Even as he thought it, his sandal turned on a slick boulder and nearly launched him into swirling blackness. But he was nimble for his age, and he managed to avert catastrophe by ramming his crook into a patch of mud and pushing off of it with his weight. How the box remained under his arm through it all he had no guess, but it did, and he was grateful.

Up he wound, scaling the rock outcroppings of Scratch Mountain to heights that never seemed to bring him any closer to the hermitage. He hadn't eaten or slept for many hours, so he was unsure what hidden reserves of strength he was calling on to proceed. It was as if the stinging rain, blustery winds, and low visibility were fuel to him now, as if his soaked cowl urged him on rather than weighed him down. Not that it should have been a complete surprise to him, this surge of willful endurance. At the heart of all that he taught and preached was a strong belief in the human spirit's ability to overcome the limits of the physical world. If he was anything more than another hypocrite in holy raiment, now was the time for God to prove it by allowing him and the box safe passage to the abbey.

Coming over the lip of rock that put him on the same level as the abbey was like stepping into a dream. Though his tired legs threatened to buckle under him and his arm ached from cradling the box mile after lonesome mile, Brother Wintrose paused in the deluge to behold the holy place that bore his name. It had never looked more perfect to him than it did now, with heavy clouds sailing in and out of the moon's persistent glow, rain lashing at its walls and steeple. On this side of the abbey, the mountain dropped down into woods, which in turn gave way to a sprawling valley. The other side was almost butted up against the final rise of the peak. The monks of Wintrose Abbey couldn't have found a more ideal location, or done a more impressive job on the architecture and construction of the edifice. They'd steadily grown in number over the years, it being easy to recruit men to dwell high on a mountain when the lowlands were every day crawling with more of hell's effluvium.

The demons refused to scramble any higher than the last thinning stand of evergreens that encircled the mountain. Wintrose believed the reason for their wariness was twofold. Brother Glendow had been the first to theorize that they didn't want to abandon the hiding places that tree cover provided, and there was likely something to the idea. The monsters were certainly smart enough to consider the consequences of such a disadvantage. But Wintrose knew in his heart that it went deeper than that. Just as he had chosen the loftiest location possible for the abbey—all the better to honor and exalt his one true God—might not the devils have feared the very same closeness to divinity? He felt sure of it, and took strength from it.

Brother Licton answered soon after Wintrose sounded one of the bronze cherub knockers adorning the main doors. He looked disheveled, agitated.

"Oh, Brother Wintrose! Praise God, it's you."

Wintrose waited a moment for the pale young man to offer to take the box and see him in. Brother Licton only stared into the abbot's eyes.

"What's the matter?" Wintrose asked. "Why do you not let me in? Have Brothers Gabbin and Drear returned?"

"Yes, yes. Oh, I'm sorry, Brother Wintrose. Forgive me. The reliquary is now complete, yes?" He gingerly took the box from Wintrose and stepped aside to let him pass. "It's just that … Well, I really should let Brother Drear be the one … He's the one who saw it."

Wintrose closed the door, lowered his hood, and drew patience from a deep well. Laying a hand on Brother Licton's shoulder he said, "Tell me where I can find Brother Drear."

"He and some of the others are down in the winery. There has been much talk amid the casks tonight."

"Mmm, and not a little tipping of the mugs, I suspect."

The uneven, spiraling stone steps that hugged the wall on the way to the basement were as treacherous as anything

Wintrose had navigated on his way back to the abbey. The men always chose to imbibe down below, thinking they went unnoticed. But such a charade was folly in Wintrose's view. The threat of a deadly fall for a drunk man climbing the demanding flight was very real.

He passed through the cellar and its stores of wine to the cozy winery beyond. At a short rectangular table sat Brothers Drear, Gabbin, and Glendow. They looked up as he entered, children caught playing an adults' game.

"Brother Licton made it sound as though I'd find more of you down here," Brother Wintrose said.

"And so you might have," said Brother Glendow in a roaring voice, "if you'd come an hour sooner. What you see here is the wheat, good Brother Wintrose. The chaff have gone to bed." He said this with a flourish of his arms, and laughter trickled around the table.

"You have the gift of humor," Wintrose said, smiling despite himself. "I hope it survives the coming days." His smile faded and a hush fell upon the monks as they stared down at their half-empty mugs of wine. "Brother Drear, may I have a word?"

As soon as the two men were out in the hall, Glendow's chatter resumed. Wintrose could tell Gabbin had wanted to greet him, but he was always so afraid of falling out of favor with Brother Glendow. Brother Wintrose smiled despite himself as he and Drear retreated upstairs in silence and stepped outside, into the cloister at the rear of the abbey.

"It's wonderful to see you again, Brother Wintrose."

"You as well, my good Brother Drear. You as well. Brother Licton has collected my relic."

"That is excellent news. We can begin."

"Brother Licton also said you have something to tell me. He seemed out of sorts about it."

"It's good news, on the one hand, I assure you."

"Let's have it, then, by all means."

"I've seen the devil prince."

Wintrose said nothing.

"Twice I've seen him. Once where the trees begin their descent and once on Kneeling Ridge."

"That's much higher than we thought they ever came."

"Just him so far, Brother Wintrose. He appears to be as bold as he is ferocious looking. He's at least half again as large as his subordinates, and his hide is a more sickly color."

"How can you call this good news, brother?"

"Perhaps the fly has come to the spider and spared her the hunt."

"We still have to catch him."

Drear fell silent, unable to deny the assertion. Rain poured into the courtyard, but the monks kept dry as they walked the covered perimeter.

"Do you think this will work?" Drear asked at last.

Wintrose stopped and turned, startled by the question. "I must believe. And so must we all. Have *you* doubts, even after the lengths to which you've gone to procure one of the relics? What, if not faith, saw you through such a difficult mission?"

"We've known each other a long time. If I express misgivings it's only because I know I can bare myself completely to you. Please, let us continue walking."

"I don't deserve your loyalty. I try to be strong for you and the others, so I pretend not to fear the worst. But we're up against a great foe, one that's grown strong alongside us these long years. I have no right to ask any of you to go one step farther in this ..."

"You needn't ask. We are beside you, and beside you we shall remain."

Wintrose clutched Drear's forearm. "Then we must melt down the relics—tonight. All must be in place before we capture their prince, as you call him."

"I'll fetch Brothers Gabbin and Licton."

"Good, we'll meet in the chapel, and all are welcome. I'll be there soon."

Wintrose took several turns around the cloister after

Drear left his side. Of the entire brotherhood, only Brother Licton seemed terrified enough. The others knew what they were up against, knew what was at stake. But they didn't feel it. Even after years of playing cat-and-mouse with the hundreds —maybe thousands by now—of hell-spawn demons that scavenged the Rocky Forest by night, the monks of Wintrose Abbey deluded themselves as to the seriousness of the task at hand.

The things could be seen in the sky just before dawn, which was a new development. They'd always had wings and occasionally left signs of recent flight—such as the horrible business with the Daggets, and Donin the Scholar—but lately murders of them were sometimes seen circling the lower flanks of Scratch Mountain. And now their crown prince, whose presence had been rumored for years, was creeping around at higher elevations. The monks should have been out of their heads with fright. God knew Wintrose was. But he had the considerable responsibility of holding it together before his flock. It wasn't quite Armageddon the holy men of Wintrose Abbey were up against, perhaps, but it was nothing less than a battle between good and evil. There was great strength on their side now, with the holy relics in place, but much was still to be done—and perhaps sacrificed—before they could pronounce themselves victorious.

The chapel was thronged when Wintrose arrived, a chattering tide of gray cowls and mostly bearded faces. Even the drunk and the slumbering had been called to bear witness. Each row of men quieted as he passed by on his way to the altar.

"Men," he said with a nod, standing before them now. "Brethren, the day has arrived. Brother Licton, the reliquary, please."

It was an awkward thing to carry. Shaped like a simple church, it was made up of panels of hammered metal soldered together. The roof was hinged along one of its longer sides and the whole thing was meticulously festooned with decorative studs and painted icons. Brother Licton carried it in outstretched arms to where Brother Wintrose stood and laid it carefully on the altar next to him.

"Open it," Wintrose commanded.

Brother Licton undid a latch at the front and swung the roof back.

"Here reside three holy relics, brothers. Brother Gabbin has retrieved a bridle from the Provinces of Ire. Brother Drear has fetched a spear point from Mount Blood. And only tonight I have returned from Witch's Hollow with the crown. All three relics are made of iron, but not just any iron. It is time you know the true significance of these sacred objects."

A swell of hushed conversation passed among the congregants but was short lived.

"Brother Licton, the bridle."

Licton withdrew a box from the reliquary and set it aside. He lifted the lid of the box and removed a dullish bridle, which he handed to Wintrose, who held the item up for all to see.

"And the spear point."

Licton removed the second box and handed Wintrose the spear point from inside.

"And now the crown."

Licton removed a crown from the third box.

Wintrose held all three items above his head and addressed the monks once more.

"These relics aren't important because they are bridle, spear point, and crown. You've probably guessed that much. They are important because of what they once were. Each of these objects, my brothers, has in its makeup one of the nails that was driven into the flesh of Jesus Christ."

He handed the relics back to Licton.

Gasps he had expected. Maybe even a cry or two. And he wasn't disappointed on either account. But there was also a startling shout of, "Blasphemy!" from somewhere at the rear of the chapel. Wintrose took a moment to find his words.

"The only proof I can offer you is in the completion of our task. Some of you know more than others about what is afoot.

We shall all have the same knowledge soon. Tonight we melt the relics down and form them into manacles. Then all that will be left is capturing the demon commander—the devil prince ...” He winked at Brother Drear in the front row. “... clamping the manacles about his wrists, and chaining him to a wall in the winery.”

“Like plucking a cherry from the mouth of a babe!” someone hollered. It took Wintrose a moment to identify the speaker as Brother Glendow.

Wintrose smiled weakly. “Yes, well, maybe not quite as easy as that. But if we can get him inside the abbey, he’ll weaken considerably. We should have little trouble shackling him and getting him down to the winery.”

“Then what?” someone asked.

“For as long as he is bound by irons forged from the nails used in the Crucifixion, this region will be free from evil. Only if someone sets him loose will evil and corruption take hold again in the Rocky Forest. We could kill him—maybe—but that would only enrage the others, not deliver them to perdition. But enough talk. Brother Licton, kindly take the reliquary down to the forge. Brother Slaggert will cast something other than cask rings and wine-making apparatus tonight.” He eyed a large man several rows from the front. “Won’t you, Brother Slaggert?”

“It will be an intense joy to do this work,” Slaggert replied.

“Fine, fine. I’ll want to know as soon as the fetters are ready.”

Brother Slaggert stood, twisting the waist cord of his cowl. “Brother Wintrose, it will take time to cool the iron if we want to avoid imperfections, weaknesses in the finished product. We should also rustle up some limestone or salt peter to use as flux. Any impurities in the—”

“You will melt down the relics, form them into a pair of manacles, and quench them in water. These bonds will have a hold over the prisoner far beyond the strength of iron. Let me know when it is done.”

The chapel was silent as Brother Wintrose took his leave.

In the narrow corridor that led to his chambers, he felt a tap at his shoulder. Turning tiredly on his crook he saw by the light of a nearby wall-mounted candle the unmistakable long hair and tall, skinny frame of Char Fasserby. He glanced around for Char's brother, Hyte, but saw no one else in the gloom.

"Welcome, Char. Do you still think you can tempt the devil onto holy ground this night?"

"I'm as sure as I was this afternoon when you and I spoke at my home."

"Your Abigail seems a fine woman. I was surprised and gladdened to learn of your good fortune. I didn't have time to express myself earlier, but I regret that circumstances have forced you and me to keep our distance from one another. It's a wedding I should have liked very much to attend."

"Attend? Had things been otherwise, it would have been you who married us."

Wintrose didn't know how to respond, so he showed Char into his room and offered him a cup of wine.

"Where is your brother," Wintrose asked.

"He's with Kurg, coaxing him higher up the mountain as we speak, I don't doubt."

"Kurg. This is the name of their leader?"

Char bowed his head, nodded slowly.

"An ugly name for an ugly beast. I wish you hadn't elected to mix with such low company for our cause. But there are few outside of the brotherhood who can be trusted these days, so I am grateful. When you and Hyte offered to accompany me on my pilgrimage to the Wizened Isle, I saw the opportunity you acted on, but I wouldn't have dreamed of asking you ... I knew we would be watched along the way, and I didn't know what to expect when I got to Donin's Temple. There was some sense in you and your brother coming back to set things in motion here. I can't deny it."

"We would do it again in an instant. We had to get them off your scent. But the biggest piece has yet to be dropped into place."

"Very true. I must ask your assistance one last time."

"It's yours for as many last times as necessary."

"Bless you. Then we best get started."

"Does everyone know—"

"Only that the time has come, and what we plan to do with Kurg once we've got him. Have you done as we discussed?"

"Yes, the rope is piled between the abbey and the mountain's peak. How do I get on the roof? I saw no ladder."

"Come." Wintrose opened a drawer, removed and pocketed the small glass spheres from Donin's chamber, and led his friend back into the corridor, "I'll show you. There's a ladder built into the wall, near the last chapel window."

The rain outside the main doors came down like guillotine blades, but compared to what the night still held in store, what was the loss of a head? They trudged through mud and chill wetness to the side of the abbey where Char's rope lay in a soppy coil.

Wintrose pointed farther along the wall, toward the cloister. "There's the ladder. Brother Slaggert forged it and attached it to the wall. I can give it no stronger endorsement than that."

Char nodded, reached down to take up one end of the rope, and climbed with it up the ladder. Wintrose stared after him for a moment before beginning his own climb up a steep path etched into the final rise of Scratch Mountain. The going was treacherous, even with his crook, but he'd practiced the route, knew exactly where to step—and where not to. In minutes he'd reached a flat-topped outcropping. There he sat down with crossed legs and looked on as Char struggled to keep his balance on the narrow stone ridge that ran the length of the roof. When he reached the steeple Char tied the rope securely to the base. He almost lost his balance once or twice on his way back to the ladder, but eventually he made it down.

The other end of the rope was fashioned into a loop, which Char picked up and carried to the front corner of the abbey. There he let if fall to the mud and, with a broad wave to Brother

Wintrose, headed straight for the drop-off fifty yards from the main doors. Wintrose watched him clamber out of sight before turning his attention to his own role in the coming drama. Char knew Wintrose would take over once Kurg was snared, but he had no idea what methods the old abbot intended to use. No one did.

Wintrose reached a hand inside an interior pocket of his cowl and fingered the two smooth orbs. He couldn't believe it was nearly time to make use of them. Since acquiring the weapons seven months ago, he had dreaded this moment as much as he longed for it. Now that the time had arrived, he found it impossible to believe that events would play out as he intended. The procession of time had made it too easy to put faith in a triumphant outcome. Now he feared that the devil would win the day. Perhaps somewhere in the middle lay the truth.

He looked to the moon for comfort and was almost surprised that it gave him some. Then Hyte was hauling himself onto the far ledge. He helped Char up, and the two of them waited, staring down into the dark drop-off below. With dramatic flourish, Kurg shot out of that darkness, some twenty feet into the air. He was massive, fully three times Char's height and Hyte's girth. He halted in the air, batting his wings powerfully against the sky, rotating his monstrous head this way and that. It was a clear display of dominance and gall, and it made Wintrose despise his enemy anew. The damned thing was laying claim to the abbey.

Finally Kurg came to rest on the ground near Char and Hyte. The brothers immediately started walking toward the abbey and Wintrose saw hesitation in the beast at last. Kurg hung back, all bravado gone from his movements, which now had something of dread in them. He was afraid of the very abbey he hoped to conquer, Wintrose noted with a chuckle.

It wasn't clear to Wintrose how, exactly, Char planned to trap his prey. Presumably he had some clever ruse in mind. Perhaps Hyte would divert the devil prince's attention while

Char came up from behind and threw the loop over his long, flat head. There would be no second chance if Char missed, so Wintrose watched with great agitation as the action unfolded below.

Hyte disappeared from view, but Char came around to the corner where he'd left the end of the rope. Kurg's head and neck, as well as the tips of his wings, were clearly visible as he followed Char. Wintrose's fist tightened around the glass orbs. His own chances with the devilish brute were limited, too. His timing would have to be well chosen.

When Char tilted an arm toward the looped end of rope, pointing it out to Kurg, Wintrose rose to his feet. A pang of suspicion coursed through him. Could Char be in league with the satanic horde after all?

Char retrieved the loop, handed it to Kurg. The creature took it in a huge claw of gnarled talons. Char appeared to be telling him something. Suddenly, in defiance of all reason, Kurg pulled the loop over his toothy snout and broad skull, then pulled it tight around his throat. Wintrose could hardly believe his eyes as Kurg turned away from Char and ran back toward the cliff's edge. He took to the air before covering half the distance, however, only to be snapped back violently when he reached the end of the rope. He managed to stay aloft, but it was a struggle. They had him. He was too dumb to realize it yet, but they had him.

Wintrose was still puzzled by what he'd witnessed, but at least his trust in Char was restored. He must have taught the monks a thousand times that trust was as binding a compact as marriage to God or spouse, that judgment against a trusted friend must always be forestalled until all evidence of his innocence has been disproved. And yet he'd needed only the most circumstantial clue to convince him, not for the first time, that Char was in service of the enemy. Hypocrisy would be the subject of his next sermon, if there *was* a next sermon.

At length, Kurg became aware he'd been tricked, and his anger was terrifying to behold. He circled and thrashed, squealing insanely. The rope wrapped around the steeple until he was almost forced to land on the roof, only to unwind again as he flew in the opposite direction. Would he tire? If not, Wintrose doubted the steeple would hold.

Wintrose plucked an orb from the palm of his left hand and cocked his arm. He glanced down at Char, who gestured wildly for him to act. He looked back at Kurg, who had yet to notice his presence against the slick black stone of the mountainside. He had no idea how much fire the spheres were capable of loosing when they struck a target. It couldn't hurt to aim for the head, in case the explosion didn't amount to much.

Though that's exactly where he aimed, the orb fell short of its whirling target entirely, instead striking the base of the steeple. Fire erupted where the ball hit but quickly subsided, leaving a tongue of flame that licked all around the steeple mount before igniting the devil prince's tether, even in the pouring rain.

"*No!*" Brother Wintrose screamed, horrified by the prospect of Kurg's being set free by such an idiotic blunder. The fingers of his right hand found the other sphere. This time he didn't bother to aim. Kurg's eyes were on him now, and filled with fire as bright and hot as what crawled up the rope. The wings beat faster. Wintrose flung the orb with every whit of strength and will he possessed.

He had no idea where it would connect, probably the far side of the abbey, maybe set Hyte on fire. But no, it caught Kurg under his right arm. Again there was a blinding flash. When it died out, Kurg's wing on that side was alive with flame. The demon flapped furiously, flying at Wintrose with terrific vengeance—*unholy* vengeance.

The rain had all but extinguished the rope fire, which Wintrose had not doubt was made stronger by some strange alchemy, but Kurg's wing burned strong, the flames there no doubt enlivened still further by his carbuncled flesh. Wintrose knew the rope wasn't long enough for Kurg to reach him, but all the demons of the Rocky Forest had such convincing, conniving eyes. Kurg's, like everything else about him, were more devilish still, and Wintrose half believed the devil prince might find a way to stretch the rope, allowing him to get his hungry jaws around Wintrose's throat and hurtle him off the mountain with a wrench of his neck. Or the rope might simply snap where it was now black and brittle from burning.

Instead, Kurg came to the end of his tether in great pain, a dozen feet from Wintrose's perch. His energy depleted and his wing useless, the leader of devils dropped like a pendulum. Following the arc determined by the rope, he crashed through one of the chapel windows. As if it had held out only long enough to do its job, the rope broke free of the steeple and trailed to the ground below like a ribbon in a breeze. Their only hope now was that the interior of the abbey would be holy enough to further immobilize Kurg until he was properly chained up in the winery.

Wintrose inched his way down the crooked mountain path to meet Char near the ravaged window. They stared at each other, both searching for words that wouldn't come. Char threw his arms around Wintrose, who returned the embrace with gusto. At arms' length once more, Wintrose finally said, "Forgive me, but again I doubted your loyalty when you showed Kurg the rope. What in the realm did you say to convince him to tie it around his own neck?"

Char laughed. "Oh, that. Well, we've been trying to convince him that his only chance for dominance in this region is to overthrow the abbey. That's why he's been venturing closer lately."

"So you mentioned this afternoon."

"Well, he thought he was going to use the rope to bring down the walls of the abbey. Little did he know it was a leash!"

"Ha! Well done, Char. Well done. And where did Hyte run off to?"

"Oh, he slipped inside to make sure no one came out during our little pageant. Kurg may have gotten wise if the monks had started filing out to see what was going on. We should make sure no one was hurt."

"Yes, come."

The inside of the chapel was a charnel house. Kurg writhed on the floor. His eyes rolled dazedly back and forth, and his ruined wing twitched in the air. Underneath the devil prince was pinned at least one of the brotherhood. Whoever it was didn't move an inch. Other monks lay scattered around, and splatters of blood decorated many pews. It was a place of groans and candlelight. And blood.

All movement and sound seemed to be slowed until Wintrose spotted Brother Gabbin, sprawled over the back of a pew, his cold, dead eyes staring upside down at Wintrose. Instead of going to the man's side, Brother Wintrose stepped briskly to the gigantic head of Kurg. He knelt, ignoring a flash of pain in his knees.

"You," he whispered angrily into the thing's ear, "have arrived at the worst night of your false life. This is a place of God, and in it you will find no pity, no love, no mercy, no hope. We have lured you here to suffer, and suffer you shall." Hauling himself up by his crook, he called out, "Where is Brother Slaggert? Tell him to bring the manacles!"

Hyte approached Wintrose from the rear of the chapel. "I know not what to say. I thought the chapel would be a safe refuge. I—"

"Your intentions tonight were good ones. But there is time for neither praise nor grief at present. All things must have their hour." He heard footsteps behind him and turned. "Ah, Slaggert, good. I see you have the manacles."

"I have them, yes. But they both cracked during quenching. I would advise against—"

"When your advice is required, Brother Slaggert, I assure you it is melodious to my ears. But now it is your duty to listen. Cuff this son of a whore and let us lead him into the basement."

Slaggert nodded, visibly shaken by the reprimand, and did as he was told.

Getting Kurg onto his feet was the worst part, but once

he was upright and the remains of Brother Hazen were peeled away from his underbelly, he was as docile as a pup. Halfway down the winding stairs to the wine cellar, Wintrose stopped the procession. The manacles were clamped tight around Kurg's enormous wrists and connected to each other by a length of chain. Wintrose pulled the connecting chain until Kurg's head swung in his direction and their eyes met.

"I think you can find the way from here," Wintrose said as he slammed the curved end of his crook into the devil prince's throat.

Kurg tried to retain his balance, but it was a wasted effort with his wrists bound. His good wing flickered to life but was incapable of preventing the fall. Down he twirled in a slow revolution that was cut short when his body connected with the hard earthen floor below, sending up a soft plume of dust.

"I'll be upstairs when you're through chaining him to the wall. I have something to tell you all."

Without another word, Brother Wintrose retraced each arduous step back upstairs to the chapel.

He was humbled to see that the bodies had already been removed, the toppled pews righted, the most garish blood stains wiped clean. Brother Licton and some others were piling timber from broken pews, but Licton must have heard the tap of Wintrose's crook, even over the wind and rain that howled through the shattered chapel window, for he spun as if startled and quickly approached the abbot.

"Was it worth all this, Brother Wintrose? Have we done any good here tonight?"

"I think so, yes. Gather everyone around, would you? I have something for all ears to hear."

He climbed to the pulpit, and soon the damaged chapel was filled with silent, sullen ranks of men.

"Why so glum?" He tried to smile. "Brothers, we have already paid dearly for victory, and we have one more price to pay. But victory *is* ours. We snared the Rocky Forest devil prince tonight, and though we've never located the sore in the earth from which he and his vermin originally seeped, I have no doubt the horde, even now, is crawling over itself to get back into its hole. We've cut off its head. It can only return to the unthinking place that eschews all wisdom, beauty, light, love, and compassion. There it can go back to dwelling on its hopeless plight—a sinking ship with stone oars."

His speech had risen to a fevered invective, yet the congregation barely stirred.

"What is this additional cost you speak of, Brother?" someone called out.

Wintrose took a moment to regain his composure. "This abbey, my brothers, has been a good home to us, and to God. For years I dreamed of its completion, and it's been all that I ever hoped. But there must be an end to all things. It is not for us to stand in the way of God's work now. Let Him train the power of this place on nothing other than the devil prince, for if that mountain of dung should ever be set free, woe to the people of this region. Woe to the people of the world.

"And there is another reason, too, that we must leave our sacred abbey to the whims of fate. Men—even men as good as all of you—are susceptible to temptation. I would sooner perish in flames than see one of the brotherhood succumb to any devilish tricks and set Kurg loose. If we leave him to his solitary throne, there's a better chance he'll remain a prisoner. Forever."

There was no rebuttal, no complaint, no challenge to Brother Wintrose's heavy words. Only quiet acceptance. *If this night marks an end to one cycle of the brotherhood's existence*, the silence seemed to say, *what plan do you have for leading us into the next one, Brother Wintrose?*

The truth was that he had no solid plan at all. For years his prayers and schemes and desires had revolved around first building the abbey, then vanquishing the infernal invaders of the Rocky Forest. There had been no future looming behind those all-encompassing objectives, no thought given to the bright new day that might dawn after such a long spell of darkness.

"First, my good brothers, let us go down into the forest and see with our own eyes what effect our work has had. Perhaps it is our calling to bear witness to this great event, to let people know to throw open their shutters again. Let them know it's okay to sleep through a summer's night with every window in the house wide open. The time has come for us to readjust our thinking. Our message has changed from one of terror and caution to one of boundless hope and rejuvenation. I say we embrace the change and let ourselves sing for once, instead of delivering warning after warning."

The silence broke apart at last in an eruption of cheers and applause as the humble brotherhood of Wintrose Abbey gave voice to its collective, though tarnished, joy. Far below, in the winery, a sickened groan could be heard but dimly.

From every corner of the forest, and from the valley beyond, the creatures took to the skies. Brother Wintrose and the others had to go no farther than Kneeling Ridge to behold the spectacle. The rain had stopped, and the wind had fallen to a calming breeze, so the moon's glint had a good reach across the wooded slopes below.

A terrible squawking filled the air as the devils circled in erratic descent. The mountain itself seemed to be swallowing them, and Wintrose eventually saw the jagged cut into which the things drained. In minutes it was over. The screeching, the flapping of wings, the ugliness ... all gone.

Wintrose fell to his knees, not out of pain or exhaustion, but out of the profoundest joy his heart had ever known. Perhaps, in an odd way, he owed the demon horde some small thanks for allowing him the deep thrill of their undoing.

Brother Drear was at his side in an instant, helping him back to his feet. Char was nearby as well. And Hyte.

"Brother Gabbin's death was not in vain," Wintrose said to Drear. "It will be answered with a million gestures of kindness and humility that wouldn't have been allowed to enter the world if the demons were still among us."

Drear's large black eyes, framed by his equally black hair,

said more than any words he might have mustered had he been capable of speech in that moment. And they spoke for everyone.

* * *

V

A Return to Wintrose Abbey

Hyte Fasserby was a simple man, but not the simpleton people often took him for. He knew the weight of his decision when he climbed back up to the mountain abbey and took it upon himself to watch over the brotherhood's charge. He felt called to it, just as Brother Wintrose had been called on to build the abbey in the first place. Just as his own brother, Char, had been called on to raise a family.

But the devil was full of tricks, and it wasn't long before Hyte was being assailed daily with taunts and confusion. It was unfair, the devil prince contended, for Hyte to have been left behind. And when Hyte told Kurg no one knew he'd returned to the abbey, Kurg only scoffed and said it was all the more reason Hyte should be upset. While the brotherhood was out in the world, collecting accolades and basking in adulation, Hyte was stuck on Scratch Mountain, looking after a devil prince who wasn't likely to so much as scratch his nose in a thousand years. While Char enjoyed the love of a good woman and the glory of rearing children, Hyte was pinned to a duty no layman ever should have been burdened with. Kurg promised that once freed he would take Hyte to see his friends and his brother's family. He said he would explain to the brotherhood that his incarceration had been the result of a terrible misunderstanding.

If Lucifer was the Father of Lies, then Kurg was the essence of those lies.

Mind, the devil prince's trickery wasn't the work of days or weeks. He was at it for years before Hyte finally wore down and did the unthinkable by setting him free. When he did, the brute pushed past him in a rage and wasn't seen or heard for days. Liberated from the creature's influence, Hyte could feel a veil lift, and it revealed to him the truth of what he had done.

There was evidence that the devil prince hadn't left the abbey for good. One evening, during a routine constitutional, Hyte discovered something odd in the cloister. Someone had built a circle of pikes, all angled in toward a space at the center, large enough for a man to stand in. A portion of the pike barricade hung open like a gate, inviting him in. The contraption chilled his blood, for it was the obvious work of a Rocky Forest devil. Kurg, in other words.

That night, while lying in bed and wondering about the young nomad who had recently taken up residence in the abbey, Hyte heard a noise like a door slamming shut. Perhaps the door to the cloister. Fear crawled across his belly as he lay there, motionless. It might have been the stranger, but Hyte hadn't heard a sound from the man since his arrival. He only seemed interested in perusing the volumes of philosophy and metaphysics left behind by Brother Wintrose and some of the others. And besides, the newcomer was early to bed without fail. This was far beyond his usual time for turning in.

Another sound echoed down the hall outside Hyte's door, this time the creak of a hinge. He'd so far avoided detection from the abbey's newest inhabitant so he could keep an eye on his movements. But maybe the man was wise to him, seeking him out in the night.

No, it had to be Kurg he now heard. He was only trying to assuage his fears by pretending otherwise. He had made a dreadful mistake in letting the devil prince go, and one way or another he was bound to pay a price. Brother Wintrose would be so disappointed in him, if the old abbot still lived. As he lay in the dark, waiting for the demon's final approach, his shame momentarily eclipsed his terror—the very shame that had kept him from fleeing the abbey after setting Kurg loose. He could never again bear the company of men. Besides, he had nowhere to go.

The door to his chamber shot inward as if caught in an explosion. Several candles burned dimly in the room, and Hyte wished he'd extinguished them. The flickering shadows they cast only made Kurg's form appear more mutated and huge than it already was. Into the room he came, limping and grunting. He held something heavy at each side. These items he deposited on the bed before leaning over Hyte's troubled features. The creature flashed something like a smile as he brought up a long, rough talon. With his other claw he pulled Hyte's tongue as far out of his mouth as it would go and then sliced it clean through with an easy swipe of the misshapen nail. Hyte heard the severed portion of his tongue strike a wall where Kurg flung it, but before he could react, the devil was holding a candle's flame to the fresh wound in his mouth, burning it closed.

He thrashed and bucked but could produce only the most pitiful gurgling sounds in his throat. Kurg turned his attention to the objects he'd brought in with him, which allowed Hyte to cover his blood-wet mouth with both hands.

But soon there was fresh pain. Kurg had clamped metal boots onto Hyte's legs and was now pushing pins into his flesh and bone through holes in the metal to secure the boots. This complete, the devil prince draped Hyte over one shoulder and carried him out to the cloister.

The gate of pikes was open as before and Kurg deposited Hyte in the center of the bizarre device. He drove several long pins through each foot, deep into the ground. Before leaving Hyte to his punishment, Kurg lashed at his face until it was free of skin. What he'd cut from Hyte he chewed on and swallowed, right before the man's eyes. Hyte moaned and cried, but his sorrow and pain only drove the beast to laughter.

Kurg threw shut the gate of pikes and hobbled to the rear of the cloister, where he disappeared through a fissure in the wall. Hyte nearly lost his balance and realized the horror of his predicament. Eventually he would tire, and his body would collapse onto the barricade. And while he had any strength or will to live, he would push himself away from the pikes, back to a standing position. It was human instinct to avoid fresh pain. But his strength would drain away. His resolve would ebb. And sooner or later he would die—impaled, faceless, and without a final scream to mark his departure from the world.

He let his head drop as he burst out sobbing, his body swaying in tiny moonlit circles.

GYPSUM AND ME

I made a wish once, and it came true. No one ever used to believe me, but I can prove it now. My dog fell into an unused, dried-up well when I was seven. It felt like it was my fault, even though it wasn't. Gypsum simply had a way of wandering off to where he had no business being. That's what made him a dog. I didn't even know there was a well back in those trees, so it couldn't have been my fault. But it felt like it was, and that amounts to the same thing.

Took me a while to find him. First I noticed he wasn't around and wouldn't come no matter how loud I called. As I closed in on the woods I could hear him crying out in pain. It was a horrible sound, maybe the worst I've ever heard. I wanted more than anything for that sound to stop. In fact, I wished it. And it *did* stop.

You probably don't believe me, either, but that's okay. You're about to. See, that was a long time ago, when I peered over the lip of that well and saw that old Gypsum wasn't dead like I'd feared when he went quiet. He was just standing down there, looking up at me like he would have wagged his tail if there'd been enough room. I threw down some kibble that I had in the pocket of my red windbreaker, the one with the white zipper, and then I went to get my pop. He'd know what to do, how to get my dog up out of that hole. Pop always knew what to do.

But I suppose you're wondering about that proof I mentioned. Well, I made another wish that day, not long after my pop broke the well apart so we could haul old Gypsum to safety—not a scratch on him, by the bye. My second wish was simple: when the time finally came along for me to shed my mortal coil, I wanted to meet up with my old pal Gypsum once more.

And here's the part you're going to have to chew on for a while before it goes all the way down. I died last April, and now I finally have permission to send this note. It's just for you, too. You can copy it down and share it with the world if you'd like, but if that's your plan you'll want to hurry some. The sheet of paper you're gripping like it was some kind of covenant will go up in smoke three hours after you first touched it.

When that happens you'll have your proof. And in case it's any comfort to you, I'll be watching over you from now on. Me and my Gypsum both.

THE SINGULAR TALENT OF NISQUALLY JOE

Tracee hated her surroundings. The constant ugliness of the world is what drove her to paint. Thoughts of war and corruption, crime and debauchery, dominated her mind, but what ended up on the canvas was always flowers in rich bloom, wildlife atwitter with the onset of spring or humanity in rapport with itself and its setting. Tracee longed to capture the plunging drop-offs of her psyche in paints, the tenebrous fens that hid themselves from her prying creativity. She *was* an artist. A damn good one. She just couldn't prevent her wintry moods and destructive passions from translating into benignity itself before emerging from the colors she splashed onto her canvas with such ferocious haste.

This morning she only stared at the incomplete creation on her easel. Brad was snoring away upstairs, as she should have been at such an hour. No light came in through the windows of her spacious art-loft apartment. The sun wouldn't rouse itself for hours. Instead she relied on the dim orange glow from overhead track lighting to make sense of her latest work. She sat cross-legged on a stool before the canvas, men's pajamas hanging loosely on her sweat-skimmed body as she ran both hands through her hair. She'd drawn a rough outline of the scene while in the middle of a field in eastern Washington and took some notes about what colors she might use. The process of adding those colors had begun here in the studio. It was shaping up to be another happy fucking painting. No surprise there.

A sudden jolt knocked her from the stool, as if something had rammed into the side of the building. She managed to land on her feet, but the easel began to shake. Before her mind could formulate the word *earthquake*, she was reaching for the painting she'd poured so many hours into. But she wasn't fast enough. The easel crashed to the floor, and with it her paints, and of course the canvas. Her palette scraped across the bright meadow landscape, leaving behind a dark trail of colors that streaked a meandering footpath. Her water can, packed with brushes, rolled across the half-finished painting, spreading a pool of running colors as it went. The shaking seemed to go on forever, but she knew it couldn't have lasted more than a minute.

"Holy shit," she heard Brad say. He peered over the partial wall of the upstairs bedroom. "That was a five or six, easy."

"My painting, it's ruined!" She dropped to her knees and began cleaning up the mess.

Brad's steps sounded heavily on the carpeted stairs, and his bare feet slapped on the hardwood floor as he came to her aid.

"Are you sure it's not salvageable, babe?"

She glared up at him. "What do you think?"

He squatted and took in the earthquake's handiwork. "Good God."

"It's completely trashed."

"I don't know ..."

"What do you mean, you don't know? Look at it!"

"You've been saying how you'd kill to create something of real substance, something that spoke from deep within you. Maybe this is it. I've never seen anything like it. Take those whorls ..." He traced circles in the air to mimic a wavelike pattern that appeared in the fresh paints that had spilled onto the overturned canvas.

"So you think I should pretend this was intentional, like Spinal Tap and their fucking Black Album?"

"I think you should show it to someone besides me. I just write about art. See what someone on the inside thinks. That's my advice. I think you've got something here. Show it to Andy at the gallery. He won't be shy about voicing an opinion."

She hated to admit it, but it was quite possible that he was on to something. Despite the absurdity of it, there did seem to be an intentional quality to the mess before her. A guiding hand, even.

"Fine," she said, still staring at her altered work, less anger in her voice. "I'll see what Andy has to say."

* * *

Andy was good enough to peddle the vapid landscapes she painted, but he pressed her to dig deeper every chance he got. She couldn't seem to convince him that she was hard enough on herself for both of them.

His condo was an alley walk-up, directly above the Crescendo Gallery. Tracee buzzed him, and a moment later he buzzed her in without asking who it was.

The dark alley entrance and somewhat dilapidated condition of the old brick building didn't exactly give the place an inviting air, but she'd been to Andy's before and wasn't surprised by the view of Elliott Bay or the lavish décor of the interior. The excess of it repulsed her. She saw no justification for wanton extravagance and prayed there was a special circle of hell for the Martha Stewarts of the world.

And yet you want people to shell out their disposable income for your art, she thought. The contradiction gave her a wickedly gleeful feeling.

"Tracee, it's so good to see you." He gave her a peck on the cheek and beckoned her inside. "You survived last week's quake?"

"Yeah," she said, taking off her coat and handing it to him. "Good to see that your building came through it in one piece."

"It took some structural damage, actually. Nothing visible, though. Nothing beyond repair."

"The earthquake's why I'm here, indirectly."

"Really? I'm intrigued. Come, have a seat. Espresso?"

"No, thanks. Where's Modest? I haven't seen him in ages."

Andy let himself drop into a banana-yellow designer chair across from the retro sofa Tracee had opted for.

"I haven't either," he said.

"What?"

"We broke up."

The matter-of-fact announcement affected her more than she would have thought. "Damn, I'm sorry to hear that. Why? What happened?"

"Oh, it's not a new story, or an interesting one. He had his priorities and I had mine. Turns out they didn't complement each other."

"When *was* this? The two of you seemed so good together."

"It came to a head last month. It was the right decision, Trace. It's not one of those breakups where we're going to keep trying to patch things up. Neither one of us has the least interest in going down that road. But enough about me and my man troubles. I hope you've come here on more cheerful business than that."

"I've brought some photographs I'd like you to take a look at." She rummaged through her bag and hauled out a large manila envelope.

"My, this *is* intriguing."

She dropped a fan of colored glossies on the coffee table between them.

"It's my latest piece. I'm curious what you think."

Andy's face elongated as he picked up one photo after another. The snapshots of her painting were definitely making some kind of impression, but Tracee wasn't sure whether it was positive or negative.

"Oh, my God. Tracee, I've been curator at the Crescendo for twelve years, and I don't know if I've ever been this excited about an artist's decision to change direction. I mean, this is exactly what you've been looking to do, isn't it?"

"It was an accident."

"What? What do you mean? Wait, you said this has something to do with the earthquake?"

She flashed a smile that was anything but.

"That's right. I was toiling away on another one of my middle-of-the-road wonders when the ground started to shake."

"You mean—"

"It's a one of a kind. Not another one like it, and not likely to be."

"Oh, you've got to try. There's no way to justify letting this go. I can market the hell out of the one from the pictures, maybe build some hype, but the hype won't last forever. Eventually you'll need to bring more work in this line to the table. Though I have to say, fans of your babbling brooks and nursing fawns are bound to be let down ..."

"I don't give a fuck about my fans if I can figure out a way to duplicate the style of this new painting."

"Well, we might want to leave that out of the press release."

She laughed despite herself. Modest would have found it funny, too.

Her gaze landed on a two-day old *Seattle Times*, open to a headline reading, *Man Claims Strange Power Result of 2001 Quake*.

"What's this?" she asked, pointing at the newspaper.

"Oh, that. Don't tell me you haven't heard about Nisqually Joe?" She shook her head. "My friend Meesha brought that over. She knows him. He's this guy who, supposedly, can make things tremble and shake by touching them, ever since the Nisqually quake back in 2001. Sounds like a couple of men I know, to be honest, but anyway, Meesha swears it's true. The *Times* tracked him down for a historical tie-in to last week's rumbler."

"You're kidding me." Tracee picked up the paper to get a better look at the accompanying photo of Nisqually Joe. "He's not bad looking for a nut job."

"You can have it if you want. I've read it. I just keep it out as a conversation piece."

"We'll call it a trade, then. You can keep the glossies."

She tucked the paper under her arm and retrieved her coat before leaving Andy to the development of his marketing campaign for her new artistic period.

* * *

For weeks she tried to reproduce the startling effects of her accidental masterpiece, but nothing came close. When she began with detailed scenery befitting her previous style, she couldn't find the means to mar the pleasant mood with any believability. When she tried flinging paint at an empty canvas —dropping it on the floor and rolling her water can across it —the result was a shoddy imitation of the original accident. Shaking the canvas to disturb newly spilled colors produced no encouraging results, either.

It might have been easier to give up on the whole damn thing if Andy's plan hadn't turned into more of a success than either of them had imagined. He'd taken out space in several high-profile art magazines and added Tracee's earthquake painting to the Crescendo's lineup. One local critic had already referred to her new mode as a "post-Ukraine-war reaction to the artist's own pre-Ukraine-war sensibilities." Stuff and nonsense, as far as she was concerned, but she welcomed the publicity drummed up by such conjecture, though it increased the pressure for her to follow up *Earthquake* with a body of equally startling work.

The futility of her pursuit became obvious when her engineer friend, Keith, built a contraption that was meant to mimic the movements of a quake. He brought it to her apartment and they bracketed one of her canvases into it so that it lay flat instead of upright. Keith threw the switch as Tracee drizzled and scraped paints across a landscape of heather-mantled hilltops. The end product was somewhat interesting but not worthy of her new phase. Work done using the machine would be recognized as a desperate attempt to try to recapture the depth and sincerity of *Earthquake*, the hellish menace of the damn thing.

Depressed one morning after nixing the machine method, she threw herself across a loveseat and massaged her forehead with one finger. She was denied even the small relief that a chat with Brad might have provided. He was at work, which meant he was trolling the city's coffeehouses, laptop in hand, for just the right atmosphere to do some writing in. Sleep started to nibble at the fringe of her anxiety and dejection when the newspaper she'd brought home from Andy's caught her eye. It lay on a nearby stool and she wondered why it was still around. She'd read the article about Nisqually Joe. It did nothing to change her mind about his being a crackpot. Yet she hadn't thrown the paper out. She was a pragmatist and skeptic by nature, but she was also an artist. She couldn't explain away some coincidences as easily as most people. If the newspaper had taken up residence in her apartment, there may have been a reason.

Pulling a phone from the back pocket of her jeans she called Andy.

"Hello?"

"Andy, it's Tracee."

"Hey, kiddo. Nothing to report on my end. Any breakthroughs on yours?"

"Um, no. Not yet. But I might be on to something."

"That's music to my ears!"

"What was the name of your friend, the one who knows this Nisqually Joe character?"

"Meesha? What do you want with her?"

"Can you text me her number? I want to meet this clown. I think that talking to him could open a door."

"Hey, who am I to question the methods of my artists. I hope this leads to something."

"I know you do. You've been beyond patient with me."

She slipped the phone back into her pocket.

It was a position she loathed being in, believing Nisqually Joe to be nothing more than a publicity seeker, while suddenly hoping he was much more. But we don't always select our own cards in life, she realized. Ferreting the man out and talking to him for a half hour or so would be a diversion if nothing else. Maybe even an adventure. If Nisqually Joe really could make things tremble, their meeting may prove to be nothing short of fateful. How could she resist that possibility?

Meesha, it turned out, was only a casual acquaintance of Nisqually Joe's, but she was able to dig up his phone number and address for Tracee. Apparently she'd been to a couple of parties at his place. As soon as Meesha read the address, Tracee knew it was an odd location, somewhere in the jumble of ugliness north of downtown Seattle. The kind of area where overpriced condos butted up against crumbling apartment buildings, making it difficult to guess which end of the economic spectrum Mr. Joe was likely to represent. Tracee was willing to put her money on down and out, based on the man's pitiful grab for media attention.

Yeah, because the wealthy would never stoop so low, she couldn't help scolding herself.

It was a long walk, but the rains were temporarily hidden away in the endless overcast, and the air was warm enough. The article hadn't gone into great detail, and by the time she reached her destination, the entire errand seemed mad. What did she expect from this man, even if he did possess an unusual ability? Did she actually think she'd be able to convince him to collaborate with her? And if he did, would his power produce the desired results? She knew she should have been more concerned about whether the guy was a dangerous lunatic, but that was the least of the questions swirling through her mind.

"Hello, Ms. Califax," Joe said over the intercom when she buzzed. "Please, come in."

He lived in an old building, but it had a certain discreet elegance that appealed to Tracee, a geographically vague architecture that pulled her out of Seattle and into a kind of make-believe realm where strange deals might be struck and men might be able to make the world tremble with a touch.

By the time she reached the stranger's fourth-floor apartment, she'd already decided to suggest they use his place instead of hers for their collaboration. She felt oddly at home.

A tall, shirtless man answered the door as soon as she knocked. He looked even better than in the grainy newspaper photo. Muscular but not to excess, he had deep, knowing eyes and a mane of black hair she suddenly longed to run her fingers through.

"Mr. ..."

"Joe."

"Okay, Joe. Thanks for agreeing to meet."

"I was intrigued by your unwillingness to tell me exactly what it is you want."

"I don't mean to be cryptic. It's just easier to talk about in person."

"Well, I can relate to that."

He led her through the main room of his apartment to a small, mostly empty spare room, the only light what filtered through an open window. Gauzy white curtains fluttered inward with a breeze.

"It's nice, this place," she said. He only stared. "As I said over the phone, I read the piece about you in the *Times*, and it seems that you may be in a position to help me."

"Believe it or not, Ms. Califax—"

"Tracee."

"Tracee, believe it or not, I didn't go public with this to attract attention."

"Why, then?"

He sat down near the window, lit a cigarette, and gestured for her to sit as well. "It's like this." He gazed out the window. "Someone mean and powerful was trying to hold this over my head. You know, blackmail me. I got tired of it, so I called the paper myself. I figured most people would assume I was just another Seattle wacko, maybe use me as an icebreaker at parties for a few weeks and forget all about me."

"What were you being blackmailed for?"

"This and that. My ability can be traced to a few ... incidents. I won't bore you with the details."

"Okay, fine. But I honestly don't see how anyone could forget about you after reading the article. I haven't been able to put you out of my mind."

"Oh?"

"I was working on a painting when the recent earthquake struck. I'm an artist. The quake knocked over my easel, paints and all. At first I thought the painting was ruined. But my ... a friend helped me to see it was actually an improvement. A *major* improvement. That earthquake turned my painting into the kind of work I've been wanting to do all my life."

"What does any of this have to do with me?"

"Well, I haven't been able to reproduce the effect. And I—"

"And you thought I might come to the rescue by making little earthquakes to knock over your half-finished masterpieces." He nodded knowingly and blew smoke from the side of his mouth. Tracee sat on the edge of a sofa, her hands pinched between her knees. "I'm afraid you've gone to an awful lot of trouble for nothing. One thing that didn't come up in the article is that I never use the power anymore."

Of course, she thought. *How convenient.*

"Why not?" She leaned forward.

"I first discovered what I was capable of when I grabbed my kid sister by the shoulders because she broke a model airplane that meant a lot to me. It was the only thing my dad and I ever worked on together that I can remember. Anyway, my hands started to tingle and burn, and suddenly I was shaking the stuffing out of her. When I backed away, she kept on shaking. Scared the hell out of me. I thought she was having some kind of seizure, but she wasn't. The shaking passed, and we both knew I had caused it. She's given me a wide berth ever since. Can't say I blame her. Sometimes I wish I could do the same.

"I was seventeen then. The Nisqually quake had just done its thing a few days before, so it didn't take a brain surgeon to associate the two things—the quake and my odd little gift.

I'd been at Discovery Park the morning it hit. Just hanging out by myself, wishing Susan Walker had some vague idea of my existence. Feeling sorry for myself, basically. But I'll tell you, it was the most amazing feeling when the earth lurched and suddenly everything was in motion—the trees, the paved footpaths, everything. It was like the world had turned into one vast sea, like stepping onto the surface of some strange planet. I got down on all fours to keep from falling over, and I really did feel a kind of kinship with the earthquake. No, with the earth itself. It was like nothing I'd ever experienced before.

"But like I said, I was seventeen, so after the incident with my sister, it was easy to convince myself to use the power inside me for mischief. Some of the things I did I won't tell you, but I rattled a few construction scaffolds, even got a whole skyscraper swaying one time, just to watch the panicked slapstick of the window washers who were hanging about twenty stories up."

"Oh my God, I remember that," Tracee said. "It was a sidebar in the paper. No one could figure out why the office workers in that tower all experienced an earthquake when no one else in the city did."

"Yup. The structural engineers were baffled. The geologists had no clue. I was the only one who knew—until now. I'd gone too far on that one, though. Making the news was kind of a slap of reality, so I toned down my displays after that. I started to wonder if I might be able to do something useful with my gift."

"And were you?"

"I finally got my chance on a train trip out to Chicago a few years ago. An old man boarded at Sand Point, Idaho. Sat right next to me. Turns out he was headed for North Dakota, but it was lucky he made White Fish, Montana. Started complaining about chest pains and shortness of breath as soon as he got on, and I didn't take him for a liar. He looked sickly. I also believed him when he told me his wife and her boyfriend had hightailed it with his motor home. He had the look of a man who knew good fortune by reputation only.

"I was up to get him water every ten minutes or so. When I got back from one of these trips to the potable water station, he was clutching his chest real hard, and shivering. Without knowing what the hell I was doing, I pried his hand away from his heart and put mine there. Then he really started to shake and shimmy."

Joe had let the ash grow long at the end of his cigarette. He pulled one last lungful of smoke from it and mashed it out in an ashtray, but not before the ash cylinder could break free and land on his bare chest. He casually wiped the biggest clumps away and continued.

"Next thing you know, his breathing normalized and he calmed down."

"You jumpstarted his ticker," Tracee said, stunned.

Joe nodded and smiled out the window. "He was all right after that. Made it to White Fish without a problem, but he got off there to be on the safe side. I made him promise to check himself in with a doctor."

"So why would you abandon this ability of yours if it's capable of pulling off such miracles?"

"Because I've always taken the side of Frankenstein's monster. There are consequences to playing God. This old man on the train, he made it to White Fish, like I said. I watched him from the train as he stepped off a curb to cross the street. But that's as far as he got. An oil truck ran over him like it would a rabbit or a coyote. The last I saw of him as the train pulled out was his head rolling away from his body, spouting a pinwheel of stringy blood. It traced a gory arc through the pool of light given off from a streetlamp."

"Jesus."

"Yeah, I put my trembling urges to rest on the Empire Builder that night. Haven't called upon them since."

"I understand." Tracee stood up but made no move to leave, only crossed her arms and stared out the window. Finally she said, "I'm not asking you to save a life, you know."

"Aren't you?" he said, his look sardonic. "Isn't that exactly what you're asking?"

"Yes, I guess it is."

She shouldered her purse and crossed to the door.

"Then I'll do it," Joe said in a calm, soothing voice.

"Thank you," she said without turning to face him. "I'll call you." She closed the door behind her and hurried to the stairs, down to the street, out into a jungle of gaudy billboards and murderous traffic. For once she was floating above all the ugliness, the decaying city that bore her up like a concrete sea, even if there was a rent in her hull. She might drown in that sea eventually, but right now it held no threat of death. It offered her, in cupped hands, a chance for a new beginning.

* * *

A week later they had begun. They spread a tarpaulin across the hardwood floor of Joe's living room and Tracee moved her painting apparatus in, being sure to leave a path to a small balcony where Joe kept a table and two chairs—perfect for morning coffee, she noted. By the end of another week they were sleeping together.

In the beginning Joe tried squatting and holding onto the legs of the easel to get it moving, but it didn't work well. As much paint ended up on him as on the canvas. He tried to make the tarp ripple enough at his touch to upend the easel, which sometimes did knock the thing over, but it never generated the momentum needed to effect the strange waves in the spilled paint that Tracee was after. He could have done as well to bring it down with a swift kick. She tried to weather the early experiments with dignity if not grace, but secretly she would seethe at every botched attempt. Joe was her last shot at turning her career around, and she feared he was blowing it. The sex was okay, but it didn't seem to be inspiring her paramour to the creative heights she'd envisioned.

Then one day Joe proposed an idea. It was a little risky, but what great endeavor didn't carry some risk? He determined to set the floor of his apartment trembling, assuring Tracee that he could pull back before the entire building started to shake. She doubted he could be sure of that but was sold on the idea in an instant.

Luckily, it went off as planned, and the results were astounding. If anything, *Earthquake 2* was darker and more evocative than its predecessor. A bond quickly formed between Joe and Tracee, and soon Brad was out of the picture completely. Andy loved every bit of it. Tracee's reversal sparked a marketing bonanza for the Crescendo. There were photo shoots and press junkets, parties and exhibitions. If all the attention didn't mean Tracee had arrived, as so many of her art friends put it, she was certainly no more than an exit or two up the road.

But fame was never more elusive than when it seemed within reach. The day before Tracee was to meet with a high-powered buyer from New York, her partnership with Joe ran aground.

"I need you to sit down," he told Tracee as soon as she walked through the door.

"Okay, I'm sitting. What is it? I'm bushed."

"I can't do it anymore."

"What are you talking about?"

"The power to make things shudder with my hands. I've lost it."

"No you fucking haven't," she said, standing and shaking her head.

"I've been trying all afternoon. I can't even make ripples in a glass of water."

She backhanded him in the jaw. *"You can't do this to me!"*

He rubbed his cheek and checked his hand for blood. There was none. "Do *what* to you? I've remade you. How is it my fault if you can't maintain the success we've created?"

"*We*? Ha! That's a laugh. You'd still be telling your pathetic story to any armchair journalist with a bendable ear if I hadn't rescued you from obscurity. Don't go putting yourself in *my* league."

She'd backed him onto the balcony without realizing it. Cool, late-afternoon air tousled her hair.

"Listen, Tracee, we can work this out. Maybe we'll come up with another way—"

"There *is* no other way. I tried everything before paying you a visit. You were my last hope. Isn't *that* pathetic? *You!*"

Her hands shot to his throat. He tried to pry them away, but her grip was iron strong. He bent backwards over the railing as she applied more pressure and leaned into him. For a moment she wasn't sure if she intended to strangle him or send him over the edge for gravity to deal with. Nature stepped in to decide for her.

This one was different than the one that had inspired her new artistic style. There was no bang at the beginning. It started off mellow but quickly escalated to a frenzy of thrusts and tremors. For a moment Tracee wondered if Joe had lied to her about losing his power, feared that this quake was his doing. But it wasn't. He looked as perplexed as she felt, and she doubted he could have caused this much motion at the *peak* of his abilities. The rumblings were enough to knock her off balance and pull her away from Joe. A wave of energy surged straight up through the building and flicked Tracee over the balcony railing, as easily as she might have shooed a languid fly from its perch. On the way down she remembered a game she used to play in gym class as a girl. One student would sit at the center of a parachute that was stretched across the floor while everyone else gripped the edge with both hands and pulled until the rider was well suspended. Then they launched the lucky child into the air repeatedly. It was a game of trust and daring. Flipping over the balcony railing had felt like one of those harmless tosses, but there was nothing harmless about her landing.

When the ground stopped shaking, she could see Joe up above, unmoving, staring down at her with vengeance that was visible even from that distance.

"Are you okay?" a voice called to her from ground level.

Footsteps followed along the sidewalk to where she lay in a crippled heap. "Ma'am, are you all right? I saw you fall."

The man was young, and he squatted beside her. She took his hand, wanting to touch one last human being before life drifted out of her.

"Just hold my hand for a bit, would you?" she said. The young man nodded.

And he didn't stop nodding. His shoulders began to shake, then his whole body. Tracee let go of his hand, but he went on shaking until at last he fell over sideways, unconscious.

From above there came the sound of Joe's laughter. She refused to meet his stare, because it was obvious he laughed at her plight. It would have been possible now to get back to work, and she wouldn't have needed any more help from Joe, or anyone. But there was a new wrinkle, of course: Tracee Califax was nearly dead.

AN OCCURRENCE AT KENDRICK OUTDOORS

With the sun peeking over the horizon, Carl Kendrick pulls his utility pickup into the parking lot of his store. Time to open for the day, but right away something doesn't feel right. He parks facing the building, several yards from the front door. That's when he sees movement at his periphery. He turns his head and sees a man stumbling toward him from around the corner of the building. The man has long hair, knotted together in places from lack of attention, and wears only a pair of cargo shorts. No shoes or anything. An uneven beard hangs from his chin. Black-ink tattoos adorn most of his arms and upper body. One across his chest reads *Rock Hard*. It would project strength on a man of intimidating size, but on this guy's wasted frame it seems a pathetic phrase to be toting around.

Carl realizes what must have struck him as off when he pulled into the lot. The property's drive runs past the side of Kendrick Outdoors where the strange man emerged from. Carl's guess is that he subconsciously noticed a broken window on his approach and that the sparsely clad man exited the building from a side door after having broken in, but not until Carl has parked.

The man is saying something, so Carl powers down his window.

"What's that?" Carl says.

The man continues his approach. "I'm really sorry about

the window, man. I'll pay you back for that."

Carl can see blood on the man's arm. "What are you doing here?"

"Have you been down below, to the City? Can you show me? They won't let me in." He reaches for the door handle on Carl's pickup and unlatches it.

"Okay, now. Hey, back up a little."

The man does as he's told and Carl steps out of the vehicle. Immediately the stranger lunges at Carl, waggling his tongue in his face and mumbling curses. Carl pushes him hard and reaches behind him for something in the pickup, then forgets what it was and turns to face the man once more. They stare at each other for a long time. Disquiet has left the man, replaced by an almost angelic look of peacefulness. He then turns and heads back in the direction he came from. Carl follows.

"I'm really sorry about that window," he says again under his breath as they round the corner. "I'm good for it, though. Just say how much and I'll have my people wire you the money, I swear. Say, do you hear that music?"

"I don't hear anything."

Carl glances absently at the window in question but continues to follow his guide to the side entrance. Did he see blood along the edges of some of the shards of glass still poking out of the frame? He doesn't bother to look back and check. In a gesture Carl finds oddly polite, the man holds the door for him as he enters the store. That's when Carl realizes he's seen the man before. A few weeks ago he spotted someone wandering among the trees at the back of the property. The man was fully dressed then, but it has to be the same person.

"You work here?" The man follows Carl inside. "I know the owner."

"Huh? No, I own the place."

"What is it?"

"It's a sporting goods store."

"Snowmobiles." The man nods toward an area behind Carl.

Carl begins to turn in that direction but realizes the man has noticed the snowmobile display. "Yeah, we carry a little of everything. Camping gear, hunting supplies. You know."

"A town the size of Dickinson, North Dakota, can support a place like this?"

A drifter maybe? Crazy? High on meth? Carl can't tell. He doesn't have any experience with this kind of thing.

"What is it you want, son?"

Instead of answering, the man walks away from Carl, toward the front of the store. Carl shrugs and follows.

The 1926 Model T he keeps in the front showroom is his pride and joy. He restored every last nut and bolt with his own hands, even gave it a top-of-the-line paint job. Highland Green for the body, with a shine like crystal lit from within by fire. Black for the fenders and running boards. Casino Red for the wheels. All of them original Model T colors, too. Most years only black was available, as the famous quote attributed to Henry Ford implies. But some years Ford broke out the color palette. Highland Green and Casino Red were on it. One of Carl's polishing rags sits on her rear driver's-side fender. That's a little odd. He hasn't wiped her down in a couple of weeks, and he doesn't leave shit like that lying around.

The man has taken a seat in a guest chair near the main entrance, which is still locked. "Have you been to the City?" He crosses his legs as if he has on a three-piece suit.

"What city are you talking about?"

"They won't let me into the fucking place. Goddamn three-headed wolf at the gate." His voice is an octave lower than it should be.

Maybe living under the sky will do that to you, Carl thinks.

"Right. Listen, I left my phone in the pickup. I'll be right back, okay?"

"Hey, you got one for me, man?"

"Uh, no. Just the one."

The man nods once and takes to chewing his fingernails. Carl doesn't give him a chance to change his mind. Unlocking the front door, he hurries to his pickup. The phone is on the dashboard where he left it. Maybe that's what he was going to reach for earlier, but he doesn't think so. Sitting with one foot in the cab and the other resting on the running board, he calls the police.

They arrive in what seems like about ninety seconds, but that can't be right. Can it? Well, he is a straight shot up Highway 22, which runs through the middle of town, and Kendrick Outdoors and the cop shop are both on the north end. Still, Dickinson's not as small as when he and his brother Duff were growing up. Nothing's like it was then.

He remains seated in the pickup, both legs hanging out of the cab now, and adjusts his trucker hat as they cuff the man and read him his Mirandas. The sonofabitch doesn't put up a lick of resistance, even as they pack him into the backseat of one of the cruisers, its light rig still sending slow strobes of blue-white-red into the dim morning sky for no discernible reason.

An officer approaches, tugging up the belt of his uniform, then rubbing each side of his jowly face, like he's checking to make sure he shaved. Do they know how many little signals of power they give off? He supposes they do.

"Mr. Kendrick?"

"Yes, sir."

"I probably don't need to tell you that you should have called us right away. You never know what these meth heads are gonna pull. Would've been within your rights to blow the sonofabitch away, too." Carl can tell that the officer is eyeing the shotgun he's got racked to the rear window of his cab. The man smirks at what's coming. "This is Dickinson, North Dakota, not Portland, Oregon."

Oregon came out *OR-a-gawn*.

"So you figure drugs, then?"

"Drugs or a head case. What the fuck's it matter?"

Carl bought the gun shortly after his brother was murdered on his own farm. Presumed killed by his friend Tuck Wagner, though nothing was ever proved and Tuck disappeared like a wisp of smoke. *Nothing's like it used to be.*

"Well, it's all squared away now," Carl says to the officer.

"Sure, until we let him out and he shows up on your doorstep again. He'll probably be back on the streets in a month, and you know what they say about returning to the scene of a crime."

"Isn't there some help he could get?"

"Yeah, if anyone gave a shit. My guess is that no living soul has included him in their nightly prayers for a good long while."

The officer looks ready to move on as he takes a deep breath and glances over at his cruiser.

"I have security cameras inside," Carl says.

"Okay. You want us to have a look?"

"Guess not. I can go through the footage, let you know if I find anything peculiar."

"That sounds real good. Don't delete anything just yet. Understand?"

Carl nods and the officer walks away. Once his parking lot is cleared he steps down onto the pavement and walks back to the building, leaving the door of his pickup wide open. For some reason, reviewing the security footage can't wait. Curiosity has him by the throat.

The command center, as he likes to think of it, is a small cubby of a room adjacent to his main office behind the sales counter. From there he can pull up footage by date and time, even zoom in and out. He wouldn't know where to begin designing or engineering the technological marvels the world now takes for granted—or worse, puts to evil purposes—but he sure as hell enjoys playing around with them.

Scanning back to the break-in, which camera two has captured as if it were shot for a movie, he lets go of the progress bar and the footage begins to play. It's eerie watching the soundless video, sitting all by himself in the tiny room. Every squawk and creak of the building, every shifting timber and complaining duct, steps in to provide the soundtrack. Sure enough, the man bloodies his left arm crawling in through the broken window but barely seems to notice. Carl switches to camera three as the man leaves camera two's range. Four cameras keep an eye on Carl's wares. Number three shows the man disappearing into Carl's office. A chill wriggles up his back. He hasn't been in there yet. Doesn't want to go now. Knows he has to.

He pauses the playback and steps into his office.

At first he notices nothing unusual. Then he sees what the man has done. It's almost shocking in its lack of vulgarity. No streaks of shit on the walls. No vomit in the corner. The man came into Carl's office, removed all of his family photos from the walls, took them out of their frames, carefully stacked the frames in the garbage can, and fanned the loose photos out on the desk in symmetrical profusion. Carl doesn't know what to make of it, but it spooks him a little. Instead of grappling with what it might mean, he turns and heads back to the command center.

Camera four is poised to keep watch over the front lobby where Carl's beloved Model T is displayed. The man walks over to the impressive automobile. Carl sees that he has the polishing rag in his hand as he makes a complete circuit of the Model T, scrutinizing every curve and cranny. On his second pass he begins polishing the fenders, doors, bumpers, and headlights, tending to each with minute care. When the job is done to his satisfaction, he drapes the rag neatly on one of the fenders—the rear driver's-side fender—and wanders out of view.

Carl almost switches off the video display but decides to take a quick look at the footage from camera two that will show the man immediately after the polishing stint. This gives Carl the clearest view so far of the man's face. He pauses and zooms in. He knows this man. From when he still had the downtown store. The man worked for him then. Jeff Conley. The name drifts into his mind like a cloud. There was no intention to rob or vandalize. This has been the act of a troubled soul, someone reaching for a hand that couldn't possibly provide the help or comfort he is in need of, but maybe it is the only hand his addled brain can conjure. Carl can only guess at the difficult path the man has walked since leaving his employ almost fifteen years ago.

Now Carl truly has had enough of the ghostly security footage. He feels the need to be outside again, so he steps out the front door and returns to his pickup truck. Before getting in he stares at the gun rack. Why does he have the urge to take down the shotgun? It's too late to do him any good. Why has he even come back to the vehicle? He can close up shop for the day. Should probably do that. But he'll need to go back and lock up first.

He brings a hand to his forehead and slowly shakes his head back and forth.

*   *   *

He couldn't remember going for the shotgun. He'd only been looking at it, thinking about removing it from the rack. Yet now he stood against the cab of his pickup, the shotgun held firmly in both hands. He let his gaze travel from the weapon to the pavement, and as he scanned the parking lot before him he was met with a grisly sight. Ten or fifteen feet before him lay the man with long, gnarled hair, clad only in shorts. A hole had been blasted out of his chest, and blood pooled around him like a carefully designed background for a grim art installation.

Carl ran a hand along the barrel of the gun and recoiled at its warmth. The distant wail of sirens told him that someone had heard the gunshot and called it in. He had found a temporary reprieve from his own guilt, but that was all. There would be no escaping the longer, sharper claws of fate. What he had done might indeed prove to have been within his legal rights, but he would forever wonder if the man had deserved to die.

An unearthly music swam into his head and grew in volume until it drowned out the approaching sirens. It sang of a city and a wolf with three heads. *I do* hear the music, Jeff. I hear it, *and I think I may be headed for the City. I'll see if I can get you in.*

He got down on his knees, placed the barrel of the shotgun in his mouth, and pulled the trigger.

THE NIGHT OF THE WOLF

*B*lizzard's comin'*, she thought as her hands worked the needle back and forth through the taut fabric, like she was stitching a world into being. She was dexterous when she wanted to be, nimble and sure. But she'd been chopping her own wood for coming on two decades, so she also knew the value of brute force.

A smile played on her lips. There'd been a time when Genevieve Ripley doubted so much as a smirk would ever find its way onto her face again. Amazing what the mind was able to put aside over time. Time was a healer, sure enough.

But healing was not the same as preventing, and even as the years wiped away past trials they carried us ever closer to the next great catastrophe. If Genevieve's spirit had been only as hard and implacable as the rounds of old wood she quartered each year for winter burning, she would have folded under the weight of such knowledge. A future as black as her past was a grim prospect, but she was ready for the bastards this time.

Storm clouds, blue and fat with snow, had sneaked up on her while she plied her needle. She watched them now through the narrow window she counted on for light. Hadn't anyone told them it's rude to sneak up on an old woman? Her smile broke into a chuckle. Spittle flew from between her teeth, slicking the embroidery in her lap.

The time had come. Rising up out of her old rocker was a good piece of work for Genevieve, but she got the job done without dropping her needlework or pricking a finger. The chair groaned with relief. Her daddy always used to call her ample-bosomed, but hell and damn if her ass hadn't caught up with her chest and then some. Aging was one of time's lesser miracles.

She deposited her half-finished needlepoint in a drawer and shuffled to the rear of the cabin as a howling wind threw a dusting of loose snow at the window behind her. At the far end of a short hall stood an ancient trunk. To the left was the bedroom, to the right a door leading out back. Genevieve swept a hand across the oily wooden surface of the trunk before lifting the lid and propping it open with a stick she left inside for that very purpose. She quickly disrobed, leaving her cotton dress and underclothes in a heap, then reached into the trunk with both hands.

It felt alive between her fingers, not like a mangy old pelt. Tonight they would come again, she thought, unfolding the wolf skin, which seemed to ripple as she let it out. This time she would not cower, would not watch them snatch her husband and rip him apart, feast on him. Tonight things would be different. Not much had changed since the night her life was cleaved in two, but one thing had. The spirit of Hobbamock had sung to her in a dream, and she'd followed him into the snow, learning his ways of protection and justice, amid the trees and forest animals.

She had only to lay one corner of the pelt on her shoulder and it crawled across her back to tighten itself. The hood of ears and muzzle pressed itself onto her head and she was forced into a stoop. A smell came on her like decaying flowers. She unlatched the door, pushed it open with her shoulder, and loped into the gathering dusk on all fours. They were just beyond the ridge now. Their scent betrayed them. This night, the element of surprise was hers.

A MILD RECOGNITION
OF IMPERMANENCE

"**I** don't suppose you put up a fight or anything. Just took their damn orders like the Private fucking Pyle you are."

Always an earful of bile with Brenda. Barney should have been used to it by then. Maybe he was but wanted an argument anyway.

"It wasn't an order, dammit. It's a little overtime. Keeps me from getting in Dutch with the boss, too. It's an afternoon's work is all."

"What are they going to replace it with, anyway? A fucking Black Lives Matter monument?"

"That's above my pay grade. Look, I'll be back in time for supper ..."

"You expect me to cook you a meal? Is that what you deserve for selling out?" She stood with her arms crossed, leaning angrily against the doorframe.

He let out a deep sigh. "No, I was going to suggest that I take you out somewhere. But forget it. I'll pick something up on the way home."

"I don't like eating out. Gettin' stared down by all the high-and-mighty maskers. If you stop at McDonald's I want a Big Mac meal with Coke." She turned away into the shadows of another room.

That's how it began. The state of Delaware wanted to uproot its last remaining whipping post dating back to slave times, and Barney had got the job. Some folks made it out to be a big deal. *Meaningful symbolic gesture* is a phrase he heard thrown around more than once. Brenda probably thought they ought to install a few more of the damn things. Barney was somewhere in the middle. He thought that if people could leave the past in the past we'd all be a lot better off. Tearing down all the Confederate statues down south and everything ... he didn't see the good in it. That was pretty much his view of the whipping post, too. What was done couldn't be undone, least of all with a meaningful symbolic gesture.

It was a hot, humid day for the work, but his Bobcat was up to it, and he had a gallon jug of water in the cab. News crews had gathered, but they kept their distance so he could do what had to be done. First he connected the chains to the back end of the Bobcat. Once they were nice and secure he dragged the other ends to the post, got down on his haunches, and tied them to the base. That might have been an end to it, but he stood up a little fast and had to reach out for something to steady himself. His hand found the only object nearby that would do the trick: the whipping post.

For a second he thought maybe the heat had gotten the better of him after all. As soon as his hand found the crown of the post, the world put on a show. That's how he thought of it in the moment. Not like curtains parting to reveal a falsehood, though. More like a shade being drawn across a false reality to show something real.

The air smells different, clean and fragrant, and Barney stands several paces away from the whipping post, yet also still touches it, as if in a dream. Turning toward the street, he sees horse-drawn carriages wheeling by, hears them, too, once he pays attention. Up the walk comes a small procession. A young black fellow with a couple of toughs on either side. It takes Barney a moment to realize they have the man in irons. They stand him in front of the post so he's facing it, then one of them strikes him hard above the calves with a switch. He drops to his knees right away, his wrists clapped behind him, so one of the other men fastens the irons to the post with a length of chain.

Then the whipping starts up. Barney has seen some violence in his life—a couple of nasty fistfights (was in a few of those himself in his beer-drinking days). He once watched a bicyclist take the front end of a Ford Explorer and go spinning through the air like two stuffed socks sewn together. But he has never seen anything like the whipping this young man endures. He can almost feel each strike of the whip himself. The man's back is raw meat by the end of the sickening display, but not once has he let out so much as a cry or a sob. Tears run down his face, sure, but he keeps his fucking mouth shut. Any of us can say we'd do the same, but Barney's guess is that not many of us actually would. He, a mere spectator, yells for them to stop. They take no notice.

Somehow Barney was able to pull his hand away from the post. It had seemed like he couldn't while the flogging was going on—like in a nightmare where you try to move and can't. But once it was over he was able to let go and the world came rushing back in. Everything was normal. It was the same muggy day he'd left behind in favor of the hallucination, or whatever it had been.

Only, not quite. He barely registers that the Bobcat is gone, as well as the chains and the news crews, when a man and a boy approach from the opposite direction the roughnecks and their slave came from. They are both black. The man is set to continue walking past Barney and the whipping post, but the boy stops and stares at the relic. "Pop?" he says. "What's this?" The man turns slowly toward the boy, then comes back and scoops him up in his arms, holds him hard against his chest. "Son, that's an old, dirty thing from a long time ago. It's got no business being here. Never did have. Can you let that be enough for now?" The boy nods into his father's neck, knowing something isn't right but trusting his pop that this isn't the time. The man continues to carry the boy and they move on, but at a slower pace. Barney watches until they disappear around a corner.

His hand had found the whipping post again—if it had ever really left—but this time he didn't have to remove it. He damn near fell over when the post vanished beneath his touch.

And suddenly it is winter, cold but not unpleasant. A white man and a black woman wearing a style of clothing Barney is not familiar with can be seen dancing at a distance, but he hears no music. As they draw nearer he can hear them laughing. They need no music, he realizes. Theirs is a private concert. Closer still they come. He almost wants to move out of their way, but he's caught in their joy, and he's come to know that these phantoms the whipping post insists on introducing him to cannot see or hear him.

Here they are, spinning on the very spot where the post stood rooted for so many long years. Kissing, laughing, kissing again. He lifts her into the chill air and snow begins to fall. She caresses his hair. Their gazes lock. Everything becomes deadly serious. The secret they share is an old one, told a million times an hour. It's the listening that is rare, and when two people hear it together, a bond is formed that only the devil can tear asunder.

Something in their earnest expressions is lovelier even than their earlier laughter as they clutch each other's hands and stroll through the falling snow, her head laid gently on his shoulder. A mild recognition of impermanence.

The post returned as suddenly as it had departed, and this time Barney did fall to the ground from the surprise of it. His muggy day was back, and so was the Bobcat. So were the news crews. He had a job to do and looked forward to doing it. At first there was enough resistance in the old stone post that he thought it might give him some real trouble, but eventually the earth loosened its grip and he pulled his prize completely free. He swallowed down the last of his water and called his friend Earl, who had the loader and was expecting his call. Earl's partner would come with a truck, and before suppertime the whipping post would be a thing of the past only.

Barney didn't stay to watch it get hauled away. He'd made his peace and he was hungry, so he loaded the Bobcat onto his flatbed trailer and headed to McDonald's. He started to shake a little while he was parked in line at the drive-through, almost felt like crying. It was more evident with each passing moment that what he'd seen today could not be written off as a fantasy, daydream, or hallucination. His memories of what the whipping post had shown him were as real as any other memories he possessed, and, he assumed, as fragile. Visions and miracles were the stuff of legend, myth, and scripture, not everyday life in the twenty-first century. Yet what else could he attribute any of it to? The poor man being whipped like a dog. The father too timid and ashamed to let his boy know too much truth too soon. The lovers enjoying their exquisite freedom. What was any of it if not divine? But this was not the way Barney thought about the world. These weren't even words he was accustomed to having pass through his brain, and now they came to him as the only words that made any sense.

"Welcome to McDonald's. May I take your order?"

The spell broken, he told the disembodied voice what he wanted, then pulled ahead to pick up his food before driving the several miles home.

His pickup and trailer barely fit in the driveway. He'd need to return the Bobcat to work at some point. Then he could unhook the trailer on the grassy lot alongside the house. He walked to the front door with a bag of fast food in each hand, Brenda's Coke precariously held between thumb and forefinger. He set her bag on the porch, then the Coke, so he could deal with the house key.

That's when it occurred to him that life was filled with options. We go through our days as though we barely have a say in the matter, but we do have a say. The men who whipped that young man had a say. The father of that boy had a say. And by God, the taboo lovers had a say. Maybe our choices weren't completely uncoupled from established realities, but Barney was suddenly convinced that he hadn't stretched the bounds of his will nearly as far as they could go.

Neither had Brenda. And maybe what was right for him could end up being right for her in the long run as well. Maybe they were blockages to each other. The two of them weren't exactly a case of opposites attracting. That would have been giving him too much credit. But it did occur to Barney that Brenda was a little far gone for his tastes. And he'd probably mellowed away from hers over time as well.

Leaving the drink and the bag of food on the porch, he made his way back to the pickup. After reversing into the street, he set off in the direction of Dabney Construction. They'd let him unload the Bobcat and park the trailer. Then … he wasn't sure. He'd head somewhere to think things through, to reflect on what he'd seen and, hopefully, learned. His life couldn't be the same as it had been before today. That was the one thing he knew for sure. He could fight it or give in, but the truth would remain. So why fight it?

Maybe I'll send her a letter in a few of days, he thought as he pulled into the parking lot, full of freedom and hope. He used to enjoy writing and receiving actual letters in the mail. He didn't suppose it would soften the message for Brenda any to receive it in a stamped envelope, but maybe some part of her would eventually understand that it was a gesture of private decency. Any help she needed beyond that was, as he was fond of saying, above his pay grade.

A PRESSING CONCERN

I t wasn't too bad until stars began to dance through his field of vision. More than stars. Some were crooked rainbows, others black lunettes with flaring nimbuses. Even then the pain wasn't excruciating, but he hadn't considered that he might lose his sight before his consciousness.

Headaches he had expected, but this was unlike anything he'd experienced before. Neither a classic stress headache that ran from forehead to temple, nor one of his migraines that often started like a deep cramp in his shoulders and crawled up the back of his skull, this unfamiliar compression brought a change to his perception that felt permanent. The world narrowed as the discomfort intensified. Cognition blurred and scurried from his mental grasp.

Bright, flashing whitenesses of agony now, ripping through his mind's eye *and* his actual vision (maybe there was no longer any difference between the two): jagged shards of light that sliced and stabbed and punctured everything in their path. He tried to cry out against the searing pain, but his mouth was affected, too, squeezed into an oval mockery of its former shape, and he could feel drool spilling out of it in unnatural quantities. Maybe there was more than drool. Surely pain this severe could be expected to come with some blood. If not now, soon.

Something in the back of his throat closed, restricting airflow. It was all getting worse by the second.

The sharp crack of a home run ball being sent out of the park by a major league batter, followed by a crushing weight and a ringing in his ears like a siren wail.

Yes, a crushing weight. That's exactly what the hydraulic press was. The woman's murder had been superb. The best of his life, probably, but it was only a memory now, bagged and tagged like all the rest. It wasn't something he could hold and analyze. It could bring him no warmth or comfort, especially now. He would take it back for an additional month of life. Hell, a week. A day.

Another bony crack convinced him that his skull was giving way. The sound of the press changed, too, having to make less of an effort now that it was through some of the cranium. He'd been right about the blood. He could taste its copper tang, and smell it over the petroleum scent of the husband's machine shop. Beneath all the other miseries was a pinching ache in his neck from having it crimped at such an awkward angle.

There was some reprieve in the end, though. A field of daisies sprang up around him, and he ran naked through their luxuriance. Even though the hill he was on sloped down toward a dark, smoking vent, he hummed and capered in lazy circles that drew him ever closer to the lip of the hole. Discolored brimstone belched out of the ground, spurting high into the cloudless heavens, where it formed teasing curlicues that depicted scenes of fornication and wanton bloodletting before drifting asunder like storm clouds come to naught.

Was this what it meant to be called home? Was this what it felt like to—

GUARDIANS OF THE LAZYRINTH

On a star-dark night, in a lonesome cove, an old woman wept with cause. Her fingers felt a dormant urge and she fell to a job of knitting. These tides of sorrow came regularly but with long intervals of mere idleness between. This was a bad one, as evidenced by the compulsion to knit her first piece in ... what, years? Her joints remembered the play of needles and yarn before her mind could fully catch up. Soon habit had control of both design and craft.

No goal moved her to create, at least not one she recognized. She felt only the source of the act, which was despair. It was need, not intention, that drove her hands into blurred motion as they hooked and pulled at the pliant maple-colored yarn. Tears fell, too, and mixed into the work as the project began to take form.

The flow of stitches grew automatic, and her thoughts turned to her pain, which was ancient and common—though in her, unusually intense. She had never carried a child and at her age never would. So she knitted and wept until her lids fluttered shut and she slept through to morning where she sat.

The woman had expected the urge to be quelled by her indulgence, but the following evening it came upon her again. The shape she'd begun was yet indistinct, but that the yarn was taking on form could not be denied. Tears came again, and again they lent themselves to the task by dampening the yarn where they fell. The great sadness largely past, her thoughts turned to a seeming mundanity. It was a lucky thing, she mused, that she had wound dozens of skeins in recent months, despite a lack of interest in knitting anything.

A *submerged* interest, she corrected herself. A sunken desire.

That second night, she would die convinced, a good portion of the work continued as she slept, for the thing had grown and had about it a vague familiarity.

The third night saw her great task completed. First an arm, then a leg, followed quickly by one more of each, and she knew what she had made for herself.

A child.

It wanted a mouth, and buttons would need to be sewn on for eyes, but there could be no doubt as to what it was. She had knitted a small boy into existence, and her heart sang like a mockingbird.

By the end of the day, her son was fitted with organs of sight (coat buttons from an old lidded box), speech (a mouth of scarlet thread) and hearing (heavy flaps of brown felt). Her masterwork complete, the woman retired to what she determined would be the best night's sleep she'd had in ages.

❊ ❊ ❊

Julian Deneuve's mission was a simple and familiar one. He'd ridden the route on a thousand bright and cheerful mornings just like this one. Down to the end of Rue des Lances, turn right toward the square and circle around to the À Ta Façon shop for Papa's cigarettes. On foot it could be a tiring excursion, but on the Red Hornet, as he called his single-speed bicycle, the whole trip was made in a matter of minutes.

"Ah, cigarettes for Papa Deneuve," said Louis in his deepest French from behind a high counter as soon as Julian entered the shop, setting off a little bell above the door.

"Yes, please," said Julian, "and a pack of gum."

"Gum, gum, gum. You never try anything else. No chocolate, no candy, no licorice. Only chewing gum. Why is that?"

Julian shrugged, a little uncomfortable with the question. "It's what I like."

"Well," Louis said, laughing a little, "that is good logic. Iron clad, as they say. Do I need to tell you how much?"

"Eight euros?"

Louis nodded sagely and Julian coughed up the payment.

"Bye, Louis," he said, running out the door and jumping onto his bicycle.

It was too early for gum, but it gave him something to look forward to, maybe after lunch when Papa would disappear to his workshop to sand and carve and finish the custom bookcases he sold.

Thinking of lunch reminded Julian that he'd forgotten to ask Mama what they'd be—

A shriek of tires as he peddled across to connect with Rue des Lances. Barely enough time to glance over his shoulder and watch the grill of a bakery truck as it claimed more and more of his field of vision. Then the small, distant sound of the Red Hornet crumpling beneath him, and a sense that parts of him were doing the same. No pain when his head first struck the pavement, only a fading of reality. Then a burst of sensation, almost pain.

He felt himself slipping—not just away, but also toward something. Was this the end? It couldn't be. Children weren't supposed to die. Not in such a fashion as this.

"Let me by," he heard someone say. "Step aside, coming through."

The voice of a man, leaning in close now, whispering, "The Lazyrinth, boy. I must tell you about the Lazyrinth, before it's too late."

* * *

The steady fire in the hearth and glint of moonlight that stole into the old woman's upstairs bedroom window were worse than total darkness. For the past ten minutes she had been lying on her back with her eyes peeled wide, doing her best to avoid witnessing the shadows scattered here and there throughout the room, praying that the sound she'd heard in the corridor had more to do with the settling bones of her house than what she feared was actually the case.

But she knew that prayer was unlikely to work in her favor. Having years ago turned her back on all the gods she could have named, what right did she have to their protection now?

Another sound came, but it wasn't the creaking of wood she'd heard earlier. There was a metallic quality this time.

The doorknob.

Was it turning? She was too afraid either to look for herself or close her eyes against such ocular proof. A click.

Skreeeeeee ...

The door swung inward. She could no longer deny the evidence of her ears. If her gut was as reliable, she was in more than a spot of trouble. Still she could not bear to turn her head in the direction of the door.

"Well, well, well," came a voice from near the foot of the bed: flat and icy. "What do you have to say for yourself, old woman?"

"Son, is that you?" Maybe if she knew for sure what she was dealing with, she'd find the nerve to look it in the eye.

"*Son*," it said, as though spitting something bitter onto the floor. "What language do you speak where *son* means this?"

She pushed herself up with her elbows and beheld the boy of yarn that she herself had brought into the world.

"My *God*," she said. It was more like a broken exhalation than speech. "You've come alive."

"You're not as surprised by that as you might be." Her creation leaped onto the bed. "How about you tell me what's happened?"

It was grotesque in this light: backlit by the hellish glow of the fire and yellowed from the side by a declining moon.

"Son, don't you see? I've given you life."

He took a step closer, between her legs. "And from where did you acquire this so-called life to give?"

"It's a kind of trade."

"A trade?" He cocked his head to one side.

"Yes, someone, somewhere, had to die that you might live."

"Someone? Like who?" The yarn of his face clenched into an ugly expression.

"I don't know exactly. A child for a child. That's all I know."

"You selfish old bitch. You have no idea how cold and empty it is in here. All hunger and rage. This is your idea of a gift?"

Through tears she replied, "Yes. Yes! I've made you out of love. You'll outgrow these early feelings. The resentment will leave you."

"No! It's sorrow that runs in these veins of yarn. Your wish was a selfish one. You wanted a companion, not a son. I was not born a mewling infant. I come with *some* understanding of my own."

"I wasn't even trying. You have to believe me. I learned such conjurations long ago, but I hadn't been practicing, I swear."

"It had become second nature, eh?" He climbed onto her belly and sat. "Well, like you, Mother, I yearn for companionship. So tell me, where is the child who breathed its last so that I could breathe my first. How do I reach him?"

"There's only one way that I know of, but what you're suggesting is impossible."

"I have no soul, woman! Can you understand that? If I'm to live, it will be as a boy. A real boy."

"Very well." Her voice had gone soft and low. "Allow me to get down."

He rolled to one side as she swung her legs over the edge of the bed and stood up. She turned to face the knitted imp.

"Well?" he said.

In a sudden frenzy of motion she threw as much of the bedclothes over him as she could clutch with her hands.

"*What are you doing?*" he screamed.

Taking him up in his bed-sheet cocoon she cried, "I'm sending you to your soulmate!"

"No!" he called out through the material, wriggling and convulsing as she hurled him into the flames.

"*Noooooo!!!*" was his last utterance as sheet and yarn caught fire as one.

The old woman turned her back on the blaze and took several steps toward the door. But she must have underestimated the magic she'd put into the boy, for the burning logs in the hearth exploded into the room, and one of them caught her at the back of the head, knocking her to the floor.

Consciousness dimmed but did not go out entirely. The stench of something singed came to her before she realized her hair and gown had been set ablaze. Too weakened from the blow to stand, she howled in agony as fire consumed her from head to toe.

* * *

Julian knew only that he was expected to wait, so that is what he did at the edge of the brackish river that ran through this strange region. Waiting here wasn't the unpleasant business it had been in the world he'd left behind, though. He felt as though he could wait here for a hundred years without complaint if he had to.

It was a realm of passage, as he understood it. Not the Underworld, and certainly not Paradise, but carrying hints of both. Even the cinnamon scent that filled the air failed to commit to being of Heaven or Hell. It was merely ... other.

Though long on patience, he had grown increasingly curious about what he was waiting for. Now, as he watched a cluster of radiant globes of energy descend the far bank, he wondered if both patience and curiosity were about to be rewarded. Drawing ever closer, the balls of light exchanged positions constantly, as if being juggled by a spirit.

"Who are you?" called a voice, seemingly from within the dancing lights.

"Julian Deneuve," he responded from across the river.

"Did you die for me?"

"I died, but I don't know that it was for a purpose." His speech was as grown up as his thoughts in this place. It was difficult to adjust to the change, but not unpleasant.

"I have a feeling it was."

Julian noticed he was able to move one foot. He wiggled the other one to confirm that he was free of the trance he'd been locked in. Maybe now he would be allowed to make his journey to the Lazyrinth.

"What is it you want?" he asked the lights.

"I wish to return to the world, but as a real boy."

"What *were* you, then?"

"An abomination. A glorified ball of yarn with a semblance of life knitted into it."

"Do you know of the Lazyrinth?"

"The—no. What is it?"

"Pity. It is said to be a way back for some. I'm headed there. You may follow if you'd like."

"Indeed I would," said the lights. "Indeed I would."

Julian said nothing further but moved off into the woods behind where he'd been standing.

The cluster of lights glided across the troubled waters and followed close by.

✻ ✻ ✻

Their travel was quick, though the distance great—like moving through a dream. Julian refused to let himself grow too curious about his new surroundings, though. He assumed that most people's primary concern upon arriving in this realm of passage was how to move beyond it, preferably to Paradise and not the Underworld. Neither of these was his destination. He aimed to achieve that which he had been raised to believe was impossible: to return to the Land of the Living from the Land of the Dead. That his travel companion had a similar goal in mind was a minor irritant, but Julian's knowledge of the Lazyrinth gave him a distinct advantage.

The forest far behind them now, a sloping meadow of small black flowers gave way to a shimmering desert before them. The distance would have seemed impossible to a small boy from France, but in his current state he was able to reach the boundary between grass and sand in what seemed like the blink of an eye. He proceeded into the vast desert without pause or ceremony. There may have been a bark of complaint from the alternating globes of light at his back, but they followed him into the heat.

When a huge cliff of brown rock came into view on the horizon, the overall quiet of the lights broke.

"Do you know where you're going?" they asked.

Julian stopped and turned, pointing with a stiff arm toward the horizon. "*That* is where I'm going."

"What are you pointing at, more desert?"

"The—" Julian smiled. "You don't see it. Of course you don't."

"See what?" The lights burned brighter and the pace of their dance quickened.

"I'm afraid I have some bad news for you. What I see in the distance, and you don't, is the outer wall of the Lazryinth. It was described to me as I lay dying in the street, dying in order to give you some kind of unnatural life, it would appear."

"Why can't I see it?"

"Because you didn't know about it in life. It can only be seen—or used—by those who have learned of its existence in life."

"I don't believe it. I *won't* believe it!"

"Then continue to follow me."

"Are you saying I'm trapped here?"

"I don't claim to know anything about your fate, only that I was to wait for you to arrive before I could move on to meet mine."

"Walk on, then," said the lights. "Let me see with my own eyes what becomes of you."

"Very well," Julian said and continued on across the desert sands, the lights of an artificial soul at his back.

The entrance to the Lazyrinth became visible only after Julian had followed the gently curving wall for some great distance. All the gigantic door of rock wanted was a touch of his hand and it swung inward to reveal a rocky passage with a sharp turn not far ahead. He guessed there would be another not far beyond that, and another after that, and so on. For he had entered the maze.

❊ ❊ ❊

What Julian didn't seem to realize was that the lights had hitched a ride, clinging to his body as he passed into the Lazyrinth. The sensation was odd. One moment there was nothing but desert all around them. The next they were following the boy through a maze of rock.

If this works, the lights thought, *maybe the old woman's magic wasn't as weak and stale as she'd thought.*

They said nothing as Julian wound his way through the maze, choosing passage after passage, seemingly without hesitation or fear. The walls gave off their own inexplicable light, so he continued on unaware of his hitchhikers' presence or influence. But when he passed an opening from which the lights had caught a glimpse of movement and heard a sigh, or low utterance, they risked unhitching themselves from their carrier. The straightaway they were on appeared to continue uninterrupted for a good distance, so the lights danced back to the passage that had captured their attention, and into it, certain they could find their way back after satisfying their curiosity.

The sound returned, louder now. A female releasing soft grunts of pleasure. They turned a corner and before them stood a naked woman, bathed in light that she herself seemed to be the source of. Her hips swayed back and forth, and long, dark hair spilled over her shoulders and breasts. Tantalizing gaps in the hair revealed rigid pink nipples and drew the lights onward. The woman's eyes had been closed as she moaned with pleasure, but now they flashed open and, giggling, she turned and ran deeper into the twisting passage.

The lights passed a number of turn-offs as they pursued the illuminated flesh that bounded before them. Finally they reached a circular area. The woman stood still in the center of the room, her back to the lights.

"Won't you turn around?" they said.

"Is that what you want?" the woman replied, her voice like warmed candle wax.

"Yes."

And so she did as they'd requested. Only her face was no longer that of a beautiful young woman, but of the hag who had knitted the lights into a perversion of nature.

"*You!*" they cried.

"Me." She grinned. "Welcome to the Lazyrinth, my son. We are now guardians, you and I."

"I don't understand."

"Of course you don't, but you have me to teach you, and all the time in the world to learn. This is a fourth place, child. Not Heaven, not Hell and not the Middle Way. This is a protected place, and protected it must remain."

The lights jostled themselves and looked back in the direction from which they'd entered the room. There was no hope of finding Julian, they realized. There had been too many bends and turns. Their fate was clear, and all that remained was to accept it.

"Let's go and give you a name, shall we?" the woman said. "There's power in a name. Come."

She turned and walked still deeper into the heart of the Lazyrinth, expecting her offspring to follow, which it did.

❋ ❋ ❋

Julian peddled away from À Ta Façon and into the traffic of the square. Distracted by hunger, he failed to notice a bakery truck until it was bearing down on him. The driver leaned on his horn and braked hard. It was a close thing, but Julian rode away intact.

At the center of the square, a statue of a man on a horse, sword held high, stood on a small landscaped plot. Something compelled Julian to pause with the Red Hornet in the shade of the statue and turn to survey the passersby in front of Louis's little shop. The feeling overcame him that someone in this crowd knew an important secret, a secret with the power to save a child's life.

No, that wasn't quite right. Not *save*. One of the faces he now watched knew how to bring a child back from the dead. He had no idea how he knew this, but he did, and suddenly the world was filled with more possibilities than he had ever dreamed of.

The sun parted a drifting cloud and brightened the square by degrees. Looking carefully in both direction, Julian Deneuve set off on his bicycle, bound for nowhere special. Just home.

ABOUT THE AUTHOR

Pete Mesling

Pete Mesling is the author of three previous short-story collections, a volume of poetry, and two novels. He composes guitar music when the mood strikes and reads as voraciously as time allows. He lives with his wife and daughter in the Pacific Northwest.

BOOKS BY THIS AUTHOR

None So Deaf

Out of print.

Jagged Edges & Moving Parts

The Portable Nine

Imperfect Lodgings: Poems

The Wages Of Crime

The Maker-Man Of Merryville